THE DESERT PROPHECY

By H. D. Rogers

To those who

have sacrificed so

much to protect and advance

religious and intellectual freedom

THE DESERT PROPHECY

CONTENTS

Prologue

When he stepped off the school bus, six-year-old Paul Swanson barely felt the raindrops that were beginning to fall from the overcast mid-afternoon sky. The handsome, dark-haired little boy with the pale gray eyes did not notice the old Chevrolet van that began to follow him as he walked home along a tree-lined street in Tampa. The rain was falling harder and the wind rising when Paul stopped in front of a vacant two-story house with a "For Sale" sign in the front yard. A tall Oleander hedge ran from front yard to back along the right property line. A gap in the middle of the six-foot-wide hedge had become one of Paul's favorite places to play. It was the secret place where he often took refuge from the afternoon sun and hunted for insects and other treasures while the Oleander leaves rustled with each passing breeze. Here, thought Paul, he would seek temporary shelter from the rain and the chilling wind that was now cutting through his wet clothing and causing the rain to feel like sleet upon his face and arms.

As Paul ran across the wet lawn toward the swaying Oleander hedge, he was distracted by flashes of lightning in the clouds of the darkened sky and then heard the rumble of distant thunder. He did not notice the old van stop beneath the wind-blown trees along the street in front of the vacant house. A pudgy, bearded man in his early thirties climbed out of the passenger side of the van while an older man nervously watched from behind the wheel, frequently turning to survey the neighborhood like a clandestine sentinel. The bearded man squinted as he ran through the pouring rain, his belly undulating above his sagging belt. He caught up with Paul as the little boy reached his hiding place in the tall hedge. Paul turned when he suddenly felt the man's meaty hand on his small shoulder.

"Hi, mister," said Paul calmly, looking up into the beady eyes of the man's fleshy, smirking face. "Is this your house?"

Surprised by the little boy's composure and directness, the bearded man hesitated before speaking. As he studied Paul's face, he felt vaguely unnerved by the child's confident demeanor and the intelligence radiating from his pale gray eyes. Then, recalling the "For Sale" sign in the front yard, he responded, "Yeah, kid. This is my house, but I'm selling it and moving away. Say, buddy, it's raining pretty hard. Why don't I give you a ride home?"

"I don't take rides from strangers," said Paul calmly but emphatically, wiping rain from his face.

"Well, buddy, you're trespassing on private property, so I'm going to have to either call the cops and have you arrested or drive you home to your parents. It's your choice."

"I'm sorry, mister. I've never seen you here before. I didn't think anyone lived here anymore."

"That's because I just come by now and then to check on the house. I come by to make sure people aren't trespassing. Well, what's it going to be? Do I call the cops, or do you let me take you home?"

"If you call the cops, will I go to jail?"

"I'm afraid so, buddy."

"OK. I'll go with you."

The bearded man firmly grabbed Paul's wrist and hastily began leading him toward the van. Paul was looking up at the man when he noticed a flock of white birds that seemed to hover high above in the rainy sky.

Pointing up at the birds, Paul said, "Look, mister, the birds are watching us."

"Yeah, how about that," muttered the bearded man, impatient to get Paul to the van.

The bearded man took three more steps. Then, he suddenly released his grip on Paul's wrist as he collapsed face down on the rain-soaked lawn.

Paul knelt, putting his small hand on the bearded man's shoulder. "Are you OK, mister?" he asked in a worried voice. Receiving no answer, Paul leaned closer to the man's ear and repeated, "Are you OK, mister?" Again, hearing no response, Paul said, "I'll get someone to help you," and he started running toward home.

As Paul ran from the yard, the driver of the van, a lanky, balding, middle-aged man, climbed from the van and rushed to his stricken companion. After turning the fallen man's body over, he could see that his companion was not breathing and that the pupils of his open eyes were fixed and dilated. "Oh, God, Lester!" he cried. Then, he attempted to hoist his dead companion's hefty body to his shoulder, but the wet body slid from his grasp, falling back to the wet grass. Now appearing desperate, he grabbed the body by both wrists and began dragging it as he backed across the wet lawn. Reaching the sidewalk, he briefly left the body and ran to the nearby idling van. He quickly backed the van underneath the trees and across the sidewalk to where the body lay. Summoning the rest of his strength, he lifted his dead companion's body into the back of the van and then hurriedly drove away.

After hearing Paul's description of his encounter with the bearded man, Paul's mother, Clara Swanson, telephoned the local police. An hour later, when the rain had stopped, Clara and Paul accompanied a young police detective to the scene of the attempted abduction. As Paul led them to the place where the man's body had fallen, the young detective appeared interested only in Clara, a pretty woman with a remarkable figure and long, strawberry-blond hair. However, as Paul discussed what had happened, describing the bearded man and the old Chevrolet van, the detective's attention returned to his investigation.

When Paul had finished, the police detective turned to Clara Swanson and said gravely, "Your son has been very lucky. His description of that man and his vehicle matches the description we received from a witness to a recent abduction near a local elementary school." Then, lowering his voice so that only Clara could hear, he added, "That child's body was found last week. I almost threw up when I saw the photographs."

"*Oh, my Lord!*" gasped Clara. Kneeling to hug her son tightly, she whispered, "Paul, I'm so sorry I didn't come to the bus stop, but I didn't know the older boy in our neighborhood wouldn't be on the bus today. And I was in the shower when it started raining." Then, standing to face the detective, she asked, "What do think caused that man to fall down?"

"Who knows. He must have blacked out and then recovered and drove away. But don't worry; we'll catch the lousy son of a . . ." The detective stifled his remark as he glanced at Paul. "Sorry, Mrs. Swanson, but this sort of thing really gets to me. If you want to help us catch this creep, please bring your son to the Tampa Police Department tomorrow. We've got a very good sketch artist."

"I certainly will," responded Clara emphatically.

* * *

The following morning, as Clara Swanson prepared breakfast for Paul and her husband, Timothy, she listened to a newscast on a nearby television. When the newscaster mentioned that Tampa police had found the body of a suspected child killer, Clara spun around, almost spilling the contents of the frying pan in her hand. "*Listen, Tim!*" she said, setting the pan down on the stove and pointing toward the television.

The newscaster continued, "Responding to an anonymous tip last night, police raided a north Tampa home where a man was seen unloading a body from a white van. Pursuant to a warrant, police searched the home of Boyd Appleton, a fifty-one-year-old registered sex offender, finding the body of thirty-three-year-old Lester Dombrosky, who had been residing in Appleton's home. According to one of the investigating officers, Dombrosky resembled a witness's description of the bearded man who allegedly abducted seven-year-old Polly Edmunds, whose mutilated body was found last week. Searching Appleton's home, the officers seized several items, including photographs, described by the officers as evidence that Appleton and Dombrosky had been involved in a series of crimes against children. Appleton is now in police custody and charged with murder, kidnapping, and aggravated sexual assault on a minor. An autopsy will be performed on Dombrosky to determine his cause of death."

Clara turned to her husband, who was now standing beside her. Timothy could see that his wife was trembling and on the verge of tears. As Timothy took Clara in his arms, she said, "They almost got Paul." Then, she began to cry.

Clara decided to take Paul to school that day, a practice she would continue for the next few years. "Paul," she said as they drove to school, "I want you to promise me that you'll never accept a ride from another stranger."

"OK. I promise."

"If that man had gotten you into his car, we never would have seen you again. God must have been watching over you, Paul."

The little boy looked up at his mother as he said, "I think God sent the birds to watch over me."

"What do you mean? What birds?"

"I saw lots of white birds in the sky when the man fell down. I think God sent them."

Smiling, Clara said, "Maybe He did, Paul."

* * *

Boyd Appleton was later convicted of the abduction and murder of seven-year-old Polly Edmunds. Although he had also been charged with the murder of his partner, Lester Dombrosky, that charge was dropped after multiple autopsy examinations could not determine the cause of Dombrosky's death.

CHAPTER 1
Dome of the Rock

Seventeen years later, a middle-aged American couple and their handsome, adopted son sat quietly among the passengers on a tour bus riding slowly through the ancient section of Jerusalem known as the Old City. For Reverend Timothy Swanson, Clara, and their son, Paul, the trip to Israel was more than a vacation; it was a quest to solve a mystery, the latest in a series of mysteries that surrounded the life of Paul Swanson. The Reverend, a distinguished looking, slightly balding fifty-seven year old, and Clara, still pretty at age fifty-four, had been quite surprised when Paul announced his intention to visit the Dome of the Rock. They thought it strange that their twenty-three-year-old son felt compelled to visit an Islamic shrine in the heart of the Jewish homeland, a place that he had only seen in pictures. Even more strange was his reason for this journey: a recurrent dream in which a disembodied voice had told him he must come here to fulfill his destiny. They knew, however, that Paul had twice before experienced prescient dreams that had accurately foretold future events. Therefore, despite their concern that Paul would be visiting a place with a history of terrorist violence, the Reverend and Clara did not attempt to dissuade him from his bizarre quest. Having long wanted to visit the Holy Land themselves, they convinced Paul to allow them to accompany him.

The Swanson family watched intently as the tour bus neared a large plaza in front of the Western Wall, a huge, ancient wall made of massive, roughly hewn stones and dotted sporadically with clumps of vegetation. The famous wall was a remnant of the great walls that had formed the sides of the Temple Mount on which the First and Second Temples of Israel had once stood. Also known as the Wailing Wall, it had become the center of Jewish mourning over the destruction of those temples and a reminder of Israel's former glory. Beyond the top of the ancient wall, which rose nineteen meters above the plaza, was an incongruous sight – a giant golden dome that gleamed in the late afternoon sunlight. Beneath the dome was the destination for which they had traveled so far, the famous Islamic shrine known as the Dome of the Rock.

As the bus passengers stared at the sights ahead, the tour guide began reciting historical facts. "The Temple Mount, called al-Haram al-Sharif by Muslims, was erected on the bedrock of a hill believed to be Mount Moriah, which is holy ground to Jews, Christians, and Muslims. To Jews it is the place where Abraham's faith in God was proven by his willingness to sacrifice his infant son and was later the site on which the First and Second Temples stood. To Christians it is the place where Jesus of Nazareth preached and chased moneychangers from the Second Temple. To Muslims it is the third most important holy site in Islam, after Mecca and Medina, and is the location of both the Dome of the Rock shrine and the al-Aqsa Mosque.

"The First Temple that stood on the Temple Mount was Solomon's Temple, which stood there from 960 to 586 B.C. when it was destroyed by the armies of Nebuchadnezzar II of Babylon. The Second Temple stood there from 538 B.C. until 70 A.D. when Roman legions destroyed it.

"Later, according to the Muslim religion, the Temple Mount was the place where Muhammad ascended to heaven to be given Islamic prayers before returning to earth. To commemorate this event, the Muslims built the Dome of the Rock between 685 and 691 A.D. when the Temple Mount was under Muslim control." Then, the tour guide added, "Many of us believe the Dome will someday be destroyed and replaced by the Third Temple, which will be built when the Messiah comes."

Soon the bus stopped, and its doors opened. The Swanson family and the other passengers debarked and began to walk toward the Temple Mount. Reverend Swanson and Clara followed their tall son, who walked with a long, effortless, athletic stride. As the tour group

10

approached the Western Wall Plaza, Jerusalem police could be seen everywhere, a reminder of the ever present potential for terrorism and violent conflicts between Israelis and Palestinians. The tour guide led the group to a security checkpoint at the bottom of a long, winding stairway leading up to Moor's Gate, one of the two gates through which non-Muslims could enter the Temple Mount. After passing through the checkpoint, the group slowly ascended the stairway and then followed the tour guide through Moor's Gate onto the lower level of the Temple Mount. Then, they walked across the lower level to another stairway and slowly climbed ancient stone stairs leading to the upper platform of the Temple Mount. At the top of these stairs, the group passed through a colonnade and began walking toward one of the porch-covered entrances to the Dome of the Rock.

As the tour group walked slowly toward the entrance of the huge octagonal shrine, the tour guide continued his discourse. "The shrine has remained essentially unchanged for thirteen hundred years, although it has undergone repairs and renovations at various times. As you can see, a mosaic of blue, green, yellow, and white Turkish tiles covers the upper portions of the outer walls of the shrine. Gold leaf covers the famous golden dome above the center of the shrine. The dome is about twenty meters in diameter and has an apex about twenty-five meters above the shrine's floor. The dome sits upon a drum with sixteen windows in the middle of the shrine's octagonal roof. The dome and drum are supported by a circular arcade of four piers and twelve columns, which you will see inside the shrine."

When the group reached the porch at the shrine's entrance, the tour guide instructed them to remove their shoes before entering the shrine. While they were doing so, the guide finished his discourse. "In the center of the shrine, directly beneath the golden dome, is the famous Rock around which the shrine was built. The Rock, which extends up through the floor of the shrine, is about sixteen meters long and twelve meters wide, and parts of it rise above the floor about one and a half meters. The Rock was the peak of Mount Moriah where, according to Muslim doctrine, Muhammad ascended to heaven. But long before that, it was where the Ark of the Covenant was placed in the First Temple and where sacrifices were offered up during Yom Kippur in the Second Temple. Below the Rock is a cave known as the Well of the Souls, where Muslims say the souls of the dead congregate. A wooden balustrade surrounds the Rock. An inner ambulatory or walkway encircles the balustrade, and an outer ambulatory surrounds the inner ambulatory. An octagonal arcade of eight piers and sixteen columns separates the two ambulatories. The Rock itself is not open to non-Muslims, but we may observe it from the balustrade."

Once inside the shrine, the Reverend drew close to Paul and quietly asked, "Well, son, have you arrived at any further insight as to your purpose here?"

Staring ahead, Paul seemed distracted as he responded, "No, but I think we're supposed to witness something here, something very important." The Reverend nodded and then turned as the tour guide began answering questions posed by some members of the group. Paul then separated from the tour group to explore the shrine.

As he walked through the green-carpeted outer ambulatory, Paul studied the marble walls and piers and the intricate tile mosaics that adorned the upper parts of the piers, soffits, and spandrels of the outer octagonal arcade. He observed the ornate designs carved into the woodwork of the ceiling.

After he had walked halfway around the outer ambulatory, Paul's attention shifted to the center of the shrine where Arab security guards watched while visitors stood at the balustrade surrounding the Rock. Passing through the red-carpeted inner ambulatory, Paul paid little attention to its elaborate decorations. When he reached the balustrade, Paul stood with other visitors, staring at the somber, irregularly shaped mass of the Rock dimly illuminated by the circular drum of windows high above. It appeared to be no more than a huge outcrop of ordinary stone jutting through the shrine's floor.

After inspecting the Rock for several minutes, Paul began to walk away, feeling somewhat disappointed. The shrine was immense and far more ornate than the small church where Paul's father preached, but he could not help feeling that he was in a tourist attraction rather than a holy place. Despite his certainty that he was supposed to come here, he was bewildered as to what his presence could accomplish. Perhaps, he thought, he had overlooked something here.

As Paul considered further exploration of the shrine, his parents suddenly approached. "The guide says the shrine is closing, so we must all leave now," said the Reverend.

"But I don't feel as if we've accomplished our purpose here," Paul responded.

"We can come back again, Paul," said Clara.

Paul silently nodded and then followed his parents and other members of the tour group as they walked to the shrine's entrance.

After putting on their shoes again, the tour group followed the guide toward the southern end of the Temple Mount. As they walked toward the gray-domed al-Aqsa Mosque, Paul noticed that the sky had become dark as if rain were imminent. The tour guide remarked that he had seldom seen rain in July.

When the group arrived at the al-Aqsa Mosque, the guide cautioned the tour group that they could not enter the mosque, a smaller and less impressive structure than the Dome of the Rock. The guide explained that Islamic authorities permitted only Muslims to enter the mosque, one of the most holy sites in Islam. He then informed the group that construction of the al-Aqsa Mosque had commenced several years after construction of the Dome of the Rock and that it had been through several building phases and major restorations. The guide mentioned that in past decades arsonists had attacked the mosque and that Israeli authorities had once foiled a right-wing Jewish organization's plan to blow it up. After waiting briefly for the group to inspect the exterior of the mosque, the tour guide announced that it was time for them to return to the tour bus.

As the group followed the guide away from the mosque, Paul felt raindrops on his face and bare arms. Looking up into the darkened sky, he saw a barely visible flock of whitish birds that seemed to be lazily circling high above the Temple Mount. Paul thought there was something vaguely familiar about the sight of the birds. Perhaps, he had seen pictures of similar flocks. He could not quite recall.

"What kind of birds are those?" asked an elderly woman in the tour group as she pointed toward the flock.

"I cannot say, madam," responded the tour guide, pausing for a moment to look into the sky. "I do not recall seeing birds like those before."

* * *

Back aboard the tour bus, Reverend Swanson patted Paul's shoulder and whispered, "We'll come back here before we leave Jerusalem."

Traffic seemed unusually heavy as the bus started back toward the Christian Quarter, where the Swanson family's hotel was located. The bus had only driven a short distance when it suddenly stopped. Paul could see a barricade ahead and several men in police uniforms. As the driver opened the front door of the bus, a uniformed man climbed aboard and spoke to the driver and then to the tour guide. The guide then announced that the bus was being detoured due to a terrorist threat. He said that terrorists had taken over a building in West Jerusalem and were threatening to detonate a bomb unless Israel met their demands.

The bus driver, who appeared quite nervous, hastily turned the bus and began to follow the heavy traffic flow away from the police barricade.

"Where are we being taken?" asked an elderly female passenger.

"The police have directed us to a nearby shelter," the guide responded.

"But, Sir, we are not in West Jerusalem. Why do we need to take shelter here?" asked bald, middle-aged male passenger.

"I'll explain when we get to the shelter," said the guide, peering nervously out the windows of the bus.

For the next several minutes, the bus moved haltingly in a massive traffic jam. Then, the tour guide, who now appeared quite agitated, said something in Hebrew to the bus driver. As the driver stopped the bus and opened the doors, the guide announced, "The shelter is within walking distance. We must leave the bus now."

"I still don't see why we need to take shelter if the terrorists are in West Jerusalem," objected the bald, male passenger.

The guide, who was now sweating profusely, replied, "The terrorists claim to have *a nuclear weapon.*"

CHAPTER 2
Consulate Crisis

At the United States Consulate in West Jerusalem, nine heavily armed terrorists had been holding the Consul General and his staff as hostages for several hours. Scores of Jerusalem police were surrounding the Consulate while hundreds more were directing traffic away from the area. One of the hostages, a Consulate guard, had been released with a message that the terrorists had brought a nuclear device into the Consulate and that they would detonate it if an Israeli assault on the Consulate were attempted.

Later, the terrorists released a second hostage, Amanda Hirsch, who was the secretary to the Consul General. Ms. Hirsch, a petite American woman in her forties, carried an envelope as she hurried to the throng of police standing outside. There a police officer introduced her to an agent of Shabak, the Israeli counter-intelligence and internal security agency. The Shabak agent drove her directly to the Shabak headquarters in Jerusalem.

After a physician had examined Ms. Hirsch, a Shabak agent led her to the office of Eli Zahavi, a highly respected and well-liked, senior Shabak agent.

"Good evening, Ms. Hirsch. My name is Eli Zahavi. I am an agent of the Israeli government." Then, gesturing to another man standing quietly in his office, Agent Zahavi said, "And this gentleman is Jack Landon, an agent of your CIA. We have been told that you have brought us a communication from the terrorists who are holding the Consulate staff hostage."

"They said I should give this to a representative of the Israeli government," said Ms. Hirsch, handing the envelope that she had been carrying to Agent Zahavi.

After opening the envelope, Agent Zahavi removed a photograph and a sheet of paper. Examining the photograph, he asked, "Mrs. Hirsch, did you personally see this bomb?"

"Yes, they have it in the Consul General's office, where the hostages are," she nervously responded. "They said I should tell you that it was a nuclear weapon and that they were trained to use it. And they made me type up that letter with their demands in it."

Agent Zahavi handed the photograph to Agent Landon. "What do you think, Jack?"

As Agent Landon inspected the photograph of the bomb, Ms. Hirsch silently studied the two agents, whom she estimated to be in their mid-forties. Had she not been introduced to them, she would have thought that Eli Zahavi, a fair-complected, pleasant-looking Israeli, was the American and that Jack Landon, a swarthy man with dark eyes and a penetrating stare, was the Israeli. She suspected that Agent Zahavi had once lived in the United States because he spoke English with no perceptible accent.

Handing the bomb photograph back to Eli Zahavi, Agent Landon sighed and said, "Looks like one of the latest generation of Russian suitcase nukes. It was probably bought on the Russian black market." Then, staring at Ms. Hirsch with an expressionless face, he asked, "Did the terrorists say anything about arming the device?"

"No, but the one who appeared to be their leader said that if they were attacked or their demands were not met, they'd *erase the Consulate and Jerusalem from the face of the earth.*"

"Could they do that with a bomb that small, Jack?" asked Agent Zahavi, sounding somewhat incredulous.

"I'm no expert on suitcase nukes, but I've heard they can do a lot of damage."

Walking over to Ms. Hirsch, Agent Landon spread several large sheets of paper on the table in front of her. "Ma'am, please look at these diagrams, which are the Consulate floor plans, and show us, as best you can, where the hostages, the bomb, and the the terrorists are located. This is the Consul General's office here," said Agent Landon, pointing at one of the Consulate floor plans.

While the Consul General's secretary examined the floor plans, Agent Landon asked his Israeli counterpart, "What are their demands, Eli?"

Shaking his head in disgust, Eli Zahavi silently handed him the list of demands typed by Ms. Hirsch.

After perusing the list for several seconds, Agent Landon looked at Eli Zahavi and remarked, "Permanent evacuation of Jewish settlements and Israeli Defense Forces from the West Bank within forty-eight hours, an official guarantee of no reprisals, and an armored vehicle to transport them, the hostages, and the bomb across the Jordanian border where the hostages allegedly will be released. About what you would expect from lunatics. Who do you think they are, Eli? Islamic Jihad? Hamas? Hezbollah? Fatah? PLO?"

"I have no idea, Jack. They have not identified themselves. Whoever they are, I think they're bluffing. Although the Consulate in West Jerusalem is in a non-Muslim area, it is still within a couple of kilometers of the Muslim Quarter and several mosques. I cannot believe they are willing to risk killing other Muslims and destroying mosques."

"Well, it wouldn't be the first time, Eli, but the device they have probably would only take out that side of the city."

"Very comforting, Jack," said Eli with a wry smile.

* * *

Walking hurriedly through narrow, labyrinthine streets of the Old City, the bus passengers followed the tour guide. Rain was now falling from the darkened sky. Eventually, the guide brought them to a building not far from the Western Wall. There they followed others who were entering the building to a stairway inside. After descending the stairway, they entered a crowded basement that was serving as a makeshift bomb shelter.

Once inside the basement, Paul and his parents found a place where they could sit together on the basement floor. In a corner of the basement, a group nervously gathered before a television to watch an Israeli newscast. Looking at the people around her, Clara could see the fear in their faces. Even her husband, whom she regarded as a brave man and strong leader, appeared nervous. Then, she looked at Paul, who sat expressionless with his eyes closed. She wondered whether he was praying – or having another vision.

After awhile, the newscast on the basement television was interrupted by a special bulletin, "A representative of the Israeli Defense Forces has just announced that the terrorists occupying the U.S. Consulate have threatened to detonate a nuclear bomb unless Jewish settlements and Israeli military personnel are evacuated from the West Bank within two days." Upon hearing this, a member of the tour group said excitedly, "That means we have two days to get out of Jerusalem. Let's get out of here now." Others in the basement voiced their agreement and started to push toward the basement stairs.

Paul, however, suddenly stood and said loudly, "*If you'll wait until the rain ends, the threat will be over.*" Those leaving the basement either ignored Paul or looked at him and shook their heads in disbelief as they pushed toward the exit stairs.

Reverend Swanson drew close to Paul and said quietly but emphatically, "We *can't* stay here. We need to leave, Paul."

"Dad," replied Paul calmly, "I have seen how this terrorist situation ends. In a short while, the rain outside will stop, and when it does, the crisis will be over. No explosion will occur. We should just wait here until the rain stops."

As Reverend Swanson stared at Paul, reflecting on Paul's statement, Clara grasped her husband's arm and said gently, "Tim, we've trusted Paul's visions in the past. There's no reason for us to stop now. Let's just rest here until the rain is over."

Reverend Swanson smiled and nodded silently. Then, as the rest of the tour group left the basement, he put his arm around Clara, who appeared to be quite tired, and led her over to the now empty couch before the basement television. There they sat and began watching a live telecast of the events unfolding outside the U.S. Consulate.

* * *

Sitting beside her husband, Clara Swanson, quietly anxious by nature, felt the fatigue of her anxiety as she rested her head against her husband's broad shoulder. Soon, her eyes closed, but she neither slept nor listened to the news telecast. Instead, her mind was filled with thoughts of her beloved son and how her life had changed since his adoption. She recalled her heartbreak at learning early in her marriage that she was barren. She and Tim, who was a lawyer at that time, considered in vitro fertilization but had eventually decided upon adoption.

For several months, she and Tim waited to adopt a newborn. Then, their adoption coordinator called about a remarkable four-year-old orphan. "I think you and Tim should meet this child," the coordinator told her. "His name is Paul. He's a handsome little boy with a charming personality. He's in a foster home that's only an hour drive from Tampa."

"Where are Paul's parents?" asked Clara.

"The administrator at the foster home told me that his parents were killed in boating accident last year while he stayed with a babysitter. The police who investigated their deaths could find no other relatives, so they placed him in the foster home."

"Oh, the poor child! Did the police tell the administrator anything else about his parents?"

"The police didn't even know his date of birth."

"Then how do you know that he's four years old?"

"The baby sitter told the police that the parents said he was three, and that was about a year ago."

"Did you find out anything else about the parents?"

"No, but they must have been religious because the people at the foster home say they often see the child praying. But don't worry; the administrator had him evaluated by a child psychologist, and he's normal. In fact, the psychologist said he's highly intelligent."

"I don't consider prayer a sign of mental illness. Tim and I would love to meet the child."

In their first meeting with Paul, the little boy immediately captivated Clara and Tim. He was a handsome child and tall for his age, but what most impressed Clara was his calm and friendly demeanor. She felt her eyes well with tears when the little boy with the pale gray eyes asked if she would be his new mother.

Tim was also quite impressed with the charming four-year-old, who seemed quite mature for his age. Clara and Tim were soon calling Paul their son.

During Paul's early childhood, Clara frequently noticed behavior in Paul that seemed unusual for a child his age. She often saw him with his eyes closed as if he were praying. He had somehow learned to read even before his adoption, and he seemed to spend more time trying to read the books that she and Tim left around the house than playing with the toys that they bought for him. Although Paul sometimes asked about the meanings of words that he was trying to read, Paul's vocabulary often surprised Clara and Tim. When they asked him how he knew the meaning of a particular word, Paul usually said that he had heard it somewhere but could not recall where. Occasionally, Clara heard Paul talking in his sleep as though he were engaged in conversation. When she asked Paul about his dreams, he usually said that he did not recall them. On one occasion, however, he said that he had dreamed that God had been talking to him but that he could not remember what God had told him. When Clara related this to Tim, he laughed and said that if Paul was going to have an imaginary friend, God was "a really good choice."

Though Paul was a good student and seemed to get along well with other children, he did not seem to share the interests of the other children. Paul was athletic, and Tim encouraged him to participate in sports, but Paul seemed more interested in reading than playing sandlot football and other games with the neighborhood children. He had no interest in comic books or children's magazines, preferring to read his parents' self-help books, novels, and even the Bible. When he watched television, Paul usually watched programs on the history and discovery channels rather than the cartoon or family channels. While other children his age enjoyed videogames, Paul was using the family computer to visit Internet sites devoted to science, history, and religion. It seemed to Clara and Tim that Paul was involved in some kind of self-directed, academic regimen. When they asked him about the purpose of his activities, however, Paul just shrugged and said he liked to read about "interesting stuff."

In grade school, Paul's teachers found him to be courteous and studious but self-possessed. He was never pedantic in the classroom and seldom volunteered to answer the teachers' questions, but outside of class, he frequently helped his classmates with their assignments. He never seemed interested in competing with his classmates but always seemed to do well at whatever he did. Although most of his classmates considered him a "brain," he was generally well liked due to his friendliness and humility. He did not associate with any particular clique and treated everyone with the same courtesy and consideration. He was neither a coward nor a bully, neither a follower nor a leader. Due to his large stature for his age, he was seldom the target of aggression, and the few fights he had were usually in defense of smaller boys.

At the church that he attended with his parents, the congregation members generally regarded Paul as a "nice, quiet kid." He seemed to be remarkably attentive during church services and sometimes questioned Tim and Clara about the pastor's sermon. After the pastor concluded one sermon by praying that God would forgive the congregation's impure thoughts and deeds, Paul, age nine at the time, asked, "Why did the preacher ask God to forgive us for bad thoughts?"

Clara responded by citing Proverbs 23:7, a verse that she had been taught as a child. "Paul, the Bible teaches us that as a person thinks in his heart, so he is."

"But, Mom," Paul responded, "everybody has bad thoughts. It's part of human nature."

After Clara and Tim exchanged glances, Tim said, "That's true, Paul, we all have sinful natures and must ask God's forgiveness."

"I think God wants us to pray for forgiveness for bad actions, not for bad thoughts," argued Paul.

After again exchanging glances with Tim, Clara asked, "What makes you say that, Paul?"

"God gave people good thoughts and bad thoughts so they could choose between them. God only judges people by whether they choose to act good or bad. As long as people act good, they should not feel guilty about having bad thoughts. God doesn't want us to feel bad about ourselves. If we don't feel good about ourselves, we can't feel good toward other people, like Jesus said we should."

Tim, now laughing, asked, "Where did you hear that, Paul?"

"I heard it in a dream when I was a little kid."

Tim and Clara both laughed, again exchanging glances. Clara started to tell Paul that Christians should be ashamed of bad thoughts. Then, she began to think about the guilt and anxiety she had experienced because of her own impure thoughts and urges even though she had not acted upon them. If those thoughts and urges were part of her God-given nature, then why, Clara asked herself, should she feel guilty for having such thoughts and urges so long as she did not act upon them inappropriately? She decided not to say anything.

Although Tim and Clara had long recognized Paul's precocity, they did not fully appreciate his uniqueness until an incident that occurred when he was eleven years old. One Thursday evening, Tim told Paul that he and Clara would be going to the local performing arts center for a Friday night concert. On Friday morning, Paul told his parents that he had had a dream about the concert. "*Don't go, Dad*," he pleaded. "I dreamed that God was warning me that something bad is going to happen tonight. God showed me a big room with lots of people; and the lights went out; and the people were screaming in the dark. It was real scary. Please, don't go out tonight."

"Now, Paul," Clara said softly, "we really appreciate your concern for our safety, but we've all had nightmares. We can't let our bad dreams prevent us from enjoying real life."

"But the pictures I saw looked so real, Mom. He's never warned me about anything before."

"So, you think God has been talking to you while you're sleeping?" asked Tim, smiling.

"Sometimes, but He's never warned me about anything before."

"What does God look like, Paul?" asked Tim, still smiling.

"He's invisible. You can only hear his voice."

"Well, don't worry, buddy," said Tim. "If you pray for us, I'm sure your friend, God, will protect us."

Paul still appeared upset when his parents left him with the sitter that evening. Paul told them that he had been praying for their safety. Tim and Clara smiled and thanked him. As they drove away, Tim said to Clara, "I didn't know he was still having imaginary conversations with God. Do you think we should take him to a child psychologist?"

"Oh, Tim," said Clara, "Paul is a happy, well adjusted child. A lot of children have imaginary friends."

"But he's eleven years old, and this apparently has been going on for years. Besides, I've never heard of a kid having God as an imaginary friend."

Later, at the performing arts center, Tim and Clara sat in an audience of twenty-two hundred, enjoying the music of one of their favorite bands. They had already forgotten Paul's warning when a power failure suddenly extinguished all of the lights in the dimly lit auditorium, enveloping the audience in total darkness. Tim and Clara heard sounds of surprise and annoyance from the audience. Remembering Paul's warning, they stood and began feeling their way to the aisle leading to a nearby exit. Most of the audience waited patiently for the lights to come back on.

Outside the performing arts center, Tim and Clara found only more darkness beneath the moonless night sky. The power failure had left the streetlights and buildings in the area without electricity; but outside in the fresh night air, they at least felt safer. Soon, they heard others trying to find their way out of the center. Within several minutes, they heard sounds of panic as people began to stumble over each other, pushing to get out of the auditorium's pitch-blackness and stale air. A few people had pocket flashlights or cigarette lighters, but these did little to illuminate the vast auditorium. Several people suffered injuries when they tripped and fell in the rush to leave the center. Hearing the cries of the injured, Tim dialed the local emergency number on his cell phone. Then, he and Clara remained outside in the darkness, dodging the hundreds of dark figures rushing past them.

An hour later, after paramedics and police had arrived, Tim and Clara joined the mass exodus from the center's parking lot. They heard a policeman say that something had destroyed a nearby electrical transformer, causing the power failure in that area. As they drove home, Clara voiced the question that occupied both their minds, *"Do you think God warned Paul about this?"* Tim, lost in his own thoughts, shook his head absent-mindedly but said nothing.

CHAPTER 3
Consulate Mystery

After Agents Eli Zahavi and Jack Landon had questioned the Consul General's secretary, members of an eight-man Dudevan unit of the Israeli Defense Forces entered the grounds of the U.S. Consulate. While the rain fell steadily and lightning flashed occasionally in the evening sky, the IDF soldiers quietly extended a lightweight, folding ladder to reach the roof of the Consulate. Six IDF soldiers scaled the ladder onto the roof while two others held the ladder steady. The first two soldiers on the roof dropped cables to the ground below where they were fastened to large canvas bags, one containing weapons and the other tools and electronic surveillance equipment. After the first two soldiers hoisted the bags onto the roof, the two soldiers below climbed the ladder to join the others.

On the roof, some soldiers began carefully prying up the rain-soaked roof tiles while others quietly removed the weapons and a tent from one of the bags. The IDF soldiers appeared to function as a well-coordinated unit, except one soldier who stood shielding his eyes with his hands as he stared into the darkened sky high above the Consulate. "Hey, don't just stand there," chided another soldier. "What are you looking at anyway?"

"You didn't see them?"

"See what?"

"Those birds . . . when we were climbing the ladder . . . when the lightning flashed."

"What birds? What are you talking about?"

"There was a flock of birds up in the rain, just sort of hovering in the sky over this building."

Squinting as he peered into the darkened sky, the other soldier said, "I don't see any birds. Who gives a damn about birds? We've got work to do. There are lives at stake."

"OK. OK. But it was so weird. The lightning flashed, and a flock of birds was just hovering up there. It flashed again, and they were gone."

Over the area where they had removed the roof tiles, the soldiers erected a small tent, fastening it to the roof by cables hooked under roof tiles. As the rain continued to fall steadily, they moved the unopened bag of tools and equipment under the tent. After switching on lights inside the tent, one of the soldiers removed a battery-powered drill from the bag. He quietly bored a small hole through the area without roof tiles and then screwed an eyebolt into the hole. He fastened a cable to the eyebolt and handed the other end of the cable to another soldier. He next removed a portable plasma cutting torch from the equipment bag, ignited it, and began silently cutting a hole around the eyebolt while another soldier stood ready with an extinguisher in case the roof caught fire. When he finished cutting the hole in the roof, the soldier holding the cable carefully lifted the detached section of roof and set it aside. Two other soldiers then lowered a small, remotely operated, MSU, mobile surveillance unit, through the roof into the attic below.

Once the MSU was on the attic floor, one of the soldiers reached into the equipment bag and removed a small console that looked like a videogame. Sitting with the console on his lap, the soldier watched the console's monitor as he used a joystick on the console to steer the MSU across the floor of the attic. Another soldier beside him held floor plans of the Consulate. The soldier at the console looked back and forth between the floor plans and console's monitor as he steered the MSU to an area estimated to be above the Consul General's office. Then, as the soldier manipulated another control on the console, the MSU extended a long, slender tungsten drill bit that silently bored a tiny hole through the attic floor and the ceiling below.

When the hole was completed and the drill withdrawn, the soldier at the monitor manipulated another control to slowly lower a tiny camera at the end of a slender cable through the hole until the camera penetrated the ceiling beneath the attic. By rotating dials on the console, the soldier adjusted the angle, direction, and focus of the tiny camera. Scanning the area below, the soldier immediately recognized that he had placed the camera not in the ceiling of the Consul General's office but in the ceiling of the hallway outside the office. As the camera swept over the hallway, he and the other IDF soldiers standing around the monitor observed a startling sight. The bodies of two men in IDF uniforms were sprawled motionless on the hallway floor with weapons lying beside them.

The soldier at the console immediately telephoned the Dudevan unit's commanding officer to report what they were seeing. The commanding officer ordered him to relocate the surveillance device above the Consul General's office. The soldier pressed a button on the console that retracted the camera cable of the MSU. He then carefully steered the MSU to a new location a few feet from the previous one. There the MSU slowly drilled a new hole and again extended its camera cable through the attic floor and the ceiling below. After the soldier at the console adjusted the camera's angle, direction, and focus, the soldiers watching the monitor gasped in astonishment at what they saw. At various places around the Consul General's office lay the sprawled, motionless bodies of armed men disguised in IDF uniforms. They appeared to be dead. On the floor in a corner of the office, eight hostages sat bound, gagged, and blindfolded but apparently alive.

After studying the scene in stunned silence for several seconds, the soldier at the console reported the situation to the unit's commanding officer.

"What could have happened in there?" asked the officer. "Do you think this is a trick? Or do you think they died from poison gas or radiation?"

"No," replied the soldier as he focused the camera in closely on the bodies of the terrorists. "The terrorists are not breathing, but the hostages are."

"We need to get the hostages out of there," said the officer. "Hold your position on the roof and maintain surveillance. I'll send in a team with Hazmat suits. There could still be poison gas or radiation in there."

Thirty minutes later, seven heavily armed IDF soldiers dressed in airtight protective suits with internal oxygen supplies entered the Consulate. They found the bodies of two terrorists and their AK47 assault rifles near the front door of the Consulate. Their Geiger counter registered no radiation, and their air analyzer revealed no toxic gasses. They proceeded to the Consul General's office where they found two more bodies outside the door. Again, their equipment detected neither radiation nor poisonous gas.

After entering the Consul General's office, the IDF soldiers observed the bodies of five terrorists but saw no signs that a struggle had taken place. Carefully inspecting the bodies, the soldiers found that the terrorists were indeed dead, but their bodies revealed no wounds or other evidence of injury. Again, their air analyzer revealed no toxic gasses. Only when two of the soldiers approached what appeared to be a large suitcase on the Consul General's desk did the Geiger Counter detect any radiation. Even then, the level of radiation was too low pose a threat. One of the soldiers removed the protective helmet from his Hazmat suit and announced to the hostages that their ordeal was finally at an end. A few of the soldiers removed the hostages' blindfolds and the plastic straps that bound the hostages' wrists and feet. The lead soldier telephoned his commanding officer to report that the hostages appeared physically unharmed and to request that the officer send a bomb disposal unit to the Consul General's office. The soldiers then began leading the hostages out of the Consulate.

* * *

In the basement where the Swanson family had taken refuge, the sound coming from the basement television brought Clara's mind back to the present. It was the sound of cheering crowds. On television, armed men who appeared to be dressed in space suits were escorting the Consul General and his staff out of the Consulate in West Jerusalem. From the televised scene at the Consulate, Clara could see that the rain had stopped.

Paul came over to the couch where his parents were sitting. "We can go back to our hotel now," he said.

The Reverend and Clara stared at Paul for a moment before Clara asked, "Do you think this is what we came here to witness?"

Gently assisting his mother as she arose from the couch, Paul said quietly, "I don't think so, Mom."

* * *

At the Shabak headquarters in Jerusalem, Eli Zahavi and Jack Landon chatted while they waited for agents to bring the hostages to them for debriefing. "Admit it, Jack. Some type of weapon system in your Consulate killed those terrorists. What was it? Poisonous micro-projectiles . . . or something more exotic, like a beam weapon?"

Laughing, Jack replied, "You've been watching too many movies, Eli." Then, becoming serious, he said, "It must have been radiation or something toxic that they were exposed to. How soon do you think their autopsies can be completed?"

"We have called in three forensic pathologists," said Eli, "so we should know something in the next couple of days. I'll contact you when we have the results."

* * *

Back in their Jerusalem hotel room, Timothy Swanson was lying in bed next to his sleeping wife. Though tired, he could not sleep, his thoughts racing as he struggled to grasp the significance of the events that he had witnessed. He felt overwhelmed by an emotion that he had not experienced since Paul's childhood, a feeling of *awe*. The events of the day had confirmed what he had long suspected – powerful unseen forces, divine forces, were guiding the life of his adopted son. How strange, he thought, that he, a former agnostic, would be blessed with a son who was closer to God than anyone else he had ever known. Yet, as much as he loved and respected his son, he had never felt that he could understand or identify with him. There had always been a mysterious quality about Paul, a calm inner strength and wisdom beyond his years. He wondered if Paul had inherited that from his natural parents or if it came from his relationship to God. How different Paul's childhood had been than his own, he thought.

Tim began to reflect on his own childhood. He recalled the beatings that he had suffered at the hands of his father, an angry man with an explosive temper. His father called the beatings discipline and said that they would toughen Tim for survival in what his father called "a dog-eat-dog world." Tim's response was hatred toward his father and rebellious, aggressive conduct away from home. Despite learning Christian principles from his mother, who had taken him to church regularly, Tim was involved in fistfights, vandalism, and street drugs by the time he entered high school. His actions, however, were not without consequence, and he struggled with a poor self-image as he bore the weight of his increasing guilt. Then, one of his friends convinced him to try out for the high school football team. Having inherited his father's size and his mother's athletic talent, he soon discovered that he was well suited for the game of football. He became a starting linebacker on his high school football team, his aggressiveness earning him praise instead of getting him in trouble.

Through his accomplishments as an athlete, Tim gradually overcame a lack of self-esteem caused by his childhood beatings. Tim's new self-confidence also carried over into academics. Knowing that his parents could not afford to send him to college, Tim realized that he would have to earn a scholarship. He knew that to increase his chances of earning an athletic scholarship, he would have to improve his grades as well as excel at football. Therefore, with the same commitment that he played the game of football, he began to apply himself to his high school studies. When Tim was not at football practice, he was studying. By end of his senior year in high school, Tim had earned a partial academic scholarship and a full athletic scholarship to Florida State University.

In college, as in high school, Tim relentlessly drove himself to excel athletically and academically. He did not join a fraternity and seldom dated or went to parties, telling himself that he would relax and enjoy life after achieving his goals. He graduated cum laude from Florida State University and gained admission into law school there. He had no real interest in practicing law but viewed a law degree as an achievement worth pursuing. Therefore, he again subordinated his other interests to the pursuit of his goal.

By the time Tim graduated from law school, he had come to doubt much of what his mother had taught him about Christianity. He had heard her say that once people had accepted Christ as their savior, they could not "fall from grace." Yet, in college and in law school Tim had met students who claimed to have rejected their once strongly held Christian beliefs. Some had even become adamant atheists. Tim had also observed the disparity between the professed beliefs of Christians and the lives they led. He began to think that self-interest was the underlying motivation for all human conduct, Christian or otherwise. He recognized that there appeared to be exceptions, as when people came to the aid of others in need. Even then, he thought, the motivation for their actions was probably their selfish need to feel charitable or to receive recognition for being charitable.

After the death of Tim's mother, he began to abandon his long-held Christian beliefs. He no longer perceived a divine purpose or meaning in the events of the world. He looked in the Bible for answers to his questions but soon felt that he would find none there. After all, he thought, in a scientific age it made no sense to search for truth in the primitive writings of ancient, superstitious people. Though he had often heard that the Bible was the inspired word of God, Tim felt that he had learned more from his college textbooks than from reading the Bible or attending church.

Despite his doubts about religion, however, Tim could not bring himself to believe that men live in a godless world. He could not accept the idea that human life had no ultimate significance and was only a random occurrence in a vast, indifferent universe. After all, Tim thought, there must be some reason for the existence of intelligent beings in a seemingly chaotic, ever-changing world. He concluded that the forces that had created man were what men had come to call "God." It appeared to Tim, however, that whatever God might be, God was not a "person" or concerned with the daily lives of people as most Christians believed. In Tim's view, "answered" prayers were probably either coincidences or the results of human intervention. So, although not entirely rejecting the concept of God, Tim settled into a comfortable agnostic apathy, seldom attending church and never discussing his religious beliefs.

During his last year of law school, Tim received employment offers from several Florida law firms of different sizes. He chose a small personal injury firm in his hometown of Tampa, believing that he would help injured people and earn a respectable income. As in his past endeavors, Tim threw himself into the practice of law with persistence and determination. As an associate attorney, he frequently worked twelve-hour days and was the last one to leave the office at night. He earned a reputation as a well-prepared and tenacious advocate for his clients.

After six years of law practice, Tim's hard work earned him promotion to partnership in his firm. However, he felt unsatisfied by his accomplishments as an attorney and disillusioned by the dishonesty that he observed in litigation process, particularly in jury trials. Opposing attorneys typically selected jurors who exhibited a lack of compassion, a lack of intelligence, or apparent antipathy toward his clients or their cases. He frequently encountered opposing expert witnesses whose trial testimony amounted to gross distortion, if not perjury. Tim concluded that fair trials by impartial juries were not the goal of opposing attorneys or the insurance companies who hired them. Tim also observed that his partners did not always pursue their clients' best interests, sometimes misrepresenting the value of cases to convince the clients to take quick but inadequate settlements. He had considered quitting the practice of law before Clara became his legal assistant.

Tim was in his early thirties when his firm hired Clara Marie Bannister to replace his retiring, elderly legal assistant. He was immediately attracted to Clara, a pretty and remarkably well-endowed woman in her late twenties. He was surprised that she was not married and knew from the moment they met that he would break the firm's policy against dating firm personnel. Although he had dated many women, the few who had captured his heart had not fallen in love with him. Tim was happily surprised when he discovered that Clara was also attracted to him. Within weeks, they were dating.

Clara, although raised in a Catholic family, had become a devout Presbyterian. When she asked Tim to accompany her to church, Tim readily accepted, fearing he might lose her if he refused. Tim eventually joined Clara's church, attended regularly, and even participated in the church's social activities. Tim never confided in Clara that he did not share her belief in a "personal" God who watched over people and answered their prayers.

After dating Clara for about a year, Tim proposed marriage. He was surprised and elated when Clara accepted, and they were soon married in their Presbyterian church. When they later discovered that Clara was unable to conceive children, the discovery strengthened Tim's secret belief that a divine being was not concerned with their personal welfare. That belief would change, however, after Paul's adoption.

As Timothy Swanson began to reflect upon how profoundly Paul's life had affected his own, he fell asleep, overcome at last by fatigue from a long, stressful day.

CHAPTER 4
Return to the Dome

On the morning after the U.S. Consulate crisis, Reverend Swanson and Clara were sitting in their Jerusalem hotel room when they heard Paul knocking at their door. After letting Paul into their room, Clara turned on the television to watch the morning news. An Israeli newscaster speaking in Hebrew was discussing the strange conclusion of the hostage crisis while narrating a video-recording of the events outside the U.S. Consulate. The video showed IDF soldiers in Hazmat suits leading the hostages from the Consulate and then showed more soldiers carrying nine body bags from the Consulate on gurneys. At that point, Reverend Swanson changed the television station to an English-language broadcast, and the Swanson family gathered around the television to listen to the interview of an IDF officer who was speaking English. The officer said that the IDF had identified the dead terrorists as Hamas guerrillas associated with a freelance cell known for taking Western hostages. He explained that two Hebrew-speaking Hamas terrorists had initially gained entry to the Consulate by posing as IDF officers. The two terrorists had then used concealed weapons to surprise and subdue the Consulate guards and nearby personnel. After binding, gagging, and blindfolding their initial captives, the two terrorists had signaled seven other terrorists, also disguised as IDF soldiers, who entered the Consulate carrying a suitcase-size bomb. Once inside, the nine terrorists had quickly subdued the Consul General and remaining Consulate personnel.

As the televised interview progressed, the IDF officer described the terrorists' bomb as a small, Russian-made nuclear weapon. He said that it had been fully functional before the IDF bomb specialists disarmed it. He indicated that he did not have precise knowledge of the destructive capability of the bomb but believed that it could have destroyed much of West Jerusalem near the Consulate.

When questioned about the deaths of the terrorists, the IDF officer stated that their cause of death was under investigation. The interviewer asked the officer if high-tech weaponry, such as the miniature, remotely controlled, flying devices that the IDF had been developing, had killed the terrorists. The officer shook his head, saying that although the IDF would like to take credit for thwarting the terrorists, he did not know what had killed them. He mentioned that the Consulate hostages, whom the terrorists blindfolded, had heard sounds suggesting that the terrorists in the Consul

General's office died suddenly and simultaneously. He then concluded the interview by stating that pathologists were performing autopsies on the bodies of the terrorists and that the IDF would announce the results later.

The telecast then switched to a discussion of the previous day's weather. A meteorologist stated that none of the local weather services had forecasted yesterday's rain and that it had been completely unexpected. After describing how seldom Jerusalem received any rainfall in July, he remarked that the rain was "just another inexplicable event in a day of inexplicable events."

As the newscast ended, Reverend Swanson turned to Paul. "Son, we've seen the Dome of the Rock, and we've survived a terrorist plot to bomb the U.S. Consulate. I know God led you to bring us here and that He has protected us. But this is not a safe place, and I'm concerned about your mother's safety. Maybe we should catch a flight home today."

Paul nodded as he said, "I understand, Dad. I don't want to put your lives in jeopardy, and I agree that you and Mom would be safer at home. But I believe that it's God's will that I stay here. That's the only way I can account for the dreams I've been having. I keep seeing that shrine and its golden dome in my dreams while a voice, the same one I've heard in the past, keeps telling me that *I must be here now.*"

Clara then interjected, "Don't worry about me, Tim. I've learned to trust Paul in these things."

After hesitating briefly, the Reverend responded, "I guess I have, too. Where do we go from here, son? Back to the Dome?"

Paul appeared to be preoccupied as he slowly nodded.

* * *

After breakfast at the hotel, the Swanson family boarded a taxicab to return to the Dome of the Rock. As the taxi drove through the crowded ancient streets, Clara's thoughts returned to Paul's childhood. She recalled how Paul's prophetic warning at age eleven about the incident at the performing arts center had a profoundly affected both Tim and her. They had discussed the experience with their church minister, who had commented that God seemed to have a special purpose for Paul and that Tim and Clara should encourage Paul's growth as a Christian. Tim and Clara became more active in their church and took Paul to church services, Sunday school classes, and Wednesday night services. Tim became a Sunday school teacher, and Paul and Tim began to study the Bible together.

By the time of Paul's fourteenth birthday, Tim had become a church elder and was assisting the church minister with communion services. Then, a few months after his fourteenth birthday, Paul had his second prophetic vision. On a Sunday morning, as Clara and Tim were preparing for church, Paul came to their bedroom and told them that he had awakened during the night. He described how, as he lay in bed with his eyes closed, he began seeing vivid images as if he were watching a motion picture. The images showed a violent storm destroying their home, while a familiar voice in Paul's mind told him that he and his parents must take shelter at their church.

Recalling Paul's last vision, Clara immediately became frightened. "When is this going to happen, Paul?" she asked.

"Today, I think."

Tim, who had been listening quietly, walked over to the television in their bedroom and turned the station to the weather channel. The broadcaster was discussing the weather forecasts for various areas of the country. Soon, however, a local weather forecast interrupted the broadcast. According to the forecast, a severe thunderstorm had developed in the next county and was heading toward Tampa. Storm warnings were in effect for the next several hours. Tim turned to Paul and Clara. "I think we'd better pack some suitcases and go to church," he said.

When they had finished loading their car, the sky was dark and the wind was beginning to howl. As they drove to church, the local radio station to which they listened began broadcasting a tornado warning. Though thunderstorms were common in Tampa, tornadoes seldom occurred.

Upon arrival at their church, they saw several church members leaving the church and walking toward the church parking lot. As another family approached the parking lot, Tim asked the father of the family why they were leaving church. The father responded, "There have been storm warnings. We're going home to put up shutters and pick up the loose stuff around the house."

"I think you'd be safer in the church," Tim said. "Please, come with us, and I'll explain why."

H. D. Rogers

Out of respect for Tim, the father reluctantly agreed, and he and his family followed the Swanson family into the church as Tim described Paul's vision to them.

Throughout the church service that morning, the congregation heard the sound of the howling winds and driving rain outside. Flashes of lightning frequently illuminated the chapel windows, and cannonade-like volleys of thunder reverberated through the chapel walls. Structurally, the church was no safer than the homes of its congregation. Yet, Clara and Tim felt secure there, believing that God was protecting their family.

Following the service, the minister and congregation remained in the church chapel until the storm had dissipated. After telephoning a local weather service, a church member announced that the storm warnings had been discontinued. The members of the congregation then left to inspect the damage to their homes.

When Clara and her family arrived at their home, they were not surprised to see that most of the roof was missing and that much of what had been inside their home was damaged or destroyed. As they surveyed the damage and salvaged some of their remaining possessions, they were profoundly thankful that God had spared their lives. Instead of sadness, they experienced elation and a sense of mystery and awe that they had not felt since Paul's previous vision.

For the rest of the year, they lived in an apartment while their home was undergoing extensive repairs. Yet, that year was a time of great happiness for Tim and Clara because God had miraculously spared their lives – and because Paul was their son.

* * *

Clara's mind returned to the present as Reverend Swanson whispered in her ear, "Look at Paul." Clara, who was sitting beside her husband in the backseat of the taxi, studied Paul, who was sitting in front. Paul had bowed his head and appeared to be praying as Clara had often seen him do. However, something was different this time because Paul's head was shaking as if he were shuddering at a frightful sight. The taxi driver seemed to notice this but said nothing. Clara started to reach for Paul's shoulder, but Reverend Swanson stopped her. "*I think he's having another vision,*" whispered the Reverend.

* * *

At a pathology laboratory in Jerusalem, three forensic pathologists were working diligently over the bodies of three of the nine dead terrorists when Eli Zahavi entered the laboratory.

"Have you completed the autopsies, Zelde?" asked Eli, addressing his old friend, Dr. Zelde Meshenberg, the head pathologist.

"No, Eli. We have checked all the bodies for radioactivity, photographed them, externally examined them, measured and weighed them, and x-rayed them. And we have completed internal examinations on three of them."

"Why did you x-ray the bodies?"

"We found no wounds, and there was no visible evidence of significant trauma. But we still wanted to rule out any possible fractures of the skull and spinal column and to determine if any of the bodies contained micro-projectiles. So, we x-rayed them. And, no, we did not find anything significant. They all appear to have been healthy, young men."

"You found no external evidence of injury?"

"No entry wounds; no burns, lacerations, contusions, or visible edema; no ecchymoses, other than typical postmortem lividity; no vomitus; no oral, nasal, or rectal hemorrhage; no cyanosis of skin, mucus membranes, lips, or nail beds."

"What did the *internal* examinations of the three bodies reveal?"

"The internal organs were normal size and weight and showed no evidence of significant disease or trauma, except one man did have emphysematous changes in his lungs. He was probably a cigarette smoker. Otherwise, gross internal inspection revealed nothing other than the usual postmortem changes. And, so far, our microscopic analysis of tissue samples from all organ systems has revealed nothing, either."

"What about poison? Do you think they were poisoned?"

"The toxicology has not come back yet on their blood, urine, gastric contents, and organ tissues. I will contact you immediately when we have the results."

* * *

The taxi carrying the Swanson family stopped within walking distance of the security checkpoint of the western gate to the Temple Mount. Before exiting the taxi, Paul turned to his parents in the backseat. "I've got to get to the Dome quickly. Maybe it would be best if you waited here for me."

Paul's parents looked worried. "But Paul, Clara asked, "why don't you want us with you? Will you be in some kind of danger?"

"I just have to deliver a warning. God will protect me. Please stay here, and I'll be back soon."

"What kind of warning?" asked Reverend Swanson, climbing out of the taxi.

"I must warn the guards to clear the Dome. *It's going to be destroyed – soon.*"

Before the Reverend could respond, Paul began to run toward the Temple Mount.

In the portico of one of the entrances to the Dome of the Rock, Paul removed his shoes before hurriedly entering the huge shrine. Once inside, he approached the first security guard he saw. "Do you speak English?" he asked. The guard shook his head and pointed to another guard. Paul approached the second guard and asked, "Who is in charge of security here?"

The guard appeared suspicious. "Why do you want to know this?" he asked.

"*I must speak with the head of security. I need to warn him about a threat to the shrine.*"

The guard was becoming agitated. "What threat? Who makes this threat?"

"Please, I must speak with the head of security. We need to get everyone out of the shrine. Something terrible is going to happen here."

Sensing Paul's earnestness, the guard pulled a cell phone from his pocket as he motioned to another guard to come over. "Are you American?" he asked.

Paul nodded. "Yes, I'm here with my parents. I see them coming in now," said Paul, pointing toward the couple entering the Dome.

Soon, two Arab guards, employees of the Waqf Islamic Trust that controlled the Temple Mount, escorted Paul and his parents to the entrance where they had left their shoes. After waiting for them to don their shoes, the guards led the Swanson family to one of the many smaller buildings on the Temple Mount. There, they met a middle-aged Arab gentleman who introduced himself as the Chief of Security for the Temple Mount.

"What is this threat you come to warn us about?" inquired the security chief, looking at Reverend Swanson.

"I'd better let my son, Paul, tell you about that."

Turning to Paul, the security chief inquired, "Well, young man, what is this threat?"

"God has led me to come here, and He has given me a vision of the Dome of the Rock being destroyed. He has told me this will occur before the day is over."

Before the security chief could speak, Reverend Swanson interjected, "Paul has had visions before, and they have always proven to be accurate."

"What kind of visions?" asked the security chief, who appeared amused.

"The last time Paul had a vision like this," said the Reverend, "he warned us that our house would be destroyed. A few hours later, it was. He saved our lives, and *he's trying to save lives now.*"

The amused expression vanished from the security chief's face, as his eyes met Reverend Swanson's. "You came here from the United States to warn us that our shrine will be destroyed? *Who* will destroy it?"

Paul then spoke in a calm, measured voice. "*God* has shown me that He will destroy the Dome of the Rock, tearing it to pieces. The nearby mosque will not be damaged, just the Dome of the Rock. I think …"

Shaking his head in disbelief, the security chief interrupted Paul. "You are deceived if you think Allah would destroy a holy place, a place that is sacred to those who worship Him. *The only ones who would destroy our shrine are the Jewish fanatics and their American supporters.* The Jews have tried to destroy our shrine and our mosque many times before. Now, I want you all to leave this place. You do not belong here, and if you stay, I cannot guarantee your safety."

The two guards that had led Paul and his parents to the security chief's office then escorted them to the stairs of the Temple Mount. The English-speaking guard whispered to the other guard in Arabic, "The young infidel thinks he is a prophet." Both guards laughed as Paul and his parents walked down the stairs. Reverend Swanson looked at Clara and shook his head, but Paul did not seem to notice.

At the bottom of the stairs, Paul began walking with his head slightly bowed as if he were praying. When they reached the street, Reverend Swanson took a cell phone from his pocket and telephoned for a taxicab. He wanted to question Paul about his vision of impending destruction, but he decided not to disturb Paul, who still appeared to be praying – or having another vision.

* * *

As they waited for a taxi, Tim pondered the impact of Paul's life on his own. From Paul's early childhood, Tim had recognized unique traits in Paul. Beyond Paul's remarkably even temperament, Tim observed unpretentious self-assurance, kindness, and unselfishness. Tim initially thought that these qualities, though commendable, were largely the result of Paul's youth and naïvete. He suspected that Paul's kindness and unselfishness would diminish as Paul experienced life's trials and tribulations and the selfishness, indifference, and cruelty of others. However, as Paul grew older and encountered injuries, illnesses, and, the cruelty of other children, his quiet self-assurance, kindness, and other noble qualities remained. Paul seemed to have an internal compass, something inside that enabled him to maintain his uncommon serenity and magnanimity in the face of life's conflicts and disappointments.

When Paul began to demonstrate remarkable insight and knowledge beyond his years, Tim searched for logical explanations but found none. Paul's first prophetic vision, which Paul described as a revelation from God, precipitated in Tim months of soul searching and reevaluation of Tim's secret agnosticism. Paul's second prophecy about the destruction of their home finally convinced Tim that God did exist and did care about Tim and his family. For the first time in his life, Tim fully embraced the principles of Christianity and experienced an inner peace and joy from truly believing that his immortal soul would someday be with God.

Tim's new faith affected all aspects of his life. He immediately became much more active in his church. After many prayers and many conversations with Clara and the minister of his own church, Tim decided to quit his law partnership and enroll in a Presbyterian seminary. In so doing, he abandoned his pursuit of worldly wealth and social status and dedicated his life to serving God by teaching others that the Christian faith was indeed the way to peace, joy, and eternal salvation.

While Tim was attending seminary, Paul, who had professed his own belief in Christianity since early childhood, became increasingly interested in his father's new career choice. Paul began studying the Bible and the educational materials from Tim's seminary courses.

The year of Tim's graduation from seminary was also the year of Paul's graduation from high school. Tim was elated when Paul announced before graduation that he would follow in his father's new career path and pursue a career as a Christian minister. In Tim's mind, Paul had the closest relationship to God of anyone whom Tim had ever known. Tim saw in Paul not ascetic piety but simple devotion to Christian precepts, not maudlin sentimentality but profound empathy, not self-importance but quiet inner strength and sense of purpose. While other youths were struggling to define themselves, it appeared to Tim that Paul was preparing himself for some mysterious, preordained role.

Following his graduation from seminary, the pulpit committee of Tim's Presbyterian church invited him to become the church's Assistant Pastor. Tim held that position for almost two years. Then, Tim learned that the pulpit committee of another Presbyterian church was interviewing candidates to replace their retiring pastor. Tim's personality and experience as an assistant pastor convinced the pulpit committee to hire him. Soon, he was Reverend Timothy Swanson, pastor of Unity Presbyterian Church in Oldsmar, Florida, a small town just west of Tampa. Several months later, the Swanson family moved to their new home in Oldsmar.

* * *

When the taxi summoned by Reverend Swanson arrived outside the Temple Mount, Paul, who had been standing quietly with his head bowed and eyes closed, turned to his parents and said, "Our work here is not done. We must go to the local police. Lives will be lost if God's warning is ignored." Reverend Swanson nodded his agreement and, after getting into the taxi, requested the driver to take them to the closest police station.

Minutes later, they were sitting in the office of Jacob Eisin, the District Police Commander in the Jewish Quarter. Commander Eisin, who spoke fluent English, introduced himself to the Swanson family and then asked Reverend Swanson why he had requested to speak with the District Police Commander.

"Sir," responded the Reverend, "we have reason to believe that within the next several hours there will be an explosion or similar event at the Dome of the Rock that will cause much destruction. People in or near the shrine will likely die. The police should clear that area for the rest of the day."

After studying the Reverend's face for a moment, Commander Eisin inquired, "Why do you believe that this will occur? Who told you this?"

Before the Reverend could respond, Paul spoke. "Sir, do you believe that God sometimes warns people about future events?"

"Why? Has God warned you that the Dome of the Rock will be attacked?" inquired Commander Eisin.

"No," responded Paul, "He has shown me a vision of it being destroyed – by Him. I know this is hard for you to believe, but I am certain that *God will destroy the Dome of the Rock before the day is over.*"

Detecting the beginning of a smile on the Commander Eisin's face, Reverend Swanson interjected, "Nine years ago, my son warned my wife and I that our home would be destroyed, and several hours later it was destroyed by a tornado. Yesterday, when terrorists took over the U.S. Consulate and threatened to detonate an atomic bomb, Paul told us that the crisis would end when the rain stopped. Two hours later, when the rain had stopped, the crisis was over. Now, he tells us that God will destroy the Dome of the Rock. He could be mistaken, but I would not want to take that chance if I were you."

Politely, Commander Eisin responded, "I can see that you and your son have good intentions and that you are sincere. And this would not be the first time that the Islamic shrine was threatened. Many Israelis would like to see it destroyed, and many believe that someday God will destroy it. But I cannot force the Islamic trust that controls the Temple Mount to close it down. I can only relate your warning to them. I will also tell my officers to warn people trying to enter the Temple Mount that a security alert is in effect for the rest of the day. Now, I must get back to my duties. Thank you for bringing this information to me." Then, Commander Eisin summoned an officer to escort the Reverend and his family from his office.

As they waited for a taxi outside the police station, Reverend Swanson noticed that the wind was changing and the sky was becoming darker. Turning to Paul, he said, "You've done your best to warn them. Now it's in God's hands."

CHAPTER 5
Supercell

By the time Paul and his parents had returned to their hotel, the mid-afternoon Jerusalem sky was as dark as night and rain was beginning to fall. Paul accompanied his parents to their room where they huddled around the television and waited for news of the events that would unfold. Eventually, a weather bulletin interrupted the regular broadcast to announce that a thunderstorm warning was in effect for Jerusalem. Later, during another broadcast interruption, a weather commentator announced, "An unusual low pressure system has formed over the Mediterranean Sea and has generated a thunderstorm that will soon come ashore between Holon and Ashdod. The storm is moving rapidly and should pass over Jerusalem in a few hours. So far, the storm has produced only strong winds, lightning, and heavy rains. However, local meteorologists have indicated that the storm appears to be developing into a '*supercell*' that could spawn tornadoes."

* * *

While Paul and his father continued to watch television for further news of the coming storm, Clara walked over to a chair and sat, looking through a window into the menacing darkness of the overcast sky. The darkness somehow reminded her of the troubled years that she had experienced in her own life. She had been raised in Cleveland, the second of three children in a middle-class, Irish-Catholic family. Her two brothers had been more achievement-oriented than she had been. Both brothers had obtained college degrees and become successful businessmen. Clara, though intelligent, had not been interested in academic achievement. She had been close to her mother and had assimilated her mother's family orientation and Christian values. During her childhood, Clara's Christian upbringing had given her life meaning and provided her with a sense of security. Later, it became the source of her guilt and shame.

Clara was a pretty child but very skinny. She did not blossom as a woman until she attended community college. By age twenty she was remarkably voluptuous and the object of many male fantasies. After obtaining her associate of arts degree, she obtained a position as a trainee legal assistant at a local law firm. She politely rejected the advances of the firm's attorneys, most of them married. She eventually met a young attorney who sometimes visited one of the partners in her firm. He was handsome and charming, and Clara soon fell under his spell. Clara was unaware of his reputation as a ladies' man. She believed that he was in love with her and wanted to marry her.

By the time Clara became aware that she was pregnant, she had learned from a friend about her lover's many infidelities. When she confronted him about them, he seemed more amused than ashamed. Clara never revealed her pregnancy to him or anyone else. Because of her strict upbringing, she believed that giving birth to a child out of wedlock would forever stigmatize her and that she would no longer be attractive to the kind of man that she hoped to marry. After weeks of agonizing over her dilemma, Clara decided to end the pregnancy. She knew that many people, including Christians, supported a woman's right to terminate a pregnancy. Clara, however, had been raised a devout Catholic, and after the abortion, no matter how much she tried to rationalize her decision, she could not escape her feelings of guilt and shame. In Clara's mind, she had not only been foolish and immoral, she had also become a murderess.

For the next few years, Clara maintained only casual relationships with men. She often prayed for forgiveness for what she considered a mortal sin, and she frequently found herself sobbing at the thought that she had killed her unborn child. Then, Clara decided that she needed a change in her life, and she moved to Tampa where one of her brothers was living. After interviewing with several law firms, she accepted a position with Tim's firm as his legal assistant. Clara felt comfortable with Tim and could see that he was quite attracted to her. Although Tim was not a handsome man, he was intelligent and strong. More important to Clara, Tim was a gentleman of integrity, a man whom she could trust. Soon they were dating, and a year later, they were married.

Clara never told Tim or anyone else about her abortion, and she continued to experience pangs of guilt over taking an innocent life. When she and Tim discovered that she could no longer conceive children, Clara believed that her infertility was God's punishment for her secret transgression. She again became depressed, fearing that God would never forgive her. After Paul's adoption, however, Clara felt as if God had lifted the curse and forgiven her, because He had entrusted her with this very special child.

* * *

At the Shabak headquarters in Jerusalem, CIA agent Jack Landon was sitting in the office of Eli Zahavi. "So, what's the word on the autopsies, Eli?"

"The pathologists have not found anything, Jack – no evidence of serious injury; no evidence of significant illness. Even microscopically, they have found nothing that could cause death. But toxicology tests are being done, and the tests may reveal a poison of some kind."

"You won't mind if we fly in some of our own people to re-examine the bodies?"

"I'm sure my government will cooperate. Would your people prefer to examine the bodies here, or have one of them flown to the U.S.?"

"I'll have to get back to you on that."

"You know, Jack, the way those terrorists died . . . I think God had a hand in stopping that terrorist attack."

Turning to leave, Jack smiled and said, "I'll believe in miracles when I see one."

* * *

Outside a small building on the Temple Mount, the Chief of Security surveyed the ominous sky. He had heard the storm warnings and recalled the events of that morning. "Arrogant fool," he muttered to himself as he reflected upon Paul's warning. The young American, he thought to himself, must have heard an earlier weather report and guessed that storms would pass through this area. The Dome of the Rock had withstood hundreds of storms, earthquakes, and attacks by infidels. One more storm was hardly a cause for concern. Still, he thought, the storm did pose a threat to the safety of visitors to the Temple Mount. Using his cell phone, the Chief ordered the security guards to close the Temple Mount for the rest of the day. Then, the Chief walked into the Dome of the Rock.

Inside the shrine, the Chief of Security told the remaining security guards that they could go home. He alone would remain to guard the empty shrine during the storm. After locking the doors to the shrine's entrances, the Chief walked around the dimly lit shrine's outer ambulatory, listening to the rising howl of the wind outside and the increasing volleys of thunder. Through the windows beneath the shrine's dome, he could see bright flashes of lightning, each casting eerie shadows across the jagged surface of the Rock below.

A half hour later, as he walked toward the balustrade surrounding the Rock, the Chief heard a loud noise that startled him. The noise reminded him of the sound of an approaching freight train. Moving swiftly toward the balustrade, the Chief noticed that the noise had become much louder and was chaotically interspersed with the sound of creaking timbers and then the sound of breaking glass. Suddenly, he felt wind swirling about him, and his eardrums popped as if he were in a descending airplane. He instinctively ran to the safest nearby place, the cave beneath the Rock, the cave known as the Well of Souls. As he stumbled down the stairs into the Well of Souls, all lights in the shrine were suddenly extinguished, enveloping the terrified Chief in total darkness. The noise above was now a deafening roar as the terrible, swirling winds tore away huge sections of the golden dome and the enormous roof of the ancient shrine. Paralyzed by fear, the Chief lay prone on the floor of the Well of Souls with eyes closed tightly and hands clasped over ears. For several minutes, he felt as if he were trapped inside a prolonged explosion as every loose object around him was swept upward toward the entrance to Well of Souls. While the Chief lay praying to Allah for his life to be spared, a giant strobe-lit funnel of wind and lightning furiously ripped apart the massive shrine, scattering its pieces into the blackness of the sky.

CHAPTER 6
Emergence of the Prophet

On the morning after the storm, television and radio stations throughout the Middle East were broadcasting the news that a tornado spawned by a supercell storm had destroyed the Dome of the Rock. Telecasts showed film footage of the piles of rubble that were the only residue of the huge Islamic shrine. Commentators expressed amazement that there were no reported deaths and that the tornado had not significantly damaged the nearby al-Aqsa Mosque or any other structure on the Temple Mount. Television meteorologists marveled at the strength of the tornado, some estimating that it had been an F-6 on the Fujita Scale, making it the most powerful ever recorded. Yet, the tornado had lasted less than an hour, and the supercell that had produced it had mysteriously subsided a few hours later.

On the English-language station watched by the Swanson family, a television reporter interviewed a local Rabbi. "Clearly, this is a sign from God," said the Rabbi, "and the long-awaited fulfillment of prophecy. God has cleared the way for the building of the Third Temple."

Then, the reporter interviewed a local Arab businessman. "I think the storm was a natural phenomenon, just like the earthquakes that have afflicted us for centuries."

The television camera suddenly turned to the reporter himself, who announced, "We now have breaking news. We are taking you live to the Temple Mount, where a survivor has been found underneath the ruins of the Dome of the Rock." The scene switched to the Temple Mount, where reporters holding microphones surrounded an Arab gentleman familiar to the Swanson family. Unshaven and disheveled, the Chief of Security for the Temple Mount was speaking excitedly to the reporters. "Through the grace of Allah, I was protected from the evil destruction that befell our holy shrine. The noise was like . . . the screams of a thousand demons. And then there was an explosion. Satan and his allies have destroyed our shrine, but Allah has protected al-Aqsa, our place of worship. And, with the help of Allah, we will rebuild the Dome of the Rock."

One of the reporters then asked, "What did you mean by your statement that 'allies' of Satan were involved in the shrine's destruction?"

"I have reason to believe that Americans were somehow involved in this. Otherwise, how could an American have told me yesterday morning that this evil would occur before the day was over? And the noise . . . I think a bomb was exploded during the storm!"

From that point, the reporters barraged the Chief of Security with questions about the American who had foretold the shrine's destruction and about the Chief's theory that explosives, rather than the tornado, had destroyed the shrine.

Paul and his parents sat in stunned silence listening to the Chief of Security. Then, Clara Swanson said, "Don't worry Paul, everyone can see that man is just confused and hates Americans."

"The Bible tells us," offered the Reverend, "that men of God have foreseen storms before. Thousands of years ago, Isaiah, Jeremiah, and Ezekiel all foretold of storms sent by God to accomplish His purposes on earth."

"Well, Paul," said Clara, "I guess we've now seen why God led you to come here. The newsman on TV mentioned there were no deaths, so your warning probably saved lives."

After reflecting momentarily, Paul said, "I think what we've seen is only the beginning of something. I believe that . . ."

A loud knock at the door interrupted Paul in mid-sentence. Reverend Swanson walked to the door and opened it. Two men stood at the door. "Hello, Mr. Swanson, my name is Eli Zahavi, and this is Jack Landon. I am with Israel's internal security agency, and Mr. Landon is an agent of your government," he said as he displayed an identification card. "May Agent Landon and I come in?"

"Why, certainly," answered the Reverend, appearing somewhat surprised. After letting the men into the room, the Reverend introduced Clara and Paul to them. "Now, what can I do for you?" he asked.

"Well, it's about your conversation with the District Police Commander yesterday," responded Eli. "He contacted us about it. He said you and your son warned him about what would happen to the Dome of the Rock. He also said that you told him that your son had predicted it and had also predicted what happened at the U.S. Consulate."

"I didn't know what would happen inside the Consulate," Paul interjected. "God just told me that we should not be afraid because He would end the crisis at the Consulate before the rain stopped."

"Have you made other predictions that came true?" inquired Agent Landon.

Before Paul could answer, the Reverend suggested, "Why don't we go some place where we can all sit down? There's not much room in here, and it sounds like you have a lot of questions."

"Ah, an excellent idea," said Eli. "Would you mind accompanying us to Shabak headquarters in Jerusalem? It would only be for an hour or so, and we would bring you back here afterward."

The Reverend looked at Clara and Paul, who both nodded. The Swanson family then followed the two agents to their vehicle.

* * *

After they arrived at the Shabak headquarters, Eli Zahavi, pointing toward a group standing outside the entrance, spoke quietly to the Swanson family. "It appears we have some tenacious paparazzi today. Looks like the same group that was here when we left. Just ignore them and follow me." He then led them past the group of reporters that was surrounding a Shabak agent who appeared to be answering their questions. One of the reporters turned and approached Eli and his companions. "*Are these the Americans?*" she asked. Eli shook his head and waived her away as he led the Swanson family and Jack Landon to the entrance of the Shabak headquarters. The reporter's reference to "Americans," however, caught the attention of the other paparazzi, some of whom began photographing and filming Paul and his parents as they entered the compound. "I'm sorry," said Eli, "but I'm afraid publicity was inevitable under the circumstances."

Once they were in his office, Eli apologized to the Swanson family for the inconvenience that he had caused by interrupting their vacation. He explained that it was his duty to investigate all possible leads concerning the circumstances surrounding the attack on the U.S. Consulate, and he thanked the Swanson's for their cooperation. Then, Eli politely began the interrogation by questioning Reverend Swanson. "As I understand it, you and your family arrived in Jerusalem on the day before the attack."

"Yes," said the Reverend, "our flight arrived during the evening before the attack. The next day we took a tour bus to visit various historic sites, including the Dome of the Rock. Actually, we came to Jerusalem because our son, who was home from seminary, felt God was leading him to visit that shrine. Clara and I had wanted to visit Israel so we came with Paul."

Turning to Paul, Eli asked, "What caused you to believe that God was leading you to visit an Islamic shrine?"

"I had been having very vivid dreams in which I was walking toward the Dome of the Rock while a voice was telling me that visiting the shrine was part of God's plan for my life and that I must go there soon."

"How were you able to recognize the shrine in your dreams?" asked Eli.

"I'd seen pictures of it in one of my textbooks at seminary."

"Did you also dream about the destruction of the shrine?"

"Not until yesterday. As we went to visit the Dome of the Rock for the second time, I had a vision in which I saw the shrine being torn apart. And the voice of God told me that I must warn the shrine guards and visitors that the Dome of the Rock would be destroyed before the day was over."

"So, young man," asked Eli Zahavi, "do you think it was a mere coincidence that on the day after Islamic terrorists attacked a U.S. Consulate, you, a U.S. citizen, accurately predicted the destruction of an Islamic shrine?"

"Mr. Zahavi," interrupted the Reverend, "surely you don't think we had anything to do with the destruction of the shrine? You know we did not cause the tornado."

"I do not suspect you of being terrorists. But Paul had knowledge of these events before they occurred, and I am merely trying to learn the source of his knowledge."

Turning back to Paul, Eli Zahavi continued, "Other than the dreams you've had, did you see, overhear, or read anything that caused you to make your predictions?"

"No, nothing, and I'd be happy to take a polygraph examination if you doubt anything I've told you."

"I don't think that will be necessary," replied Eli Zahavi. "Has God told you why the events of the past two days occurred?"

"Not specifically, but . . . when God told me to warn people that the Dome of the Rock would be destroyed, He said I must deliver that message to save men's lives. Then, He said that I would soon deliver another message that would change men's lives. He has not yet revealed that message to me, but I believe He soon will."

"I hope you will call me if you receive any further warnings concerning Jerusalem," said Eli Zahavi, handing Paul a card with his name and telephone number. "Do you have any questions, Agent Landon?"

"Tell me, Paul," asked Jack Landon, "has God told you what happened to the terrorists inside the Consulate?"

"No. After we heard about the bomb, God just told me that He would protect us from it and that the crisis would end by the time the rain had stopped."

"I see," said Jack, his face expressionless.

Extending his hand to shake Paul's, Eli said, "I think we're done here."

As Eli stood and extended his hand to Reverend Swanson, the Reverend asked, "How did the terrorists die?"

"We don't know," said Eli. "Follow me. I'll take you out through a back entrance of our compound. One of our agents will drive you back to your hotel."

* * *

When the Shabak driver left the Swanson family in front of their hotel, paparazzi were waiting. "What should we do about them?" asked Clara as a group of reporters and photographers approached.

Before the Reverend could answer, Paul said, "If I'm going to deliver a future message to change the lives of men, I may as well get used to talking to the media. This is as good a time as any."

Reverend Swanson just smiled and nodded. He then escorted Clara into the hotel while Paul stayed outside, surrounded by cameras and microphones, answering questions about the revelations that he had received from God.

* * *

Back in his office at the Shabak headquarters, Eli Zahavi was conversing with Jack Landon when a woman in a physician's smock entered the office. "Hello, Eli, I understand you want to speak with me," she said.

"Yes, come in Zelde. I'd like you to meet Agent Jack Landon. He's the CIA agent investigating the Consulate incident. Jack, this is Dr. Zelde Meshenberg, the chief pathologist who is supervising the autopsies of the terrorists involved in the Consulate attack."

"I'm pleased to meet you Dr. Meshenberg."

"And I you, Agent Landon," replied Dr. Meshenberg. "I assume you gentlemen want to discuss the status of the autopsies."

"You assume correctly, Zelde," said Eli. "Jack and I would like to know if you've made any further progress in determining the cause of death."

"We've done microscopic examinations of specimens from every major organ system of all nine men," replied Zelde. "We've also performed toxicology screens of blood, urine, and stomach contents of all nine. We've screened for every known pathogen and toxin. *We've identified nothing that would account for their deaths.* I've never seen anything like it. I have no explanation."

"So, you're telling us that nine healthy men suddenly dropped dead for no reason?" asked Jack.

"No, sir. I'm sure there is a reason . . . of some kind. What I'm saying is that very thorough autopsies have not revealed that reason. We did find pathologic conditions in three men. One had a duodenal ulcer, and two others had emphysema. But we could not identify a cause of death in any of them."

"Thank you, Zelde," said Eli. "Any questions, Jack?"

"No, but I do have a request. I've been discussing the situation with my people. We'd like to have a couple of the bodies flown to a path lab in the States. It won't hurt to have two labs working on this."

"Fine," said Eli. "Have your lab contact Dr. Meshenberg to make the necessary arrangements for transport." Then, turning to Dr. Meshenberg, he said, "I think that's all we need for now, Zelde."

After Dr. Meshenberg left his office, Eli and Jack resumed their prior conversation. "The Swansons seem like nice people to me, Jack. I don't think they had any involvement in the Consulate incident."

Jack smiled and said, "So, you think Paul Swanson is a prophet."

"Don't be so cynical, Jack. There have been Jewish and Christian prophets in the past."

"I don't think 'cynical' is the right word. 'Realistic' is more accurate. All of those supposed prophets seem to have had the same modus operandi. They made lots of vague predictions that were projections based upon past events. Then, they took credit for the few that turned out to be correct and pretended that they never made the rest. That's what we don't hear about – all the bogus predictions that never came true."

"Well, my cynical friend," responded Eli, "as usual, you see the glass as half empty. Apparently, you don't believe in divine inspiration." Then, changing the subject, Eli asked, "Have your people done a background check on Paul Swanson?"

"We've checked out the whole family. They seem to be upstanding citizens although some of the people we've interviewed think Paul Swanson is a little on the weird side."

"Why, because he made predictions that were accurate?" asked Eli.

"People who knew the kid in grade school told us that he got really religious and quit hanging out with the other kids. Some of his college classmates told us he had a real babe for a girlfriend but recently broke up with her. The girlfriend told one of our people that the kid told her that he loved her but that God had chosen him for a mission that could put him and those close to him in danger. That sounds to me, Eli, like the profile of a paranoid, religious nut and possible terrorist."

"So, being religious makes him a potential terrorist? If that were so, most Christians and Jews would be potential terrorists. I think you have a problem with religion, Jack."

"Well, look at the people who are causing most of political unrest and violence in the world today – religious fanatics who think they are doing God's will."

"Fanatics, yes. Godly, no. Those people, consciously or unconsciously, are using religion as an excuse to perpetrate violent and criminal acts to achieve their own selfish objectives or the geopolitical agendas of their leaders. They are not godly people."

"That we agree on, Eli. But, in Paul Swanson's case, you have to admit that his auditory and visual hallucinations and his grandiose, delusional ideas sound psychotic."

"I suppose that you think that Jesus and the prophets of the Bible were delusional and psychotic."

"Well, Eli, you have your beliefs, and I have mine. In any event, my people are watching the young prophet, and we're also doing a further background check on him. He's an adopted child, so we're trying to identify his natural parents. Maybe insanity runs in the family."

* * *

Back in their hotel room, Reverend and Clara Swanson were talking to Paul. "If we stay here now, Paul," said Clara, "we'll be hounded by Israeli reporters wherever we go."

"Besides, Paul," said the Reverend, "after what the Chief of Security for that shrine said on television, the Muslims around here may think we're somehow involved in their shrine's destruction. So, your mother and I think we'd all be safer if we returned home."

In the background, a television news anchorman announced that the evening newscast would include a recorded interview with the American prophet who had predicted the destruction of the Dome of the Rock. This caught the attention of Clara, who suggested to the Reverend and Paul that they continue their discussion after the newscast.

Gathered around the television, the Swanson family watched a telecast of Paul's earlier interview in front of their hotel. Surrounded by reporters, Paul was patiently answering their questions about his reasons for coming to Jerusalem, about rumors that he had predicted the end of the crisis at the U.S. Consulate, and about how he had predicted the destruction of the Islamic shrine. Then, the questioning turned to Paul's interpretation of God's purpose in causing these events. "I don't pretend to know God's purpose," said Paul, "but I see that His warnings were intended to save lives – not just the lives of Christians and Jews but the lives of Muslims, as well. Even His taking of the lives of those who attacked the Consulate was to save the lives of many more people."

"Yes," shouted one reporter, "but what about the destruction of the Dome? Was that not the first step in the fulfillment of the prophecy that the Messiah will come and the Third Temple be erected?"

"I don't know why God destroyed the Dome of the Rock but protected the nearby mosque. God has not spoken to me about that. But, as to the future, men have often predicted the coming of the Messiah and the end of the world – and they have always been wrong."

"Have you made any further predictions?" asked another reporter.

"No, God has not revealed anything else to me – but I believe that He will."

"What about the strange weather that we've been having?" inquired yet another reporter. "Will we have more tornadoes?"

"I really don't know. I'd tell you if I did. Well, please excuse me. I need to rejoin my family now," said Paul, as he held up his hands to cut off further questions.

CHAPTER 7
Revelation

In the darkness of the moonless night, while the Swanson family slept in their hotel rooms, a helicopter descended toward the southern end of the Temple Mount. The descent of the helicopter ceased about one hundred fifty meters above the dome of the al-Aqsa Mosque. Hearing the noise from the helicopter, Arab security guards in the mosque came out to investigate. The guards shined their flashlights into the sky, futilely attempting to determine whether it was a news or police helicopter that hovered above the mosque. Suddenly, there was a bright flash from the helicopter, and the guards heard the sound of an anti-tank rocket grenade as it streaked over the roof of the ancient mosque barely missing its gray dome. When the rocket grenade exploded on the Temple Mount behind the mosque, the startled guards dove to the ground. Sprawled on the ground, they fearfully listened for the sound of another rocket grenade. Instead, they heard the deafening roar of a second, much larger explosion that shook the ground violently and produced a giant, blinding ball of fire in the black sky above the mosque. The explosion obliterated the helicopter, causing a shower of fiery debris, which fell on and around the mosque but caused only superficial damage to its roof. Soon, the Jerusalem police arrived on the scene and began questioning the Arab security guards.

* * *

Later that night, as Paul slept in his hotel room, he began to have a very vivid dream. In the dream, he was touring the Temple Mount, led by a guide whom he could hear but not see. The guide's voice was deep and resonant but barely louder than a whisper as it drew Paul's attention and created a feeling of intimacy. Paul recognized the guide's voice from his previous dreams. God was his guide on this tour.

As Paul climbed the stairs to the Temple Mount, God said to him, "Man is a work in progress, Paul. Of all the creatures in this universe, man alone was created with the capacity to discover the laws that govern the physical world, to contemplate the purpose of his own existence, to ponder My existence and his relationship to Me, and to honor Me by subordinating his instinctual urges to obey the moral laws that I have revealed to him. These moral laws are to protect man, to prevent him from destroying himself, and to enable him to continue on the path of his enlightenment until he attains the goal that I have set for him.

"To exist in the physical world, man must have a physical body as must all other creatures of the physical world. Instinctual urges are inherent in the physical body as gravity is inherent in the matter of the physical world. The instinctual urges themselves are not sin, but the failure to control them in accordance with My laws is. Man's failure to control his instinctual urges has often caused man to detour from the path to My goal for man. However, I have given man the ability to control his instinctual urges and the ability to discover the physical and moral laws that will lead him to My goal.

"It is necessary that man find his own way to My goal. For this reason I have seldom intervened in the affairs of this world. However, mankind is now on a path to destroy itself and this world, and I will not allow that to happen. Though I created this world and the laws by which it operates, I am not part of it. I have intervened in its affairs through other men to whom I have spoken, and I once entered it through My conduit, Jesus of Nazareth. I now speak to you, Paul, because you must carry a message to men so that they can continue their progress toward the destiny that I have planned."

In his dream, Paul and his invisible guide reached the top of the Temple Mount. Surveying the buildings before him, Paul saw the al-Aqsa Mosque to the south. North of the mosque was another building, a temple marked with a large Star of David. To the north of the temple was a church that was marked with a large cross. The three buildings were of equal size and connected by arcades. Crowds of people were walking freely through the arcades from one building to the other. There were no security guards or police. As Paul studied this scene, he heard God's voice saying, "These are places where men come to learn about Me and My moral laws. Through Jesus of Nazareth, I told men that My moral laws require that men treat others as they want to be treated by others. Yet, seldom do men guide their lives by this law. Even leaders of religions, who are supposed to teach My moral laws, have forgotten this law and now teach hatred and intolerance toward men who follow other religions. Men should never use religion as an excuse for violence toward other men or their religions. No religion possesses all of My truths, and men of all religions have often strayed far from the path to My goal. Any religion that truly honors Me deserves the respect of all other religions. The three religions that you see represented before you on the Temple Mount must learn to coexist in peace and to honor Me by refraining from violence against men who follow other religions. Those who advocate violence in My name or the name of any religion are violating My moral laws. I will no longer allow men to commit violence in My name or in the name of religion. This is the message that you, Paul, must bring to the world."

* * *

The next morning, after Eli Zahavi arrived at the Shabak headquarters, he received a visit from District Police Commander Jacob Eisin. "As you have heard," said Commander Eisin, "last night there was incident at the Temple Mount. This morning we began recovering debris from the helicopter that exploded over al-Aqsa. The evidence corroborates the eyewitness accounts that the helicopter was attacking al-Aqsa when something caused the helicopter to explode. One eyewitness said

that a bolt of lightning struck the helicopter, but that appears unlikely. We think something else caused the explosion by setting off the rocket grenades that were onboard. Before it becomes public information, I thought you should know that debris from the helicopter leads us to believe that it was an IDF attack helicopter. The Waqf is already raising hell and threatening retaliation. I need to know whether the helicopter was stolen or the IDF had a renegade pilot."

"One of our attack helicopters is missing, and so is an IDF pilot," Eli responded. "I've learned that the pilot was a member of the Temple Mount Loyalists, who, as you know, advocate taking back the Temple Mount. But he had a good record with us. We had no reason to suspect he was capable of a terrorist act against a civilian target."

"So, where do we go from here?" asked Commander Eisin.

"I'll have one of our people contact the Waqf and issue an apology. We'll tell them that the pilot was apparently mentally unstable and took the helicopter without authorization. And we'll assure them that we will take precautions to prevent such incidents from ever occurring again. All of which will be true. When you're contacted by the news media, just tell them the same thing. There's no point in trying to cover this up. If we did, the truth would eventually come out, and we'd look like conspirators."

"Very well," said Commander Eisin. "I've instructed the investigating officers to direct the media to me with their questions." Then, shaking his head, he added, "By the way, the Arabs are saying that the helicopter was destroyed by Allah."

"Lately," said Eli, "there have been a lot . . ."

Suddenly, the door to Eli Zahavi's office opened, cutting him off at mid-sentence. Eli's secretary stepped into the office and said, "Please excuse my intrusion, but there's something on television I think you'll both want to see."

As Eli and Commander Eisin followed the secretary into a nearby room, they heard a familiar voice coming from the television. Paul Swanson was telling a group of local reporters that he had received another vision in which God had entrusted him with an important "message for mankind."

"Mr. Swanson," asked one reporter, "What is this message that you say God has asked you to deliver to us? Is something else going to happen at the Temple Mount?"

"As I slept last night, God spoke to me about His reason for bringing me here and about His reasons for causing the events that have been occurring here. This morning, when I heard the news about the attack on al-Aqsa, I knew that God had stopped that attack just as he stopped the attack on the U.S. Consulate. God told me that men must never again use religion as an excuse for violence toward others. He told me that although He seldom interferes in the affairs of this world, He would no longer allow men to commit violent acts in His name or the name of any religion. He is intervening because He sees that mankind has strayed from the path to God's goal for man and is on a path to destruction. He is not going to allow that to happen. I believe that is why God intervened at the Consulate and at the al-Aqsa Mosque.

"God told me that He is the God worshipped by Jews, Muslims, and Christians. He showed me a vision of the Temple Mount in the future. Al-Aqsa was still there; next to al-Aqsa was a Jewish temple where the Dome of the Rock once stood; and next to the temple was a Christian church. Arcades connected the churches, and worshipers were moving freely through the arcades without the presence of security guards. This was God's way of telling us that the followers of these religions must learn to coexist in peace. To achieve that peace, God has commanded that we follow a simple principle that He conveyed to us through Jesus Christ thousands of years ago: We must learn to treat others as we want them to treat us."

While Paul was speaking, all the reporters were listening in stunned silence. For several seconds afterward, the silence continued as they considered his words. Finally, one asked, "Does this mean that God will protect Israel against Islamic terrorists?"

Before Paul could answer, an Arab reporter asked, "And will Allah protect the Palestinians against attacks by the Jews?"

Paul responded, "God has revealed that He will not tolerate religiously motivated aggression from anyone. He wants Jews, Muslims, and Christians to peacefully pursue the path toward spiritual enlightenment as to God's goal for man. You have seen what God can do to those who attempt violent acts toward others in the name of their religions. Unfortunately, those who are filled with hatred toward other religions and those who use their religious beliefs as an excuse to pursue their own selfish ends will likely reject the message that I have brought to you. Their acts of violence will bring about their destruction. That is all I can tell you. Thank you for giving me this opportunity to deliver God's message. Please broadcast it to the world." Paul then raised his hands to cut off further questions before he made his way through the reporters toward the elevators in the hotel lobby.

"If only it were all so simple," mumbled Eli Zahavi, turning away from the television on which he had been watching Paul's interview. Then, gesturing to Commander Eisin to accompany him back to his office, he said, "Looks like the young prophet is having his fifteen minutes of fame."

* * *

During the telecast of Paul Swanson's interview, a Waqf maintenance crew at the Temple Mount was removing the debris from the helicopter explosion. The maintenance workers were discussing the miraculous way in which Allah had protected the al-Aqsa Mosque from the aerial assault. One of the workers climbed a ladder to the roof of the Mosque and began tossing debris from the roof. As he worked his way around the roof, the worker came upon a nearly transparent object that resembled the tip of a large bird's wing. After climbing down from the roof, the worker showed this object the other workers. One suggested that it might be part of the *wing of an angel* sent by Allah to protect the mosque. Others expressed their agreement with this explanation. Having decided the object was a divine relic, the workers took it to the Temple Mount's Chief of Security for safekeeping. Recognizing the uniqueness of the object, the Chief's first inclination was to turn it over to the Waqf. After reflecting upon his meager salary and the object's potential value, the Chief elected to place it in his office safe while he contemplated the manner of its eventual disposition.

CHAPTER 8
Shield of God

Later that morning, Paul was packing his suitcases in his hotel room while his parents stood nearby. "We're proud of what you've done here, Paul," said Reverend Swanson, "but we must return home, and we just cannot afford to pay for you to stay here indefinitely."

"Oh, I understand, Dad. I've done what God asked me to do. I've delivered His message. I don't see any further reason to stay here."

"We're so glad you're returning with us, Paul. This place just seems so unsafe," said Clara.

As Paul finished packing, the Reverend said, "Well, the taxi should be here soon. We'd better go down to the lobby. I just hope we're not mobbed by reporters again."

When the Swanson family entered the hotel lobby, a crowd of reporters and photographers was waiting for them. While the Reverend and Clara stood nearby, Paul patiently responded to their questions by stating that he had told them everything that he could recall about what God had revealed to him. He repeatedly stated that he was neither psychic nor clairvoyant and knew nothing more about the future than what God had revealed. When the taxi arrived, Paul stated that if he received any further revelations, he was certain that the reporters would be hearing about them. Paul then extricated himself from the reporters and joined his parents as they departed in the taxi for Ben Gurion International Airport, forty kilometers northwest of Jerusalem.

* * *

As the taxi drove through Jerusalem, the Swanson family was unaware that two other vehicles, a small van and a car, were following the taxi at a distance. Soon, their taxi entered Highway 1 and headed toward Tel Aviv. In the traffic behind them, the van began to move up closer to the taxi. When the taxi passed the exit to Latrun, the van was only two hundred meters behind. About a kilometer before the exit to Ben Sheman, the van accelerated and began to overtake the taxi from the inside lane of Highway 1. As the van drew within fifty meters of the taxi, a passenger in the van stood up, extending his torso through the van's retracted sunroof. The car that had been following the taxi at a distance began to accelerate to catch up with the van. Before the car could reach the van, the passenger standing in the van had lifted a grenade-launcher through the van's sunroof and was aiming it in the direction of the taxi carrying the Swanson family. Suddenly, the man with the grenade-launcher appeared to collapse into the van as he fired a rocket-propelled grenade. The grenade-launcher fell from the roof of the van while the grenade flew past the rear of the taxi, exploding alongside the highway. The van veered sharply toward the outside lanes, its driver slumped over the steering wheel. The van crashed through a barrier near the exit to Ben Sheman, flipped over and slid to a stop on its side. The car that had been following the taxi pulled into the exit lane and drove up to the crashed van.

When the explosion occurred, Reverend Swanson, who was sitting with Clara in the back seat, instinctively grabbed Clara and pulled her toward him. Paul turned to look in the direction of the explosion and then in the direction of the crashing van. He asked the taxi driver if they should stop to see if the occupants of the van had been injured. The driver responded, "No, they may be terrorists," and kept driving to Ben Gurion International Airport. The Reverend and Clara expressed their agreement with the driver and assured Paul that other cars had exited the highway and were in better position to check on the accident scene.

* * *

Later, while Ben Sheman police interviewed witnesses at the scene of the accident, the driver of the car that had been following the Swanson family telephoned Jack Landon. "You aren't going to believe what just happened," he said.

"Don't keep me in suspense," replied Jack.

"The kid and his parents are leaving Israel. Apparently, they're flying home today. So, I'm following them to the airport when I notice a van accelerating to catch up with their taxi. Then, I see a guy stand up through the van's sunroof and aim a grenade-launcher at the taxi. As I'm trying to catch up to the van, the guy with the grenade-launcher appears to collapse as he fires a rocket grenade. Then, the van suddenly swerves to the right and crashes off the freeway. So, I pull off to check out the perpetrators, and they're both dead."

"What happened to the Swansons?" asked Jack.

"Nothing. The rocket missed. They're probably at Ben Gurion by now."

"Have the assailants been identified?" asked Jack.

"Before the police arrived, I checked out the bodies in the van – two Arab males. I looked in the driver's wallet, wrote down his name and license number, and got the tag number."

"Good. What caused the crash?"

"Beats me. There're no flat tires. And, that's not the only screwy thing about this."

"What else?" asked Jack.

"Other than superficial bruises and abrasions, *the bodies don't have any visible injuries.*"

* * *

At Ben Gurion International Airport, the Swanson family had to pass through the extensive airport security before boarding their flight back to the United States. As a result of Paul's television interviews, several bystanders recognized him. Most of them just stared and whispered to each other. A few asked to shake Paul's hand, and one asked for his autograph.

During the long flight back to the United States, Clara Swanson sat between her son and husband. Leaning close to Paul's ear, she said quietly, "I don't think what happened on the way to the airport was a random terrorist attack, Paul. I think the men in that van were trying to kill us."

"I know, Mom. They shot a rocket at us. I saw it hit the embankment along the highway. But God was protecting us, just like He did in Jerusalem."

Now obviously upset, Clara said, "After what that Arab from the shrine said about you on TV, you may be a target now, even at home."

"Maybe so," said Paul calmly, "but I know that God will protect us."

* * *

At the IDF compound in Jerusalem, Jack Landon had just arrived at Eli Zahavi's office. "Come in, Jack. I've got some information for you about the incident near Ben Sheman."

"Have you been able to identify the would-be assassins?"

"Members of the al-Aqsa Martyrs' Brigades, the armed wing of Fatah. They have been responsible for suicide bombings in Tel Aviv and Jerusalem as well as attacks on settlements in the West Bank and Gaza Strip. The Muslims are outraged by Paul Swanson's prophecy that a synagogue will be built where their shrine was destroyed, not to mention his prediction that a Christian church will be built nearby."

"So, they've decided to kill the kid for having hallucinations?"

"Not exactly. We've been informed by representatives of Waqf Islamic Trust, which controls the Temple Mount, that Muslims consider Paul Swanson's prophecies to be part of a conspiracy by the U.S. and Israel to justify seizure of the Temple Mount."

"Don't they understand that if Israel wanted to seize the Temple Mount, it would have done it already?"

"Yes, but Muslims also know the Jewish prophecy that the Third Temple will be erected there when the Jewish Messiah comes. According to the prophecy, the Third Temple will then stand forever. Some Jews believe the Temple will suddenly appear out of fire from heaven, but others believe that Jews, led by the Messiah, will build the Temple. They believe that this will occur during a time of incomparable miracles, greater than the miracles that occurred when Moses led the Jewish people out of Egypt. They also believe that the one who anoints the Messiah as king will be a prophet of God. There is already talk that Paul Swanson is that prophet and that the events he predicted are the first miracles."

"Yeah, but what about the kid's prediction that your Temple will be connected to a Muslim mosque and a Christian church?" asked Jack, who seemed amused by this idea.

"I suppose that idea offends most Jews, Muslims, and Christians since we've spent millennia fighting among ourselves as to which of our religions represents God's truth. Now, a young Christian tells us that God wants the three religions to coexist in peace. Yet, as far as I know, nothing in the teachings of Christian Bible, the Torah, or the Koran tells us that we should tolerate other religions, much less treat them as equivalent to our own. For this reason, I would have to say that Paul Swanson is either a false prophet attempting to foist his own ecumenical pseudo-religion on us . . . or, as you believe, he is just a delusional young man."

"Well, I'm glad to see we agree on something," said Jack, smiling. Then, suddenly becoming serious, he added, "Too bad, though, that Jews and Muslims can't live in peace. The world would be safer if they could."

"We're not initiating the violence, Jack, but it does seem that violence is inevitable. After we were attacked in 1967, we recaptured the Old City. As a peace offering to the Arabs, we unilaterally turned over control of the Temple Mount to the Muslims, allowing them unfettered access to their shrine and mosque. But when a former Israeli Prime Minister merely visited the Temple Mount in the year 2000, it triggered a wave of Muslim violence and bloodshed that lasted for years. And, now," Eli added, "thanks to the destruction of the Dome of the Rock, groups all over Israel, including members of the Knesset, are calling for Israel to take back the Temple Mount and build the Third Temple. Just imagine the Muslim riots that will occur if we try to build a temple on the ruins of that Islamic shrine."

"Yeah," said Jack. "But there may be Jewish riots if the Muslims are allowed to rebuild the Dome. And, since the Muslims don't believe the kid's prophecy, the Muslims *will* rebuild the Dome."

.

CHAPTER 9
Homecoming

The Swanson family had anticipated that Israeli media would communicate the news of Paul's television interviews and his departure from Israel to the United States. Therefore, they were not surprised to see a group of local reporters waiting for them as they entered the main terminal at Tampa International Airport. Besieged by reporters, Paul began explaining that he had announced all of God's revelations during his previous interviews and had nothing further to convey. Then, he saw a very attractive young woman standing behind the reporters. "Please excuse me," he said. "It's been a long flight, and my parents and I are tired." Moving through the group of reporters, Paul walked up to the young woman, who greeted him with open arms. "Rachel," he said, embracing her passionately, "you came all the way to Tampa to see me!"

As cameras flashed, Rachel Lindsey kissed Paul and whispered, "You didn't think I'd quit caring about you, did you?"

"But, Rachel," whispered Paul, "you've put yourself at risk by being seen with me."

"Good," she responded, smiling as she looked into Paul's eyes. "Now you can't protect me by pushing me away again."

While Reverend Swanson fended off the reporters, Clara walked over to Rachel and hugged her. "I'm glad to see that my son hasn't scared you off, Rachel. You're welcome to stay with us while you're here; we have an extra room."

Walking over to them with reporters following, the Reverend said, "Hello, Rachel. It's nice to see you again." Pointing toward a down escalator, he said, "I think we'd better move down to the baggage claim area and pick up our luggage." Then, turning back to the reporters, the Reverend said, "We have to leave now. If you want to hear about our experiences in Jerusalem, then come to Unity Presbyterian Church in Oldsmar this Sunday at 9 a.m. Now, please excuse us."

After loading their luggage into the family station wagon, which they had parked at the airport, Reverend Swanson and Clara began the drive home, and Paul and Rachel followed in Rachel's car. While Reverend Swanson listened to music on the car stereo, Clara sat with her eyes closed, reflecting on the amazing events that she had witnessed in Israel. Then, her thoughts turned to her son being reunited with Rachel. She recalled that she and the Reverend had first met Rachel while visiting Paul during his sophmore year in college.

Although Rachel was quite attractive – some would say beautiful – what had most impressed Clara was Rachel's gregarious and unaffected personality. In the years that followed, she had become quite fond of Rachel and thought that Paul and Rachel made a lovely couple. She was surprised and upset when Paul announced that they had separated. Paul stated only that God had revealed to him that he must soon travel to an Islamic shrine in Israel, a place where he thought Rachel might be in danger. Clara had hoped the separation was temporary, and she was now happy that Rachel was apparently in Paul's life again.

* * *

Rachel Erin Lindsey had been pursued by many men, some of whom had been as handsome as Paul. But when she met Paul in a college psychology class, she was captivated by his guileless charm and friendliness. She noticed that Paul seemed to have little interest in talking about himself but seemed genuinely interested in her and what she had to say. As she came to know Paul, she recognized that he possessed a quiet self-assurance and integrity of character that made her feel safe with him.

Rachel was not surprised when Paul mentioned that he planned to attend seminary after graduation from college. She was surprised, however, to find that she was still attracted to him, because she had seldom dated "religious" men. As a child she had attended church with her parents, but she had come to believe that religion was not particularly important to her existence. In college she had quit attending church altogether and had found that she could also live comfortably without prayer. She continued to believe in God but felt that God had become irrelevant to her life. Nevertheless, Rachel had been taught enough about Christian principles to recognize someone who truly exhibited them. And Paul, she thought, exhibited kindness and genuine concern for others, which she considered to be the finest Christian attributes. But unlike other Christians whom she had observed, Paul was neither judgmental nor intent upon convincing others to believe as he did. Rather, he seemed content to live in accordance with his beliefs, treating others with kindness and respect but without trying to impose his beliefs on them.

Desiring to become closer to Paul, Rachel began attending church with him. Eventually, Rachel came to embrace the Christian faith, experiencing an inner peace and sense of security previously unknown to her. She also came to realize that she was deeply in love with Paul.

Like everyone else who knew Paul Swanson, Rachel marveled at his remarkably even temperment and humility. She could not recall ever seeing Paul nervous or fearful. Though he could be passionate, she had never seen him lose his temper. Despite being handsome and charming, he never seemed vain or egotistical. Initially, she had thought these qualities were hereditary traits, but later she came to believe that they were manifestations of his closeness to God.

Rachel was shocked when Paul had told her that God was leading him to go to Israel and that he would have to leave her indefinitely. He had told her that he loved her and that if it was God's will that they be together, he was sure that God would bring them together again.

Coming from anyone else, these statements would have felt like a rejection to Rachel. But Rachel knew that Paul would not say that he loved her unless he did, and she was certain that he would return to her when his mysterious mission was concluded.

* * *

After a late dinner, Reverend Swanson and Clara, tired from the long flight home, soon retired for the night, leaving Paul and Rachel alone. As they sat together on a living room couch, Paul described God's recent revelations to him. He also told Rachel about the rocket attack on his parents and himself and then said, "That's the type of thing that I wanted to protect you from, but now you and my parents may be targets in the future."

"But Paul," asked Rachel, "don't you think God will protect your parents and me, like He has protected you?"

"I am praying that He will. God has not warned me about any danger to you, but He didn't warn me about the rocket attack either."

"But He did protect you and your parents. It must be wonderful to be told by God that He is protecting you and guiding your life. I wish I knew what that was like, but God has never spoken to me. Why do you think He speaks to you and not to other Christians?"

"Rachel, I have no idea why God has chosen me as His messenger. And, although He has told me that He has plans for me, I have no idea what will happen to me next. I just have faith that God will guide me in the right direction."

"I wonder why God is so good to some people and lets others suffer so much. Think of all the Christians you know who have been killed in car accidents or had other tragic events in their lives? Why do you think God was not protecting them? Do you think God planned for them to have tragic lives?"

"I guess we all wonder why God lets so much tragedy exist in this world. I have often prayed about that, but God has never spoken to me about why He allows bad things to happen to good people. Maybe the tragic events in this world are meant to help us appreciate the peace and joy that we will experience in the afterlife. Or, maybe they are meant as a test of our faith to see if we will continue to believe in God despite life's tragedies and the apparent randomness of the world around us. I really believe that we are all part of God's plan for mankind and that we all have been given a chance to be with Him after death. But I also believe that in this world, some of us have specific roles in God's plan, while the others play a collective role."

"I wish I had your faith, Paul – and your self-confidence."

"Without my faith in God, I doubt I'd have much confidence at all." Then, looking into Rachel's eyes, Paul said, "I am confident of one thing though. I love you, Rachel, and I've missed you." And he embraced Rachel passionately as he had so often done in his dreams.

* * *

On Sunday, the Unity Presbyterian Church was filled to capacity for the morning service. Several reporters were among the congregation while others and their cameramen waited outside. Reverend Swanson led the congregation in a prayer and hymn and then announced that before the sermon, he would briefly describe the recent experiences of his family in Israel. For the next several minutes, he recounted Paul's predictions and their fulfillment. Then, after describing God's last revelation to Paul, he began the sermon.

"We live in an age in which many people believe that God is dead or never existed. To many, science is the new religion, and many think that science disproves Christianity. For example, look at the evolution-versus-intelligent-design controversy. Many believe that the theory of evolution and the Christian belief in creationism or intelligent design are mutually exclusive concepts. They say science supports the theory of evolution and disproves the concept that man is the product of intelligent design, that is, that God created man. But these people are not looking at the world or life as a whole. They have focused their attention upon one aspect of life, that is, how living things can adapt to their environment, and they have completely overlooked the uniqueness of life on earth.

"The religious skeptics accept the fact that the universe operates according to physical laws. One of those laws, the Second Law of Thermodynamics, basically states that in an isolated system, concentrated energy disperses over time until it reaches an inert equilibrium in which there is uniform distribution of energy and no further change occurs. Within our universe, stars are dispersing their concentrated energy, burning out, and collapsing into dwarf stars. Planets, such as earth, are gradually losing the heat from their cores. On every known planet, including earth, the dissipation of energy is causing the gradual degradation of matter. Yet, somehow, here on earth, inert molecules, instead of simply degrading like everything else, have mysteriously combined to form highly complex living organisms, including man. Nowhere else in the known universe have the forces of nature produced the unique combination of matter and energy necessary to create and sustain life. The creation of life on earth, whether it took place over a day or over millions of years, appears to be an exceptional event in the grand scheme of our universe. And to me that exceptional event implies purpose. And purpose implies intelligence – the intelligence of our divine Creator.

"The skeptics also tell us that man is no more than a highly intelligent ape. According to evolutionary theory, man's intelligence is a random product of selective adaptation. Evolutionists say that intelligence is such an advantageous evolutionary trait that it has become part of man's genetic makeup, passed on through generations of humanity. But if intelligence is such a beneficial evolutionary trait, why has the intelligence level of apes not increased over the past several million years? What is the probability that among millions of species that have existed over millions of years, only man would develop high intelligence, a trait so adaptive and beneficial that it has enabled man to dominate all other species on this planet? Why is there no evidence that any of the other species besides man has become even a little more intelligent during the period that man has supposedly evolved from an ape? Is it truly scientific, or even logical, for evolutionists to teach that random events alone have created the one living creature in the known universe with the capacity to contemplate the meaning of his own existence and the existence of God? Is it not more logical to conclude that something besides random probability is responsible for man's unique status in the universe? Is it not more logical to conclude that there was a purpose behind the creation of such a uniquely intelligent creature? Again, purpose implies intelligence – the intelligence of a Creator whom we call God.

"Should we reject science? Certainly not – science is the tool that we use to learn more about our physical bodies and the physical universe that God has created. Our physical selves are, after all, biological organisms, similar to other creatures on this earth. And, as God's recent revelation to my son has indicated, it is our physical bodies and the instinctual urges inherent in our bodies that, although necessary to our survival, also give rise to man's sinful condition.

"With the gift of man's intelligence, came the responsibility to control man's instinctual urges so that we do not destroy ourselves and can survive to fulfill God's plan for us. Each of us must constantly use our intelligence to balance our desire to pursue our own selfish urges and goals against the rights of others to pursue their urges and goals. This is the essence of the dual nature of man – the constant battle to balance our own self-interest against the interests of others. To help us accomplish this, God has given us moral laws to govern our instinctual urges and selfishness, that is, to help us determine right from wrong.

"Man has always been driven by his urge to dominate and control the world around him. This urge has helped man achieve some of his greatest accomplishments. But it has also caused man to steal, murder, and wage war. When life was more primitive, there may have been a place for war in this world. The Old Testament records wars between Israel and its heathen enemies. 'An eye for an eye and a tooth for a tooth' may have made sense then. But as man has become more knowledgeable, his weapons of war have developed to the point that he is now capable of global self-destruction. For this reason God has given us a message, a warning that God will no longer tolerate aggression in the name of religion. Men must now consider religious tolerance to be one of God's laws for mankind. This is not really a new law. It is an extension of the 'golden rule' taught by Jesus. As you know, that rule is recorded in Matthew 7:12, which states: 'Therefore, whatever you want men to do to you, do also to them, for this is the Law and the Prophets.' For thousands of years, Christians have known that this rule should guide their conduct. Now, we see that mankind's very survival will depend upon man's adherence to this simple rule.

"So, as Christians, let us always be guided in our battle to control our instinctual natures by this 'golden rule' set forth by God through his son, Jesus Christ. To that end, let us now pray. "God, our heavenly father, please be with us through the coming week. Please guide us in our battle against unrestrained selfishness and protect us from the ever-present temptation to yield to selfish instincts in ways that would cause harm to others. Please help us be examples of Christian conduct in our dealings with our families, coworkers, neighbors, and even our enemies. Although we do not accept the tenets of other religions, please help us recognize the right of others to follow their religions, as you help them recognize our right to follow the teachings of your Son. We give praise to You and thank You for the many blessings that You have provided us. These things we pray in the name of your Son, Jesus Christ. Amen."

CHAPTER 10
Voices of Discord

At the Shabak headquarters in Jerusalem, Eli Zahavi had summoned Jack Landon to his office. "I apologize for interrupting your day, Jack, but I need some information."

"If it's about autopsies on those bodies you shipped to us, our people haven't been able to find the cause of death yet. But they're still running tox' screens for rare poisons. We'll find the cause."

"I hope so, Jack, because we seem to be having an epidemic of unexplained terrorist deaths. Have you been watching the news lately?"

"Yeah. I heard about your renegade pilot attacking al-Aqsa. Was his helicopter really struck by lightning?"

"I don't know, Jack, but that was just the beginning of a series of unexplained incidents. We still haven't been able to determine the cause of death of the two Palestinians who attacked the Swanson family. Three days ago, Palestinian police in North Gaza found the bodies of four other terrorists associated with the al-Aqsa Martyrs' Brigades. They had set up a Qassam rocket launcher to fire on Israeli communities, but they apparently died suddenly before firing a single rocket. Their cause of death is unknown. We've had only one suicide bombing in Israel during the past month, but during that time we've recovered the bodies of several apparent suicide bombers. They died suddenly before they could detonate their bombs. We cannot determine the cause of death. Yesterday, Jerusalem police found the bodies of two Israelis who were suspected members of the Jewish underground. Their bodies were found outside al-Aqsa. They were carrying explosives. We cannot determine their cause of death. This morning we received a report of an explosion in the West Bank town of Jenin. IDF agents have determined that it came from a facility suspected of being a bomb factory for Islamic Jihad. Palestinian police have been unable to determine the cause of the explosion."

"I've seen the reports, Eli – dead suicide bombers, dead roadside bombers, and no known cause of death. Every TV newscast I've seen in the past couple of days, even on Al Jazeera, has suggested that we're seeing the fulfillment of the 'Swanson prophecy.' The gullibility of the public never ceases to amaze me. I have to admit, though, the kid is either a damn good guesser or he's psychic."

"So, you no longer think he's psychotic," said Eli, smiling.

"Maybe not, but I don't think he has a hotline to God, either."

"Spoken like a true atheist, Jack. By the way, what have you found out about his background?"

We've learned that he was orphaned at age three when his parents died in a boating accident. Apparently, he has no living relatives, so he ended up in an orphanage. Then, a year later, he was adopted by Timothy and Clara Swanson. Strange thing is . . . we haven't been able to identify his real parents or find his birth certificate. But we will."

* * *

In Qom, Iran, several Islamic leaders met to discuss their response to questions from Islamic clergymen about the unexplained deaths of Islamic martyrs and about the prophecies of the infidel American. "We know that Allah, the Lord of the universe, does not reveal Himself through American infidels," said a senior Grand Ayatollah. "Before the time of the great prophet Muhammad, Allah did reveal His existence to the prophets of other religions. But the revelations to those religions were superseded by Allah's revelations to Muhammad, the last true prophet. We know from the Qur'an and the Sunnah that, in the eyes of Allah, Islam is the only true religion. Allah himself has told us, 'And whoever desires a religion other than Islam, it shall not be accepted from him, and in the hereafter he shall be one of the losers.' Sura 003.85. Those who honor and obey Allah will never defile Islam by recognizing Judaism or Christianity as Allah's truth and will never defile al-Haram al-Sharif by allowing the Jews and Christians to build their churches there, as the infidel prophet has foretold."

"Yes," agreed the eldest Grand Ayatollah, "I believe the false prophet to be an instrument of Satan and his prophecies to be the work of Satan, who intends to undermine Islam by creating doubts in our minds as to Allah's true plans for mankind. We must not cease in our fight against the infidels who oppress us in Palestine, Iraq, Lebanon, and Afghanistan. As it is written, 'The punishment of those who wage war against Allah and His Messenger, and strive with might and main for mischief through the land is execution, or crucifixion, or the cutting off of hands or feet from opposite sides, or exile from the land; that is their disgrace in this world, and a heavy punishment is theirs in the Hereafter.' Sura 005.33."

"I, too, believe the American to be a false prophet," said another. "However, I suspect that he is part of an Israeli-American conspiracy to seize al-Haram al-Sharif and to subvert the spread of Islam. These deaths of our martyrs started at the American consulate in Jerusalem, and I believe they are the result of a new secret weapon the Americans are using in a campaign of genocide against Islam. But we must not desist from our holy cause for we are told, 'Think not of those who are slain in Allah's way as dead. Nay, they live, finding their sustenance in the Presence of their Lord.' Sura 003.169."

Nodding in agreement, a younger Ayatollah offered, "The scientists of the Great Satan have devised many insidious weapons with which they have afflicted the world – atom bombs, stealth fighters, smart bombs, beam weapons, and now some deadly weapon they are keeping secret from us."

"Perhaps," said the eldest Grand Ayatollah, "but that would not explain how the young infidel was able to predict the destruction of our holy shrine. I still believe that his prophecies are inspired by Satan, although I agree that he may also be part of an Israeli-American conspiracy."

After further discussion and debate, the Islamic leaders resolved to inform Islamic clergymen that the prophecies of the American were likely the work of Satan and also part of an Israeli-American conspiracy to undermine faith in Islam. They further resolved that to fulfill the will of Allah, they must not cease their advocacy for the spread of Islam through Jihad. Then, they adjourned their assemblage, satisfied in knowing that they would bring truth to the Islamic world about the Satan-inspired prophecies of the American infidel.

* * *

In Jewish and Christian communities throughout the world, religious leaders debated the legitimacy of the prophecies of Paul Swanson and the concept that God desired the peaceful coexistence of the world's three great monotheistic religions. Most orthodox Jews and fundamentalist Christians were adamant in their belief that religions other than their own were invalid and unsupported by the Holy Scriptures. Some fundamentalist Christians accused Paul Swanson of being one of the antichrists or false prophets mentioned in Matthew 24:24. Nevertheless, most Jews and Christians at least accepted the concept that

God did not want men to use their religious beliefs to justify violent aggression against the followers of other faiths.

* * *

Among the non-religious, many explanations, some quite bizarre, were put forth to explain the events following Paul Swanson's prophetic announcements. *Truth about Man* magazine, published by a self-professed expert on man's extraterrestrial origins, ran a cover story claiming that the mysterious deaths of terrorists were the result of intervention by an alien race of superior beings that had created man through genetic modification of prehistoric apes. According to the author's perspective, the alien race was intervening in human events to prevent a nuclear holocaust that would prematurely end the aliens' human-genetic experiment. Some readers of the article recalled an old science fiction story about an extraterrestrial alien who traveled to earth in a flying saucer and stopped electrical devices throughout the world to gain attention for a speech warning mankind about the dangers of nuclear warfare.

* * *

At the Swanson family's home in Oldsmar, Florida, Paul frequently received telephone calls from reporters requesting interviews, particularly after reports of terrorists dying from unknown causes. Such reports now appeared in newspapers and newscasts on an almost daily basis. He politely declined such interviews, stating that he was only a messenger and had already delivered the message of God's revelation to him. He also received hundreds of letters each week, most questioning him about the future, some accusing him of being an antichrist, and some from female admirers expressing their desire to meet him.

Outside the Swanson family's home, the paparazzi frequently pursued Paul, invariably asking him if he had any more predictions about the future. He patiently repeated that he was not clairvoyant and had already delivered the messages entrusted to him by God. He assured them that if he received any further revelations, he would announce them to the media.

Because of the media circus that now surrounded his life, Paul decided not to return to seminary. He did not want to be a distraction to the seminary and its students. He also wanted to spend more time with Rachel, who had moved to Oldsmar to be with him. While Rachel began her new employment as a part-time, elementary school teacher, Paul prayed and waited for God's guidance as to his own future.

CHAPTER 11
A Fearful Peace

During the next several months, the body counts of dead terrorists continued to rise throughout the Middle East as hundreds of Islamic jihadists died mysteriously during attempted acts of terrorism. By the following spring, civilian deaths from terrorist attacks in Israel had almost ceased. Still, however, a few suicide bombers succeeded in their murderous missions, and Islamic fundamentalists cited these successful suicide bombings as evidence that God was not causing the deaths of Islamic martyrs. Rumors were rampant in Muslim communities and on Muslim websites that American and Israeli forces were using some new secret weapon to kill jihadists. Muslims, however, had no explanation for the sudden deaths of Sunni and Shi'a militants who died mysteriously during attacks upon each other.

In Palestine, Islamic fundamentalists frequently discussed the "satanic prophecy" of the young American, whom they perceived as part of a Jewish-Christian conspiracy to seize possession of the Temple Mount. The Palestinian Authority repeatedly issued warnings to Israel that a "bloodbath" would result if Israelis attempted to erect a synagogue on the Temple Mount. The Palestinian Authority commissioned Muslim architects and engineers to develop plans for a new and larger shrine to replace the Dome of the Rock. The President of the Palestinian Authority announced that construction of the new shrine would commence within the year.

In Israel, Temple Mount activists, whose efforts to gain control of the Temple Mount had been frustrated for so long, were gaining political support for a plan to construct the Third Temple. Bowing to public sentiment, the Knesset was considering plans to renegotiate the 1967 Arab-Israeli agreement that had placed the thirty-five-acre Temple Mount solely under Muslim control. The Israeli government was also reconsidering its prohibition against non-Muslim prayer on the Temple Mount, and leading Orthodox rabbis were reconsidering their ban against Jews ascending the Temple Mount. One reason for the ban had been the lack of facilities for ritual purification before entry upon areas of the Temple Mount where the Arc of the Covenant had once rested. Another reason had been the rabbis' interpretation of the Scriptures as indicating that construction of the Third Temple would have to await the arrival of the Messiah. However, after the mysterious destruction of the Dome of the Rock and the miraculous abatement of religious terrorism, many Jews and their rabbis now felt they were seeing the fulfillment of Messianic prophecy. Many had come to believe that Israel should build the Third Temple in anticipation of the Messiah, not after his arrival. They reasoned that because God had used Jewish manpower to build the first two temples, He would use Jews to build the Third.

* * *

While debate raged about building the Third Temple, Shabak and CIA agents were continuing their investigation into the cause of terrorist deaths. At the Shabak headquarters in Jerusalem, Jack Landon and Eli Zahavi discussed a breakthrough in the investigation.

"Have your pathologists confirmed our findings?" asked Jack with uncharacteristic gravity.

"Yes, we have found identical lesions in all of the bodies examined so far. But we have no explanation, no theory whatsoever, as to how this could occur. How did your pathologists even discover a lesion that small inside the brain stem?"

"They didn't," said Jack. "It was a radiologist. When autopsies showed nothing, we asked a radiologist to do head-to-toe x-rays on a couple of the bodies. He did x-rays and found nothing. Then, he decided to do CT scans on the brain and spinal cord of one of the corpses. That's when he found it. But, listen to me," said Jack, leaning forward in his chair, "this information should not be made public . . . at least not until we have a better handle on what's going on."

"What's going on! A *miracle* is going on! Dr. Meshenberg says that nothing she's ever seen or heard about could have caused the type of lesion we are finding in the brains of those terrorists. I asked a neurosurgeon if there was any way to reproduce the lesion without opening the skull, and he just laughed. Face it, Jack, *nothing human did this.*"

"So, what are you saying, Eli? You seriously believe a supreme being is hunting terrorists down and killing them?" asked Jack, his voice heavy with sarcasm.

"Well, what's your explanation, Jack? How do men suddenly develop a small void inside the brain stem without perforation of the skull or the membranes surrounding the brain stem? We have tried lasers, radiation machines, and high-frequency sound without success. Face it, Jack . . . there is no technology that can do that, much less do it to terrorists who are walking on a crowded streets or driving in automobiles . . . or standing inside your Consulate."

"I've seen a lot of things that people thought were miracles, Eli. They always turned out to be something else. We haven't figured out how it's being done, yet. But we know these injuries were inflicted with surgical precision, apparently from a distance. That sounds like some kind of weapon to me. And until we've had time to learn more about it, we want to keep this information quiet."

"A high tech weapon? You Americans have all the high tech weapons. If you don't have a weapon that could do this, no one does."

"Nevertheless, my friend, we need Israel to keep this quiet, at least for a few more months. If this is a weapon, we'll have a better chance of catching the perpetrators if they don't know we've figured out what they're doing."

"*Perpetrators?* You think stopping terrorists from murdering innocent civilians is a *crime?* Do you want to interfere with something that is bringing peace to Israel for the first time since we declared our independence in 1948?"

"No, Eli, but if there are vigilantes out there who possess a weapon that gives them the power to decide who lives or dies, then we need to find them. They could decide that religious terrorists are not the only ones that they should exterminate. They might decide that Israeli and American soldiers are fair targets. The point is that we cannot let an unknown group or individual have sole possession of the *power of life or death* over the rest of us. And if such a weapon does exist, just think what would happen if the jihadists captured it?"

"Your last point is well taken. But, I think we are seeing something that is beyond man's control, and I am beginning to believe in the young prophet and his vision of the future. After all, how could he have predicted these things unless the future truly had been revealed to him?"

"I don't buy it, Eli. Experience tells me that people are behind all of this, and I think the kid is part of some sort of counter-terrorist network."

"Always the cynic, Jack. How could this twenty-three-year-old American seminary student be part of a global, counter-terrorist conspiracy?"

"I don't know. But I do know that *he has no birth records, and we can't identify his real parents.* The story about his parents dying in a boating accident came from an old woman who was baby-sitting for the kid when his alleged parents disappeared. The old woman, who was their next-door neighbor, told the police that the couple claiming to be the kid's parents had recently rented the house next to hers. They asked the old woman if she could sit with the kid for a few hours while they went out on their boat. A couple of hours after they left, the old woman got a cell-phone call from the kid's father, who said his boat was stranded with engine trouble and the Coast Guard had been called. That part of the story checks out. The Coast Guard has a record of the incident. But when a Coast Guard boat got to the coordinates that the kid's father had given them, all they found was debris from an apparent explosion. The bodies of the kid's parents were never recovered."

"So, what is so suspicious about that? Their remains could have been carried away by ocean currents or eaten by fish."

"What's suspicious is that the parents' identities cannot be traced. They paid cash in advance to lease the house for the summer and left no pictures, identifying information, or even fingerprints in the house. They paid cash for a small second-hand boat that they bought from a private owner who had advertised it in a newspaper. They might have bought their car the same way, but we don't know because their car was never found. The police were unable to locate anyone who knew them. They'd only been living there for two weeks before they disappeared. We don't even know if Paul was really their kid. He may have been kidnapped."

"That is all very mysterious, Jack. But how does it make Paul Swanson a suspect in a counter-terrorist conspiracy? After all, he was only three years old when all of that happened."

"Again, I don't know, but I don't believe it's a mere coincidence that the kid has a suspicious background. I think he's part of something very well organized, and I intend to find out exactly what that is."

"You might start by reading the Bible, Jack. But that's only my opinion."

* * *

Later that day, Eli Zahavi met with Dr. Zelde Meshenberg, the pathologist who had supervised the terrorist autopsies performed in Israel. "Tell me, Zelde – can you conceive of any means by which these fatal brain injuries could have been caused by a weapon of some kind?"

"My colleagues and I have been discussing this for some time, Eli. As you know, the fatal lesions are precisely located in the medulla oblongata – also called the brainstem – where they sever the neural communication pathways controlling several autonomic functions, such as respiration, heart rate, and blood pressure. If the lesions had been lower, as in the cervical spinal cord, they likely would have produced quadriplegia, but they might not have been lethal. And if the lesions had occurred in the cerebral cortex or cerebellum, they probably would have caused neurological deficits but not death unless they also caused significant hemorrhage or edema in which case death could have been slow and painful. However, these lesions caused no hemorrhage because whatever created them also cauterized the tiny blood vessels in the brainstem. It appears to me that whoever inflicted these lesions intended to cause *sudden, painless death* rather than painful death or disabling injury.

"It is also remarkable that there are no entry wounds. The brainstem, where the lesions occurred, lies deep within the base of the brain. The brainstem is protected not only by the skull but also by three meninges or membranes that surround the entire brain and spinal cord. Yet, whoever killed these terrorists did so without causing entry wounds in the skull, without rupturing any of the membranes around the brain, and without causing significant bleeding or edema. Nothing that I know of can do that."

"Nor I, Zelde. But I am trying to be objective and to consider all the possibilities in analyzing this situation."

"Well, Eli, there is another aspect of the deaths that I find interesting."

"Which is?"

"I think these lesions were intended to do more than cause death. It would have been much simpler to cause sudden death by perforating the heart or aorta, thereby inducing a massive fatal hemorrhage. It appears to me that whoever caused the deaths of these terrorists intended their deaths as a demonstration of *power* ... the power to reach directly into the most protected part of the human anatomy and snatch the life away from those who would take the life of others. *To me, the mechanism of death appears to have been designed to send the message that a higher power has decided to enforce a death penalty for terrorism and there is no place for terrorists to hide.*"

CHAPTER 12
Investigation of the Prophet

In Langley, Virginia, the Director of Central Intelligence, Maxwell Colson, spoke at a special meeting of CIA Station Chiefs from countries throughout the Middle East. "Gentlemen, next month I have to meet with the Senate Select Committee on Intelligence to discuss our investigation of the hundreds of terrorist deaths reported over the past several months. As you know, brain scans performed during autopsies on some of the bodies have revealed precisely located brainstem lesions that apparently were the cause of death. The news media are fascinated by the idea that these deaths are miraculous and, for all I know, they may be. But we cannot ignore the possibility that these deaths have been caused by some type of weapon system – a weapon system against which we have no defense. Virtually every intelligence agency in the world is investigating the situation. If some type of weapon system is responsible for these deaths, we must obtain that technology before it falls into the hands of our enemies and before it is used against us. I want you to assign your best agents to this investigation and to tell them to use every available intelligence modality. Tell your agents to report any pertinent discoveries to you immediately, and I want you to transmit that information to me through secure channels on a daily basis. When I go to that meeting next month, I want to have something of substance to report. Okay, gentlemen, this meeting is adjourned. I want the Station Chief from Jerusalem to come to my office."

Later, in his office, Director Colson spoke with the Station Chief from the CIA's Jerusalem office. "What is this mysterious object that you mentioned in your last report?" asked the Director.

"One of my agents was told by a maintenance worker at the Temple Mount that the object was found among the debris from the helicopter that exploded while attacking the al-Aqsa Mosque. Apparently, it was so unique that some of the workers decided that it was a piece of an 'angel wing' and took it to the Waqf Security Chief for safekeeping. As far as we know, the Security Chief still has it in his office at the Temple Mount. It may just be part of the helicopter. Or it may be part of whatever destroyed the helicopter, so I thought you'd want to know about it."

"Let's get it. Tomorrow, I'll have one of our specialists flown to Jerusalem."

* * *

After learning that Paul Swanson was taking a leave of absence from seminary, the elders at Unity Presbyterian Church offered Paul the position of Ministry Intern. Paul initially declined due to his concern that his presence would bring unwanted media attention to the church. Reverend Swanson, however, convinced Paul to accept the internship, assuring him that the position would provide valuable experience to someone aspiring to become a minister. Paul soon found that he enjoyed his new duties, which primarily involved assisting the church's ministry staff with programs and activities for the youth of the church.

The income from Paul's new position enabled him to rent a small apartment in the same complex where Rachel lived so that they could be together more often. The apartment complex, a tall building in Clearwater, had a keyed security entrance. Rachel had chosen the complex for personal safety and to keep reporters from intruding on her privacy, particularly when Paul came to visit. By the time Paul moved into the complex, however, he was seldom approached by reporters due to his repeated refusals to grant interviews.

Soon after Paul moved into his new apartment, another new tenant moved into an apartment on Paul's floor. It was not long before the new tenant, a young man in his mid-twenties, introduced himself to Paul. The new tenant, Daniel Mosby, was quite affable and soon became acquainted with Paul and Rachel. Daniel, who never mentioned Paul's recent publicity, told Paul and Rachel that he was working as a stock broker but aspired to become a mutual fund manager.

Eventually, Daniel convinced Paul and Rachel to have dinner with him and his girlfriend, who prepared the meal in Daniel's apartment. The food was excellent, and Daniel kept everyone entertained with amusing stories about his family and childhood. Later that night, after Rachel and Paul had left his apartment, Daniel and his girlfriend, a forensic specialist, carefully collected and packaged the drinking glass and tableware used by Paul. On the following day, a special courier delivered the packaged items to a CIA forensic laboratory in Langley, Virginia, for DNA and fingerprint analyses.

* * *

At the Shabak headquarters in Jerusalem, Jack Landon had just entered Eli Zahavi's office. "Hello, Eli. Your telephone message was rather cryptic and mysterious." Then, sitting down, Jack asked, "What is this important information that you have for me?"

"I thought that you should hear it from me first. The Prime Minister is about to announce the decision of the Knesset to renegotiate the present Temple Mount agreement to allow Israel to share control of the Temple Mount with the Muslims . . . and to allow construction of the Third Temple where the Islamic shrine once stood. In exchange for these concessions,

Israel will offer to provide economic assistance to the Palestinian economy, particularly in the Gaza strip, and to help develop infrastructure in the West Bank and Gaza. Of course, we expect the Palestinian Authority and militant groups, such as Hamas, Islamic Jihad, and Fatah, to reject this proposal since they do not even recognize our right to exist. Nevertheless, recent events have convinced most Israelis that the time has come to build the Third Temple on the land that belonged to Israel before it was seized by the Romans and later by the Ottoman Empire."

"So, I guess we should prepare for protests and riots. I knew the recent peace wouldn't last."

"Don't be so cynical, Jack. Most of us have come to believe that this peace is the work of God and that God will continue to prevent terrorist aggression against Israel."

"And terrorist aggression by Israelis, it appears. I've seen recent reports of the deaths of some Jewish fanatics who attacked al-Aqsa."

"Your point is taken. We must be prepared for conflict over our decision to build our temple, particularly when the Muslims are planning to rebuild their shrine on the same spot. There is other space on the Temple Mount for their shrine, but they will want to build it over the Rock. We will soon see if it is God's will that the Third Temple be built."

"I suppose your Prime Minister will request the U.S. or the U.N. to participate in the negotiation process."

"That is being done as we speak. But there is another matter that I wanted to discuss with you. The Prime Minister will also be announcing the terrorist autopsy findings. Rumors are rampant in the Arab community that we are killing terrorists with a new secret weapon, even though Jewish terrorists have also died. The Prime Minister thinks that it is important to explain that no weapon is capable of killing men this way – that only God can reach into the brains of men and disconnect the nerves to their hearts and lungs."

"I wish he'd wait a little longer. The CIA is in the middle of an investigation of these deaths."

"I am sorry, Jack, but we are certain that you will find no secret weapon. Shabak and Mossad have thoroughly investigated many of the terrorist deaths. These deaths, like the destruction of the Islamic shrine, are acts of God. There can be no other explanation, my friend."

"I wish I could believe that, Eli. But doesn't it seem strange to you that since the deaths started, some terrorists have carried out successful bomb attacks or fired fatal gunshots before they were killed? If God killed those terrorists, why didn't God kill them before they killed innocent civilians?"

* * *

At a CIA forensic laboratory in Langley, Virginia, a technician was reporting a surprising discovery to the laboratory supervisor. "Using PCR-based analysis, I processed the DNA of Paul Swanson. I next had the system run his DNA profile against samples in CODIS. It didn't match the DNA profile of any terrorist or criminal in CODIS. Then, out of curiosity, I ran it through the DNA database for federal employees. I got no match on the paternal side. However, when I ran a maternal kinship analysis, I found that Paul Swanson and a former federal employee shared alleles at all selected loci. I re-analyzed the DNA using RFLP and got the same result. *I can say with greater than 99% certainty that Paul Swanson is the son of Dr. Suzanne Marie Barnett, a former Director of the Lawrence Livermore National Laboratory.*"

"Excellent work," said the supervisor. "I'll notify the Director immediately."

CHAPTER 13
Temple Mount Conflict

In the West Bank city of Ramallah, the President of the Palestinian Authority met with leaders of Fatah, Hamas, and Islamic Jihad. The Fatah leader was speaking. "We must not allow the Jews to seize al-Haram al-Sharif and desecrate the Rock and the Well of Souls by building their temple over it. They are trying to violate Israel's agreement with us. If we give in to them this time, soon they will seize all of al-Haram al-Sharif, including al-Aqsa."

"And all they offer us in exchange," added the Hamas leader, " is economic assistance to Gaza and the West Bank to ease the economic hardship caused by their policies."

"Yes," responded the President, "but this is not the time to engage in warfare with the Israelis . . . not when we are already under attack by something that is killing our martyrs. If we do negotiate for the land they want for their temple, I think we should demand a higher price than they are offering. Perhaps, they would be willing to give more land to Palestinians and finance the rebuilding of the shrine if we give them a small section of al-Haram al-Sharif on which to build their temple."

"That would still be a desecration of al-Haram al-Sharif," said the Islamic Jihad leader. "I think we should move ahead with rebuilding the Dome of the Rock and let the Israelis be the aggressors if they wish to stop us. Then, the world will see their aggression and support our cause."

"The Christian world will never support our cause, my friend," said the President. "But I agree that if we reject negotiations with Israel, we must move ahead with construction of our shrine so that the Israelis will be the aggressors if they try to stop us."

"What about the secret weapon of the Americans that is killing our martyrs?" asked the Hamas leader. "They could use it to kill our workers when they are rebuilding the shrine."

The Palestinian Authority's President reflected for a moment and then said, "Whoever is killing our martyrs is attempting to create the illusion that the false prophecies of the American are being fulfilled by Allah. But the American has prophesied that Allah desires peaceful coexistence between Muslims, Christians, and Jews. Therefore, if the Jews attack us when we rebuild the shrine, they will be the aggressors. If the American's prophecy is true and the Jews are the aggressors, it is they who will be struck dead. If they are not struck dead, the world will see that the American's prophecy is false and is merely a ruse to justify Zionist aggression."

"Then," offered the Fatah leader, "the Palestinian Authority must reject the Israeli proposal and move ahead with construction of the new shrine as soon as possible."

"I agree," the President said, "but while we rebuild the shrine, you should be working to discover the weapon that has been killing our martyrs."

"It must be some sort of death ray developed by the Americans," said the Hamas leader. "But how can we find a weapon that no one can see?"

"Perhaps, you should start with the American prophet," suggested the President. "The use of this weapon began when he came to Israel, and its use has continued in order to support his false prophecy. Even if he is not the one using this weapon, he must at least be aware of its existence."

The leaders of Fatah, Hamas, and Islamic Jihad nodded their agreement with the President's suggestion.

* * *

Soon, newscasts throughout the world carried reports of the Palestinian Authority's rejection of Israel's proposal for shared control of the Temple Mount. The reports mentioned that the Palestinian Authority would commence construction of a new Dome of the Rock before the end of the year. A few news commentators speculated about the possibility that an Israeli-Islamic conflict over the Temple Mount might precipitate a war between Israel and the neighboring Islamic nations.

* * *

At his office on the Temple Mount, the Chief of Security received a telephone call from a Waqf administrator. "One of our maintenance workers asked my secretary if the Waqf had received a holy relic from you. He said a worker found it on top of al-Aqsa after the Israeli helicopter attack and that the worker turned it over to you for safekeeping. Why did you not contact me about this?"

"Oh, the piece of debris from the helicopter . . . I had forgotten about it. A piece of an angel's wing, the worker called it. The worker's imagination had played a trick on his mind. I didn't think to bother you about it. I just put the debris in my safe to satisfy him, and then I forgot about it. I will bring it to you if you like."

"That would be advisable. I would like to examine it – today."

The Chief shuddered as he hung up the phone. It was fortunate, he thought, that he had not sold what could be a religious relic. He might not have lived to spend the money. But, as he hastily opened his office safe, he was horrified to discover the safe was empty.

Meanwhile, at a laboratory in Langley, Virginia, a scientist employed by the CIA was performing tests on an almost transparent object that appeared to be the tip of a small wing.

CHAPTER 14
The Desert Prophecy

During his first few months as the Ministry Intern at Unity Presbyterian Church, Paul discovered that he truly enjoyed helping to organize and administer the church's programs for children and young adults. He particularly enjoyed teaching children's Sunday school classes and speaking to youth groups. Although some parents had initially expressed skepticism that a "prophet" could be a proper example for Christian youth, Paul's humility and friendliness eventually won over even the most skeptical members of the congregation.

For almost a year, Paul had no further visions. Though he prayed regularly for God's guidance, he did not sense a divine presence leading him in any particular direction. Paul began to feel that he had fulfilled his role as God's messenger and that God was now leaving it up to Paul to find the future course that his life would follow. Then, one night, Paul's sleep was interrupted by another prescient dream.

The next morning, Paul made an unannounced visit to his father's office at the church. His voice and demeanor conveyed an unusual sense of urgency as he said, "Hello, Dad. I hope I'm not interrupting your work, but I have something important to tell you."

"I'm just finishing my preparation for Sunday's sermon. Come on in, Paul. Have a seat. What do you need to tell me?"

"I thought you should be the first to know. This morning I had another vision. God has told me that I must return to Jerusalem."

Reverend Swanson paused for a few seconds as he reflected upon Paul's statement. Then, he asked, "Why? Is it because of the conflict over the Temple Mount?"

"I think it goes beyond that, Dad. God told me that His plan for mankind requires that men have both religious freedom and intellectual freedom. He wants men to be free to discover the universe and the laws by which it operates. He wants men to be free to improve the quality of their lives on earth. He even wants men to have the freedom to either accept or reject God's very existence, although those that reject Him will never know the blessings enjoyed by the faithful. To the extent that the teachings of any religion or ideology prohibit or interfere with the exercise of religious or intellectual freedom, those teachings interfere with God's plan for mankind. Because freewill is so important to God's plan for mankind, God will not continue his current intervention in human affairs any longer than necessary. God wants men to choose peace rather than having it forced upon them. For the time being, God has stopped religious violence, but religious hostility remains. God has told me that there will not be lasting peace until men understand that God truly desires that men have freedom of religious choice and that men of all religions live together in peace. To convince men of this truth, God has chosen reward over punishment. And last night He asked me to deliver a message to Israel and Islam that God will reward them for peacefully settling the conflict over the Temple Mount."

"But, Paul," interrupted the Reverend, "why do you have to go to the Jerusalem to deliver this message? You could hold a press conference here."

"I don't know, Dad. I just know that I was told to go to Jerusalem to announce how God will reward the Israelis and Muslims for negotiating a peaceful resolution of the Temple Mount conflict."

"How will God reward them?" asked the Reverend.

"He told me that He would transform the deserts of Israel and Palestine into lands filled with lakes and rivers."

* * *

In Langley, Virginia, several CIA Station Chiefs and a scientist from DARPA, the Defense Advanced Research Projects Agency, were meeting with Director Colson. "Gentlemen, I was very embarrassed to report to a Senate committee that this agency has made no progress in determining who is killing terrorists and what they're using to do it. I know that some of you believe that these deaths were acts of God, but every act of God that I've ever seen had a scientific explanation. Now, I want to know if any of you have made any progress in this investigation."

"Sir," said one Station Chief, "we have numerous eye witness accounts of terrorists suddenly dropping dead, but none of the witnesses observed any evidence of a weapon. We have obtained contemporaneous satellite reconnaissance of the areas in which these incidents occurred. But they show nothing unusual in the sky above these areas. We have even obtained a videotape taken by an Iraqi citizen of a suicide bomber who dropped dead before he could blow himself up. But there is no indication of any type of weapon being involved in his death."

"What about this familial connection between Paul Swanson and the former head of one of our nuclear-weapons research facilities?" asked Director Colson.

"My people have been exploring that," announced another Station Chief. "Dr. Suzanne Barnett resigned from her position as Director of the Lawrence Livermore National Laboratory when she was forty-three years old. That was nine years before Paul Swanson was born. There is no record of her having any children, much less having one at age fifty-two. I think the lab boys screwed up the analysis of Paul Swanson's DNA sample."

"Considering the lab's track record and how many times they ran Swanson's DNA, I doubt they made a mistake," responded the Director. "So, what else can you tell me about Dr. Barnett?"

"Well, she was married from age twenty-five to age thirty-three to another nuclear physicist, Dr. Alexander

139

Carr, then she divorced him. They had no children. She remained single until the year before her resignation from Livermore when she married an immigrant from Lebanon, a computer scientist and entrepreneur, Dr. Omar Bardoon. A former colleague of Dr. Barnett described Dr. Bardoon as a 'billionaire genius.'"

"Is that it?" asked the Director. "You don't have any more than that? Didn't you interview Dr. Barnett?"

"Well, that would be difficult, Sir, since *she died seven years ago.*"

"What about her husband?"

"We haven't located him yet."

"Look, the best leads we have are Paul Swanson, Dr. Barnett, and this Dr. Bardoon," said the Director. "I want your people to follow those leads as far as possible. Maintain the surveillance on Paul Swanson. Get interviews from everyone who knew Dr. Barnett and her husband. Interview her first husband and her last one, if they're still alive. Get a sample of their DNA, too, since one of them may be Paul Swanson's father. Get Dr. Barnett's medical records. There must be records of her prenatal care and delivery somewhere. I want to know why a top nuclear physicist quit her career, secretly had child in middle age, and then secretly abandoned the child. Put as many agents on this as you need. I want a full report with detailed interviews in two weeks. As for the rest of you, use all of your contacts to find out if any private U.S. groups have been conducting secret nuclear-weapons research over the past several years, particularly groups that Dr. Barnett was associated with."

Then, turning to the DARPA scientist, the Director asked, "What about the object found at the Temple Mount? What can you tell us about that?"

"I can tell you that it was not part of the helicopter that exploded over the al-Aqsa Mosque. And I can tell you that it was not part of an angel's wing, if there is such a thing. It's shaped like a wing tip, and it may have come from an object that was flying near the helicopter when it exploded, maybe a small plane of some kind. I cannot tell you what it's made of, because the stuff doesn't ionize well enough to be analyzed with mass spectrometry. It's very light-weight and very strong. It doesn't reflect radar. It's almost transparent when dry and becomes whitish-translucent when wet. And, under a microscope, we found embedded throughout the entire length of the object" – the scientist paused to clear his throat – "what appears to be part of an *incredibly* complex integrated circuit, a circuit that might have been part of an even more complex network of microcircuits. *None of our scientists has ever seen anything like it before.*"

* * *

After explaining to Rachel and his mother why he must return to the Jerusalem, Paul made reservations by telephone for a flight to Israel and a hotel room in Jerusalem and then began packing for a long stay. Although he had no specific plan as to how he would make his fateful announcement of God's latest revelation, Paul was certain that God would guide him in carrying out his appointed task.

On a Saturday morning, Rachel drove Paul and his parents to Tampa International Airport. They were unaware that when Paul had telephoned for his flight and hotel reservations, the CIA had been monitoring the calls. They also were unaware that a car with two Hamas agents was following Rachel's car.

At the airport, Paul's parents and Rachel stood in line with Paul while he waited to check his luggage and pick up his boarding pass. They noticed people in the line who appeared to recognize Paul and then whisper excitedly to each other. They did not notice the two Hamas agents who had followed them into the airport and who now stood several feet behind them in line.

Later, before boarding the airport shuttle that would transport him to the departure gate, Paul stood outside a security checkpoint with Rachel and his parents to exchange good-byes. While Paul kissed Rachel and his mother and hugged his father, the two Hamas agents passed through the security checkpoint and stood in the waiting area for the shuttle. Paul then passed through the security checkpoint and soon boarded the next shuttle with the Hamas agents. Unknown to Paul and the Hamas agents, a CIA agent was already at the departure gate waiting for the flight to Israel.

CHAPTER 15
Return of
the Prophet

During the flight to Israel, Paul decided that upon reaching Jerusalem he would check into a hotel and then visit Eli Zahavi, whom Paul considered to be an official of the Israeli government. Paul planned to seek Eli Zahavi's advice as to how best to obtain audiences with the Israeli Prime Minister and the President of the Palestinian Authority. Although he had neither experience in politics nor training in diplomacy, Paul had no doubt that God would somehow enable him to convince Israeli and Islamic leaders to negotiate a peaceful resolution of the Temple Mount conflict.

Upon his arrival at Ben Gurion International Airport in Tel Aviv, Paul followed the other passengers to the heavily guarded baggage claim area. While Paul waited to pick up his luggage, the CIA agent who had been aboard Paul's flight met a fellow agent who had been waiting at the airport. Unknown to the two CIA agents, one of them had been recognized by an agent of Hamas, who had been waiting at the airport for the two Hamas agents on Paul's flight. When a taxi later drove Paul away from the airport, two other vehicles followed.

It was late evening when Paul's taxi arrived at the hotel where he had made a reservation. The three Hamas agents, having followed the CIA agents' car and Paul's taxi to the hotel, simply drove past the hotel. They planned to return later. While Paul was checking into his hotel room, one of the two CIA agents entered an adjacent hotel room, which the CIA had previously reserved. The other CIA agent drove home for the night.

Although he wanted to telephone Rachel, Paul remembered that the time at home was seven hours earlier than the time in Israel and that Rachel was probably teaching her elementary school class. He had dinner in his room, took a shower, and went to bed. Exhausted from a long day of travel, he soon fell asleep.

Paul had not slept long when he began having a very vivid dream in which he was walking through darkness toward a brightly lit horizon. A familiar voice, deep and resonant, whispered to him as he walked, "Although man is said to share some of the attributes of his Creator, man is an imperfect creation because he is part of an imperfect world. Man's imperfection affects all that man does and all that he will do. It clouds

man's judgment and often blinds man to My truth.
Yet, I have imbued man with a need to find My truth
and endowed him with the ability to someday realize
My goal for mankind. Through the ages of man, various
religions and philosophies, some more than others, have
embraced some aspects of My truth. To that extent, they
deserve the respect of other religions and philosophies.
However, no religion or philosophy has yet embraced all
of My truth or fully realized My goal for man. Men will
not achieve My goal for mankind so long as men attempt
to force their religions and philosophies on other men.
In ages past, I have condoned violence against followers
of evil religions and philosophies that corrupted man
and led man away from the path to My truth and My goal
for man. Although such religions and philosophies still
exist, they will eventually fail in their natural course. I
will no longer condone violence against the followers of
any religion or philosophy except in defense of human
life. Violence begets violence, and escalation of violence
begets escalation of violence. The chain must now be
broken before mankind destroys itself. Remember
my words as you deliver the message of My promised
reward for peaceful resolution of the conflict between
the religions of this troubled place. Fear not to proclaim
My message boldly to their leaders for I will shield and
protect you while you are in My service."

Paul had been asleep for only a few hours when he
was roughly awakened. The three Hamas agents who had
earlier followed him from the airport had Paul firmly in
their grasp. Two of the men held Paul's arms, pinning
him to the bed, while the third placed duct tape over

Paul's mouth. Startled and disoriented, Paul struggled to break free. Then, the man who had placed tape over Paul's mouth switched on a bedside light and showed Paul something in his hand. "This, young American, is a hand grenade. I have pulled the pin from it so it will explode if I drop it. If your American secret weapon should kill me, I will drop the grenade and we will die. If you do not come with us quietly, I will drop the grenade and we will die. We are martyrs for Palestine, and we do not fear death. Now you can get up and take the tape from your mouth; but if you shout or try to escape, you will die."

Removing the tape from his mouth, Paul slowly arose from his bed. Looking into the eyes of the man holding the grenade, he stated calmly but emphatically, "I have come to bring a message to Palestine and to Israel. It is a message from God – a promise of reward to Palestine and Israel if they will peacefully resolve the present conflict over the Temple Mount. I will soon visit the President of the Palestinian Authority to deliver this message. Now you must leave. You must not interfere with God's work. I do not want you to die as so many others have in recent months."

Stunned by Paul's words and fearless demeanor, the three men stared momentarily at Paul and each other. Then, the man holding the grenade in one hand reached for Paul's throat with his other hand. Before his hand touched Paul, he collapsed awkwardly at Paul's feet, his other hand still gripping the live grenade. One of the other two men raised his assault rifle as if to shoot Paul. He also fell dead. The third man, whose eyes were wide with terror, stood as if paralyzed. To him Paul said,

"You have seen God's punishment of those who commit violence in the name of religion." Then, pointing toward the door of his room, Paul said, "Go tell others about what you have seen here, and tell them I come to bring a message that God will reward the Palestinians if they choose peace over violence against Israel. It is a far greater reward than the plot of land sought by the Israelis to build their temple." The Hamas agent, now visibly shaking, ran from Paul's room. As he fled the hotel, he heard what sounded like a flock of birds flying from the hotel's roof.

Feeling relieved but exhausted, Paul slowly picked up the telephone by his bed and called the front desk. He requested the hotel clerk to telephone the Jerusalem police.

* * *

Later that morning, Paul was sitting in the office of Jacob Eisin, the District Police Commander in the Jewish Quarter of Jerusalem.

"So, we meet again, Mr. Swanson. The investigating officers tell me that you claim God killed the two men whose bodies were found in your hotel room."

"Yes," said Paul calmly. "Three men came into my room while I was sleeping. They were trying to abduct me when God struck two of them down. The third ran away."

"The last time we met, I was skeptical of your prediction about the destruction of the Islamic shrine. This time I am not so skeptical of what you say. But I would like to know how God killed those men. And I would especially like to know how one of them fell dead without dropping a live grenade. His grip was hard to break, even after death."

"I don't pretend to understand how God caused their deaths. I just know that He is protecting me while I am here to deliver His message to Israel and to Palestine about the Temple Mount. I must speak to the Prime Minister and to the President of the Palestinian Authority."

* * *

After Commander Eisin finished questioning Paul, Jerusalem police drove him back to his hotel. Paul then telephoned Shabak headquarters to speak with Eli Zahavi but was told that Agent Zahavi was away from his office. Due to the time differential between Israel and Florida, Paul waited a few hours before calling Rachel and his parents to tell them of his attempted abduction. Rachel and Clara begged him to reconsider his decision to stay in Jerusalem while delivering God's message. Paul thanked them for their concern but assured them that God would continue to protect him. Then, Paul telephoned Eli Zahavi's office again.

* * *

Following Rachel's telephone conversation with Paul, she struggled to cope with her fear of losing Paul and with her sadness at the thought of being away from him indefinitely. She had difficulty sleeping and teaching her elementary school class. In her despondency, she turned to the person who had become her closest friend.

Rachel had come to think of Clara Swanson as an older, wiser sister and, despite their age difference, she felt they had much in common. They shared the same Christian values, and they were both pretty and accustomed to the attentions of men. Although she was not as voluptuous as Clara, Rachel did have an equally attractive, long-limbed, curvaceous figure to compliment her delicate features. What most caused Rachel to feel comfortable around Clara, however, was the empathy and concern for others that she sensed in Clara. Rachel would never know that Clara's empathy was born in part from the years of guilt and shame that she had suffered following her secret abortion. Though Paul's adoption had helped relieve Clara's pangs of remorse, she had not found true peace until she had focused her attention on helping others instead of worrying about her personal shortcomings.

As she sat with Clara in the Swanson home, Rachel tearfully explained the reason for her visit. "I'm so worried about Paul that I can't sleep. I've prayed about his safety, but I guess I just don't have enough faith to quit worrying."

"I used to worry about Paul, too, Rachel. When Paul was six years old, a man almost kidnapped him, and I worried about him for years after that. But as Paul grew older, I came to believe that he was put into this world for a special purpose. I believe his destiny is to accomplish that purpose and that his trip to Israel is part of his destiny. Although we sometimes can't help worrying about the ones we love, you and I needn't worry about Paul. His fate is in the hands of God."

* * *

At a hideout in the West Bank, the terrorist who had fled Paul's hotel room was excitedly reporting to other members of the Izz el-Din al-Qassam Brigades, an armed wing of Hamas. "The American is not like others I have met. He has no fear of death. He says he is a messenger of Allah. He says he brings a message to Palestine of a great reward that Allah will give Palestine and Israel if they will peacefully resolve the present conflict over al-Haram al-Sharif."

"He is a false prophet whose words cannot be trusted," responded one of the men. "This, our clerics have often told us."

"But he is protected by a great power," said the excited terrorist. "I have seen it myself. Whether his power is of Allah or Satan, I do not know. But it is undeniable. We must warn other martyrs that he is protected."

* * *

Later that day at the Shabak headquarters in Jerusalem, Jack Landon was speaking to Eli Zahavi. "So, the kid prophet is requesting a meeting with the Prime Minister. What does he want to talk to the Prime Minister about?"

"He told me that God has sent him to Israel to deliver a message to us and to the Muslims about the Temple Mount situation. Considering the accuracy of his previous prophecies, I relayed his request to my commanding officer, who then contacted the Prime Minister's office. Due to the present political situation and the public's fascination with Paul Swanson, I was not surprised that the Prime Minister agreed to meet with him tomorrow. The Prime Minister could use some positive publicity . . . and some divine intervention, as well."

"Amazing! The kid's becoming an international celebrity. By the way, have your people autopsied the bodies of the two terrorists who attempted to abduct him?"

"We quit doing formal autopsies on the bodies of dead terrorists," responded Eli. "We just do MRI scans on their brain stems to find the fatal lesions."

"What about the terrorist who died with a death grip on a live grenade? How did that happen?"

"Exactly the question I asked Dr. Meshenberg. She told me that voluntary and involuntary muscle contractions are controlled by deep brain structures called basal ganglia. Knowing this, she requested the terrorist's MRI scan to include views of his basal ganglia. The scan showed lesions in both his basal ganglia and his brain stem. Dr. Meshenberg believes the lesion in his basal ganglia occurred just before the fatal brain stem lesion, so his hand was paralyzed before he was struck dead. Again, as always, there were no visible signs of trauma and no entry wounds. Face it, Jack – no weapon could do that."

"No weapon we've ever seen. But I still can't believe God's pulling the plug on terrorists. There has to be another explanation."

"Now, I would like to ask you a question, Jack. Why did you not warn us that Paul Swanson was coming back to Jerusalem? We could have provided security for him, which we will do from now on."

"We had him under daily surveillance in the U.S. We had an agent living in his apartment complex and had a tap on his phone line. We had an agent on his flight to Israel, who followed him to his hotel in Jerusalem. We even had an agent in the hotel room next to his. But somehow, in the middle of the night, the terrorists got into his room while our agent was sleeping."

"I understand completely, Jack. Now you can see why we have so much trouble protecting our own people from these fanatics. They are deceptive as well as ruthless."

"Tell me about it," said Jack. "I just got my ass chewed out for half an hour by my Station Chief because the sneaky bastards werc able to attack the kid while he was under our surveillance."

"Why does he blame you for that?"

"Because he put me in charge of the kid's surveillance," replied Jack.

"I see. But why did the Station Chief ask a senior agent like you to perform surveillance?"

"Our Director believes, as I do, that the kid is connected to a counter-terrorist conspiracy. The Director has an entire CIA Station investigating the kid's background. And what they're finding out is pretty bizarre."

"Why? Because his parentage is unknown?"

"No, we've identified his real mother."

"Well, don't keep me in suspense. Who is she?"

"An American nuclear physicist named Suzanne Barnett. She was once the head of nuclear weapons research at our Livermore Laboratory."

"And what does she say about this?" asked Eli.

"Nothing. She died seven years ago at age sixty-nine."

"So, she would have been seventy-six now, but Paul Swanson must be about twenty-four now. You think this woman gave birth to Paul Swanson at age fifty-two? That would be rather miraculous."

"No, we've interviewed her first husband and her former employees, neighbors, and friends. They all tell us she was not pregnant during the year before the kid prophet was born. Her first husband says she miscarried twice during their marriage and then never became pregnant again. She divorced him when she was thirty-three. According to court documents, the divorce was due to 'irreconcilable differences.' Some of her friends refer to her ex as the 'philandering physicist,' so we suspect infidelity was the real reason for the divorce. In case you're wondering, her ex was not Paul's father. He and Dr. Barnett were federal employees with security clearances so we had their DNA on file. The DNA was how we found out the kid is Dr. Barnett's son and is not related to her ex-husband."

"Very interesting, Jack," said Eli, stroking his chin. "But, again, do you think this woman had a secret child at age fifty-two?" asked Eli with a slight smile.

"The ex-husband tells us that he and Dr. Barnett had used a fertility clinic in their attempts to have a child. We suspect that the fertility clinic obtained her ova and froze them, although the clinic could find no record of doing that."

"What?" said Eli, now obviously amused. "You suspect ova twenty years old were implanted in another woman? This gets more fantastic by the minute."

"Look," said Jack, somewhat annoyed, "DNA doesn't lie. If you have a better explanation for the match between Dr. Barnett's DNA and the kid's, I'd like to hear it."

"Relax, my friend. I'm not questioning the DNA evidence. But I do think that if one of Dr. Barnett's ova produced Paul Swanson, the ova were more likely obtained from her closer to the time of conception . . . even though most women have gone through the change of life by that time."

"Yeah, that makes sense. That would probably be after she met Bardoon."

"Bardoon? Who is Bardoon?"

"Dr. Omar Bardoon. So far, he's a mystery. We haven't located him, yet. He could be the kid's real father. He's a retired computer scientist who emigrated from Lebanon to the U.S. He made a fortune in various computer software and Internet ventures. He married Dr. Barnett ten years before Swanson was born and disappeared after Dr. Barnett's death. Here's a picture of Bardoon and Dr. Barnett. Quite a striking couple."

"Bardoon," said Eli, looking at the photograph. "I have never heard that name before."

"Yeah, weird name for a weird guy."

"Weird in what way?"

"Some of the physicists we interviewed at Livermore occasionally socialized with Bardoon and Dr. Barnett.

We may be smart, Eli, but those folks make us look like retards."

"Thanks for including me in the retarded group."

"Just a figure of speech, Eli," said Jack, laughing. "Anyway, the bottom line is that every one of those physicists described Bardoon as some kind of super genius – the smartest person they've ever met. But they also said he was an oddball. They said they heard other scientists refer to him as 'Dr. Bardoom' or just '*Dr. Doom*'."

"Dr. Doom?" asked Eli.

"Yeah. They said after his wife died, Bardoon became obsessed with the idea that the human race would end by global thermonuclear annihilation. He thought we were living in the last days."

"It sounds like he was depressed about Dr. Barnett's death, Jack."

"Sounds to me like a paranoid genius with a death wish."

CHAPTER 16
Promised Reward

During Paul's second day in Jerusalem, a Shabak agent escorted him from his now heavily guarded hotel room to the Prime Minister's Office in Jerusalem. There he met the military secretary who was the Prime Minister's liaison with the Israeli Defense Forces. The military secretary accompanied Paul to a conference room where the Prime Minister, Attorney General, and Cabinet Secretary were waiting. After introductions, the Prime Minister, smiling benignly, motioned to a chair and said, "Please have a seat, Mr. Swanson. We understand that you have come here at great personal peril to bring us a message."

"Yes, Prime Minister. I have come here only as a messenger. I do not pretend to be able to foretell the future, nor do I claim to have any psychic powers. As you know, God once warned me that He would destroy the Dome of the Rock, and He did. Then, He warned me that He would no longer allow religious terrorism, and He has not. Now, God has asked me to convey the message that if Israel and Islam will peacefully resolve their differences and negotiate a resolution of the conflict over the Temple Mount, God will reward both by transforming the desert areas of Israel and Palestine into lands with lakes and rivers."

After exchanging glances with the Attorney General and Cabinet Secretary, the Prime Minister responded, "Mr. Swanson, we have already offered to negotiate peacefully with the Palestinian Authority for shared control of the Temple Mount, but they refuse to negotiate with us. As you are probably aware, Hamas and other Palestinian Muslim groups do not even acknowledge Israel's right to exist. Their attacks upon us have ceased only because of the recent deaths of their jihadist terrorists. You do not have to convince us to negotiate peacefully, Mr. Swanson. But you have a formidable task ahead in convincing the Palestinians to do so."

"Then, Sir, I must meet with the President of the Palestinian Authority to convey God's message to him."

"I doubt that the Palestinian Authority or any of the Palestinian groups will ever consent to such negotiations, even if God will reward them for doing so. And, Mr. Swanson, you could be exposing yourself to great danger by attempting to persuade them to enter such negotiations."

"Please do not be concerned about my personal safety, Sir. God will protect me as He has before. Could you arrange for me to meet with the President of the Palestinian Authority?"

"I will have my office contact his office and request a meeting for you. Leave a telephone number where my office can contact you. If he will meet with you, I will have our Shabak agents take you to his office in Ramallah. If you do meet with him, please tell him we are prepared to offer very substantial concessions to the Palestinians for the right to share the Temple Mount. May God be with you, young man."

* * *

That evening the Palestinian Authority President conversed with leaders of Fatah, Hamas, and Islamic Jihad. "I received a telephone call from the Israeli Prime Minister's secretary. I was told that the American 'prophet,' Paul Swanson, claims to have a message from Allah about al-Haram al-Sharif and that he wants to deliver it to me in person."

"The American prophet? This is absurd," said the Fatah leader, shaking his head. "Surely you are not going to meet with him."

"Do not dismiss this young man so lightly," said the Hamas leader. "Yesterday, three members of Izz el-Din al-Qassam Brigades encountered him alone in his hotel room. They attempted to take him hostage to interrogate him about the deaths of martyrs. He was unarmed and did not fight them. Yet, the two men who tried to subdue him fell dead to the floor. One held a grenade from which he had pulled the pin. It did not explode. The American told the third man that Allah was protecting him and that he brings a message to Palestine of a great reward that Allah will give to Palestine and Israel for peacefully resolving the present conflict over al-Haram al-Sharif."

"His God is not Allah but Satan," the Islamic Jihad leader interjected.

"How can one judge a prophet but by the truth of his prophecies?" the Hamas leader asked rhetorically. "The American foresaw the destruction of the shrine and the deaths of martyrs, and he is protected by unseen forces."

"His power to foretell the future is satanic," insisted the Islamic Jihad leader.

"But he is a man of peace," said the President. "He is trying to bring peace between our people and the Israelis. Is this something that an evil man would do?"

The Fatah leader then spoke. "I have no answer to the riddle of this man. But I do not trust him. Maybe he seeks fame or political power."

"I do not think so," said the Hamas leader. "I am told he avoids publicity though the media wish to make him a celebrity. But he could be part of an American-Israeli conspiracy. And he does not understand our cause."

"It will not hurt us to hear his message," said the President. "Then, we can better judge who and what he is."

"Yes," agreed the Islamic Jihad leader, "to defeat an enemy, it is best to learn as much as possible about him."

* * *

Two days later, Paul attended a meeting in Ramallah with the President of the Palestinian Authority. Also present were leaders of Fatah, Hamas, and Islamic Jihad, whom the President introduced as representatives of Palestine and Islam. "Mr. Swanson, I am told that you are a prophet who brings a message for the people of Palestine," said the President to Paul.

"I do not claim to be a prophet or a psychic. I personally cannot foresee the future. However, God has entrusted me with a message for Palestinians and Israelis. You have seen that God will no longer tolerate terrorism in the name of religion. God has shown me that He wants Muslims, Jews, and Christians to coexist peacefully. God desires that the Temple Mount, which you call al-Haram al-Sharif, become a symbol of peace among the three religions that profess to worship Him. God has told me that He will reward the Palestinians and Israelis if Islam and Israel will peacefully negotiate an agreement to share control of al-Haram al-Sharif so the Jews can build their temple where the Dome of the Rock stood."

"And what is this reward that Allah will give the Palestinians if Islam allows this?" asked the President.

"God has told me that He will transform the desert areas in Palestine and Israel into lands with lakes and rivers. I have read that only twenty-seven percent of the West Bank, twenty-four percent of the Gaza Strip, and seventeen percent of Israel is arable land, so this would be a great reward to the people of Palestine and Israel."

"So, young man," said the President, who was now smiling, "you are asking Islam to allow the Jews to build their temple on our holy ground based upon your representation that Allah will bring lakes and rivers to our deserts?"

"The Prime Minister of Israel has told me that if Palestine will negotiate with Israel, it will offer very substantial concessions to Palestine for the right to share the Temple Mount. If such negotiations are successful, God will fulfill his promise. I am sure that you, as a Muslim, know that God can do anything."

"Yes, but many men have falsely claimed that Allah has spoken to them," replied the President. "Once an American named James Jones convinced many others to take their own lives because he thought Allah desired it. I am sure that you will agree that he was mistaken."

"The message I deliver is a message of promise for a better way of life for both Jews and Muslims. In recent months, you have seen the power of God. You have probably heard how He has protected me. I now ask you to help your fellow Palestinians by trusting the message I bring and negotiating with Israel. God will help you negotiate a mutually satisfactory agreement with the Israelis. Perhaps Israel would agree to trade other land that it occupies for the space to build its temple on the Temple Mount."

"Why should we trust the Israelis to honor such an agreement? Have they not taken our land, demolished our homes, destroyed our air and sea ports, and replaced Palestinian workers in Israel with foreign workers?"

"I am sure that Israelis and Palestinians have a long list of grievances against each other. But God is offering Muslims and Jews a new beginning – a chance to overcome the problems of the past – a chance to change barren land into gardens. I understand your skepticism. I might be skeptical too if I myself had not seen the power of God. Please convince your people to seize this opportunity for a better future. To demonstrate my sincerity and my faith in God's ability to deliver what He has promised, I make this personal promise to Islam: If Islam will resolve the Temple Mount conflict as God has requested, I will live in Palestine, under guard if necessary, until the world has seen that your deserts are being changed as God has promised."

"But what if this never happens? How long will you live in Palestine?" asked the President.

"God will honor His promise, and I will honor mine."

"Ah," said the President, "you are a man of faith. But tell me, young man, do you think the Israelis have enough faith in God to make a similar promise?"

"What do you mean by 'similar promise'?"

"If the Israelis truly believe that your message is true, then they should be willing to agree that if we let them build their temple but God does not bring lakes and rivers to our deserts, then they must return all of al-Haram al-Sharif to us, including the temple they build on our holy site."

"If Israel will agree to that condition in writing as part of the negotiations, will the Palestinian Authority and Islam negotiate with Israel?"

"I seriously doubt that Israel would ever make such an agreement, but I will discuss this with representatives of Islam. I will contact you when I have their answer."

After Paul had left his office, the President of the Palestinian Authority conferred with the Fatah, Hamas, and Islamic Jihad leaders, who had remained silent during the President's conversation with Paul. "Gentlemen, we have been presented with a rare political opportunity," said the President.

"You mean an opportunity to denounce this false prophet publicly?" asked the Islamic Jihad leader.

"Ah, my friend, it is much more than that. We have an opportunity both to prove to the world that he is a false prophet and to put the Israelis in a political dilemma. Do you not see? If we agree to negotiate with the Israelis on the terms I have proposed, we cannot lose. If the Israelis refuse to negotiate on our terms, they are showing the world that they know the American's prophecy is false. If they are foolish enough to accept our terms, they will build a temple only to lose it to us when the prophecy proves to be false. We then keep our holy site and the Israelis' new temple and everything else they have traded for the opportunity to build their temple."

"And what if the American's prophecy is true?" asked the Fatah leader.

The President smiled and said, "For thousands of years our deserts have been deserts. If Allah had wanted them to have lakes and rivers, they would have had lakes and rivers long ago."

"I personally would be willing to trade the site of our former shrine for lakes and rivers that would bring fertility to our land and quench the thirst of our people," said the Fatah leader.

"Those are blasphemous words," said the Islamic Jihad leader.

"Not if the trade is truly the will of Allah and it is He who creates the lakes and rivers," responded the Fatah leader.

"Gentlemen," said the President, "let us not quarrel about the benefits of something that will never happen. Let us seize this opportunity to gain politically and economically at the expense of the Israelis. If they refuse to negotiate on our terms, it will force an end to their attempts to build their temple on our holy site and will show the world they have no faith in the prophecies of the American. If they negotiate with us, we will end up with our holy site and their temple and whatever other concessions we have negotiated with them."

"Yes," agreed the Islamic Jihad leader, "we will look reasonable to the world. And the world will know that we are rightfully entitled to take back our sacred property when this foolish infidel's prophecy is shown to be false."

Nodding his agreement, the Hamas leader said, "And do not forget the American's promise to live in Palestine until Allah turns the deserts into lakes and rivers. He may be with us for a long time." This statement brought laughter from the others.

After the laughter had subsided, the Fatah leader spoke. "The American offered to be our hostage. But holding him as our hostage would give us a bad political image and could bring the United States into the situation. I say that we just watch him closely while he lives in Palestine."

"Yes," said the Hamas leader. "We can watch him closely to see if he communicates with those who are killing our martyrs. Perhaps, we can discover their weapon."

"At least," said the President, "the American will have an opportunity to observe firsthand the hardships imposed on Palestinians by the Israelis." Then, after the others had nodded their agreement, the President said, "Let us now discuss how we will explain to Islam the reason that we should agree on behalf of Palestine and Islam to participate in this negotiation."

* * *

For weeks the President of the Palestinian Authority and the leaders of Fatah, Hamas, and Islamic Jihad conferred with other leaders throughout Islam about their plan for negotiation with the Israelis. Paul, on the other hand, undertook the formidable task of convincing the Prime Minister that Israel should accept the contingency proposed by the President of the Palestinian Authority. Eventually, the Prime Minister and the Knesset agreed that an act of faith was preferable to negative publicity from an act of faithlessness. Besides, they reasoned, the only alternative was seizure of the Temple Mount site, which would be an act of religious aggression likely to precipitate war with Islam and, perhaps, provoke the wrath of God. Moreover, as the Prime Minister told the Knesset, by constructing the Third Temple, Israel would be preventing construction of a new Dome of the Rock and giving Israel time to convince the world that it had a right to keep the the temple that it was building.

* * *

Two months later, the Israeli Prime Minister and Palestinian Authority President jointly announced the commencement of the Temple Mount negotiations.

Throughout the world, Paul's 'Desert Prophecy' and his role as initiator of the negotiations was widely publicized. Public perceptions, as always, varied greatly. Some Jews and Christians perceived Paul as a heroic messenger of God; however, most thought he was a well-meaning but delusional young man. A few fundamentalist Christians suspected that he might be the antichrist of Revelations. Most Muslims viewed him as a false prophet who either was a tool of Satan or was part of a Jewish-American conspiracy to confiscate sacred Islamic property. To atheists he was just another foolish religious fanatic. Nevertheless, although skeptical of the 'Desert Prophecy,' most people were convinced that Paul truly believed that if the Temple Mount negotiations were successful, God would transform the deserts of Israel and Palestine. After all, Paul had promised to live in Palestine until the desert transformation occurred.

* * *

At Eli Zahavi's office, Jack Landon conversed with Eli about the impending Temple Mount negotiations. "I still can't believe Israel would agree to return that Temple Mount site to the Muslims if the kid's prophecy is bogus. Deserts changing into lakes and rivers? Come on, Eli – you can't believe that."

"What other choice did we have, Jack? Some Israelis believe his prophecy is true. Others just want peace. And, as you know, it would be politically untenable for us to use military force to seize the Temple Mount in violation of our previous agreement with the Arabs."

"Yeah, but to acquire that land, your Prime Minister is reportedly going to offer to withdraw from strategic positions in the West Bank, which could leave Israel more vulnerable to attacks from Palestinian terrorists. And for what? Surely he can't believe that God is really going to turn the Negev and Judean deserts into lakefront properties."

"The Knesset and Prime Minister have considered all contingencies. In the worst-case scenario, we will have traded military positions in the West Bank for peace. According to Paul Swanson's prophecy, fulfillment of the prophecy is contingent upon negotiating an agreement to share the Temple Mount, not upon building the Third Temple. Therefore, we will not have to spend a lot on construction or even start construction of our temple until we know whether the prophecy is true."

"Israel is still paying a high price to find out if the kid's delusional."

"Not really. We had planned to withdraw from some of those West Bank positions anyway. Besides, as Paul Swanson predicted, the terrorist attacks have been stopped, so some of those positions are no longer necessary to our security."

"You still think God is killing terrorists? How long do you think that will last?"

"In all these months has the CIA found another explanation for these deaths?"

"Not yet, but we think the kid's background will lead us to the truth."

"Have your people located Dr. Omar Bardoon yet?"

"No, but we've found out more about him. We know that he was born Omar bin Nuha al-Bardoon in Beirut seventy years ago. At the age of twenty-six, he immigrated to the U.S. and changed his name to Omar Bardoon. Bardoon's parents, an Arab father and Jewish mother, were professors of medicine at the American University of Beirut. He was either home schooled or privately schooled until age twelve, when he became the youngest student ever admitted to the American University of Beirut. At age sixteen, he earned doctorates in both mathematics and physics and became the youngest professor of mathematics and physics at American University's Center for Advanced Mathematical Sciences. At age twenty, he left the University to start a company that produced specialized computer hardware and software systems, which he later relocated to the U.S. after the deaths of his parents. Our agents in Beirut tell us that Bardoon's parents, Nuha and Tahira al-Bardoon, were outspoken advocates for peaceful coexistence between Islam and Israel. We believe they were assassinated as a result of their political views."

"Interesting, but how does all of this relate to Paul Swanson's ability to predict future events?"

"We're still working on that. But I don't think it's a coincidence that Swanson is the secret son of a top nuclear weapons physicist who was married to a man known as Dr. Doom, who has now disappeared. Do you?"

* * *

Although Paul had daily telephone conversations with Rachel, she longed to be with him again. She urged Paul to reconsider his plan to live in Palestine if the Temple Mount negotiations were successful, pointing out that God had not asked him to do so. Paul, however, was adamant that he could not rescind his promise. He explained that he had given his word to live in Palestine to show the Palestinian people that he truly believed that God would honor His promise to transform the deserts. When Rachel suggested that she come to Jerusalem to visit Paul, he urged her not to endanger herself by coming to a place where terrorists had twice threatened his life. Despite his best efforts, however, he could not dissuade Rachel from visiting him during the Temple Mount negotiations, and she soon took a leave of absence from her teaching position to fly to Israel.

On the day of Rachel's arrival, Paul and the Shabak agent assigned to protect him drove to Ben Gurion International Airport to meet Rachel. Paul's arrival at the airport, as usual, drew considerable attention. By the time Paul greeted Rachel with open arms, curious spectators and paparazzi were surrounding them. Paul's passionate embrace of Rachel resulted in cheers and camera flashes. Somewhat embarrassed by the unwanted attention, they both smiled broadly before hugging once more. Paul held up his hands to the group of reporters and requested, "Please, no interviews today." Gesturing toward Rachel, he said, "She is tired from her long trip, and we must leave." He then introduced Rachel to his Shabak companion before they pressed through surrounding spectators and paparazzi on their way to the baggage claim area. With the assistance of airport security guards, the Shabak agent managed to keep the reporters away from Paul and Rachel while they retrieved Rachel's luggage. Then, the Shabak agent led Paul and Rachel as they again pressed through onlookers on their way to the agent's car. On the way back to Paul's hotel, where a room had been reserved for Rachel, Paul asked the Shabak agent if he could guard Rachel's room rather than his own. The agent assured him that multiple agents were already guarding both rooms against terrorists and paparazzi.

* * *

In Qom, Iran, a senior Grand Ayatollah was speaking to an official of the Iranian government and commanding officers of Hezbollah. "Many are opposed to this plan to negotiate with the Jews. It would be blasphemy to allow them to desecrate al-Haram al-Sharif by building their temple on the site of our holy shrine."

"Do not worry," a Hezbollah officer interjected. "If an agreement is reached, the world will soon know that the infidel's prophecy is false, and Islam will regain the site of its shrine."

"I doubt the Jews are foolish enough to believe this prophecy," continued the Ayatollah. "If an agreement is negotiated, I suspect they will not honor it by withdrawing from al-Haram al-Sharif when the infidel's prophecy fails. The infidel's prophecy may also be a trick. Maybe the Jews and their American allies will start irrigation projects in the deserts and claim that they are doing Allah's work in fulfillment of the prophecy. To prevent such trickery and to stop the desecration of al-Haram al-Sharif, Islam must negotiate a deadline for fulfillment of the false prophecy, and we must be prepared to drive the Jews from al-Haram al-Sharif as soon as the deadline passes. The Palestinians are not strong enough to do this. But the nations of Islam and Hezbollah have the military might to force the Jews from al-Haram al-Sharif. When the falsity of the infidel's prophecy is exposed, the eyes of the world will see that we are justified in taking back the site of our sacred shrine. And when we drive the Jews from al-Haram al-Sharif, we will have our long-awaited opportunity to take back all that the Jews have taken from Islam."

"Are you asking us to attack Israel?" asked a Hezbollah officer. "What about this secret weapon that is killing Islamic martyrs? And remember, the Israelis have a formidable army and air force."

"This secret weapon has not stopped some of our martyrs from exploding their bombs," replied the Ayatollah. "We pursue a holy cause. Allah will not permit any weapon or the Israelis to stop us. The might of the nations of Islam will drive the Jews from our land forever. A man of faith would know this."

"And," added the Iranian government official, "our Islamic brothers in Lebanon, Syria, and Jordan have agreed to participate in a coordinated attack on Israel."

"What if the Jews decide to use their weapons of mass destruction against us?" asked one of the Hezbollah officers.

"Good," responded the Iranian official, "then Iran will be justified in retaliating with its full nuclear arsenal."

"We have heard of your weapons," said the Hezbollah officer, "but can Iran deliver them with accuracy to targets within Israel?"

"Thanks to Russian missile technology," the Iranian official responded with a smile, "we now can. And do not forget the hundreds of rockets we have provided to Hezbollah and to Hamas. Those, too, can be equipped with nuclear warheads. And they will not have to travel far from their hidden bunkers in southern Lebanon and the West Bank to find their targets."

After the Hezbollah officers had left his office, the Iranian official addressed the senior Grand Ayatollah. "Our agents in the United States have assured us that the Americans are going to great lengths to investigate the deaths of Islamic martyrs. A source inside the CIA – a very reliable source – has revealed that a physician hired by the CIA was the one who discovered the brain injuries that are causing these deaths. The source also has reported that both the CIA and Shabak have been conducting investigations to find the weapon causing the brain injuries, but they have found nothing. The CIA has investigated the American prophet's background. Their agents have tried to discover if he is part of a secret group responsible for the deaths, but they have found no such group. The Americans and the Israelis know no more about these deaths than we do. If there is no American secret weapon, could these deaths be the work of Allah? Could the prophecies of the American be true?"

Staring angrily at the official, the Ayatolah responded, "Have you lost your faith? Do you no longer believe the word of Allah that He gave to the blessed Muhammad, the last true prophet? How could you believe that a Christian infidel from America, the Great Satan, could be a messenger of Allah? If Allah had wanted peace between Israel and Islam, do you not believe that He would have revealed this to His faithful servants in Islam?"

"Yes, Ayatollah, I see the truth in what you say. But how do you explain the infidel prophet's ability to predict the destruction of our shrine and the deaths of our martyrs?"

"Do you not think Satan knows the future? Do you not think Satan has the power to take men's lives as well as their souls? If men are not causing the deaths of Islamic martyrs, who do you think is causing them – Allah or Satan?"

"Ah," said the Iranian official, his eyes widening with comprehension, "then we must fight not only Israel but Satan himself."

"You have spoken wisely, my friend. Islam is always under attack from Satan. If the infidel prophet is not willingly possessed by Satan, then he may be the unwitting tool of Satan, who is using the infidel's prophecies to attack our faith in Islam."

"But how can we fight against Satan? How can we prevent Satan from killing our martyrs?"

"We fight Satan by defeating his plan for the Jews to desecrate the site of an Islamic shrine by building a temple there. The more we limit the time for fulfillment of the infidel's prophecy, the sooner its falsity will be exposed. And when the world sees that the deserts have not been transformed as the infidel has prophesied, we will attack, driving the Jews from the Temple Mount and from Jerusalem, as Muhammad once drove the Jews from Medina. Then, we will drive them from the rest of the land they have stolen."

"What if the Americans come to the defense of Israel?" asked the Iranian official.

"That will not happen if we strike before the American military can be brought across the world to fight in Israel. We must attack quickly, as soon as the infidel's prophecy is shown to be false."

"Yes," said the official, "I will see that your words are passed on to those who negotiate with Israel and to our military and to the leadership of Syria and Jordan and to the leaders of Hamas and other Palestinian resistance groups. We shall prepare to bring the might of Islam against Israel and the infidel prophet."

CHAPTER 17
Doomsday Committee

In Langley, Virginia, an agent of the National Security Agency was speaking to Maxwell Colson, the Director of Central Intelligence. "As you know, Director Colson, the security of Livermore and our other nuclear research facilities is something the NSA monitors carefully. When I heard from a Livermore physicist that your agency was investigating the late Dr. Suzanne Barnett and her husband, I asked our NSA Director about the purpose of the CIA investigation. I think I may have some information that will be useful to your investigation."

"Information about what?" asked the Director.

"Part of our job is to monitor the communications and affiliations of all of our top-level scientists, particularly those involved in nuclear weapons research and development. For example, we know that Dr. Barnett and her husband were members of the Global Union of Scientists for Peace, which is a legitimate organization."

"Yes. We've interviewed several Global Union members who knew Dr. Barnet and Dr. Bardoon. But they haven't seen Dr. Bardoon since his wife's death. He's a person of interest in our investigation. But we've been unable to find him, and there is no record of his death."

"Well," said the NSA agent, "I have some additional information about the mysterious Dr. Bardoon. As you may know, he was a pioneer in artificial intelligence and cybernetic robotic systems. One of his companies, a company he sold for billions to AmBotics, designed the most advanced cybernetic machine control system on the market. One of his other companies created a cryptography software system that was so powerful that we considered it a threat to national security. The damn thing could crack every code we had, no matter what the level of encryption was. To protect the security of U.S. information systems, we had to buy his company and make him sign a secrecy agreement. We are still using his software to monitor communications throughout the world. Although Dr. Bardoon signed a secrecy agreement, we had to consider him a potential security risk. After all, the man could have created another decryption system and sold it to our enemies. That's why we had to tap his phones. And since I was a rookie agent at the time, I got stuck with monitoring his calls."

"During what time period did the wiretapping occur?" asked the Director.

"It was after he married Dr. Barnett – about twenty-five years ago."

"So, how is all this relevant to our investigation?"

"Well, I thought you'd want to know about Dr. Bardoon's membership in some sort of *secret group.*"

"What type of group?" the Director asked with sudden interest.

"While I was monitoring his calls, I heard him talking to dozens of retired scientists about meetings of a secret group they belonged to. I checked all of them out. They all had good reputations, and some even had security clearances, so eventually my Director ordered me to drop the investigation. I thought that was a mistake, but orders are orders."

"Why did you want to continue the investigation?"

"Well, as I said, some of those scientists had security clearances. The way they were sneaking around made me uneasy; and in some of his telephone calls, Dr. Bardoon referred to the group as the '*Doomsday Committee.*' He seemed to be the leader of the group. I never found out what they were up to." Then, handing a document to the Director, the NSA agent said, "But when I heard you were investigating Dr. Bardoon, I thought you might want this. It's the list I made of the scientists who were members of Dr. Bardoon's 'Doomsday Committee.' Unfortunately, the list is twenty-five years old, and most of the scientists on it were retired when I made the list. I doubt that many of them are still alive."

* * *

At the outset of the Temple Mount negotiations, which were held in Jerusalem under heavy security, the parties stipulated that the Israeli contingent would be led by the Prime Minister and that the Islamic-Palestinian contingent would be led by the President of the Palestinian Authority. They agreed that each lead negotiator would have with him a team of advisors, including attorneys, with whom he could consult during the negotiations. The parties further stipulated that if an agreement were reached, its terms would be reduced to writing and would not become binding until it was signed by the lead negotiators before the General Assembly of the United Nations.

During the first week of negotiations, the negotiators focused primarily upon Israel's agreement to withdraw from the Temple Mount if the miraculous desert transformation, now known as the 'Desert Prophecy,' did not occur. For days, the negotiators argued over what would constitute fulfillment of the prophecy and what the deadline for its fulfillment would be. The Palestinians initially proposed that fulfillment would require that within twenty-four hours after execution of a written agreement, lakes and rivers must occupy half of the desert areas of Israel and Palestine. Following a discussion with his team of advisors, the Prime Minister made the counter-proposal that fulfillment of the prophecy be defined as the existence of new lakes and rivers in five percent of the desert areas within two years of the agreement's execution. On the fourth day of negotiations, after several more proposals and counter-proposals, the parties finally agreed that the prophecy would be fulfilled if at least one tenth of the surface area of the deserts was covered by new lakes and rivers within three months after execution of a formal Temple Mount agreement.

* * *

While the negotiations continued, Paul and Rachel decided to explore historic sites in Jerusalem. Accompanied by two Shabak agents assigned to provide their security, they first visited the Western Wall and the Temple Mount. Soon after their arrival at the Western Wall, Paul and Rachel found themselves besieged by paparazzi and curious spectators. While the reporters among the paparazzi attempted to interview Paul, the photographers focused their attention on Rachel's graceful beauty and radiant smile. The Shabak agents attempted to keep the reporters at bay, but eventually Paul agreed to speak briefly to them. They immediately asked Paul if he had any more predictions about the future, particularly the future of Israel and Palestine. Paul patiently repeated what he had said many times before – that he was only a messenger, not a clairvoyant or psychic. He then stated that he had already delivered all of the messages entrusted to him by God and did not know whether he would be given any future messages. When asked about his relationship to Rachel, Paul requested the reporters to respect Rachel's privacy and then asked the reporters and photographers to excuse him while he accompanied Rachel to the Temple Mount. This, of course, did not dissuade the paparazzi from following them and continuing to photograph them as they toured the Temple Mount.

On the following day, photographs of Paul and Rachel appeared in newspapers throughout the world. One of the photographs captured Paul showing Rachel the ruins of the Dome of the Rock. A Muslim cleric in Palestine, one of many opposed to the Temple Mount negotiations, saw the photograph and became enraged. In the cleric's mind the photograph depicted a demon-possessed, infidel prophet who was gloating over the destruction of a sacred Islamic shrine. Unaware that the Temple Mount negotiations were part of a secret Islamic plan to attack Israel, the cleric contacted a group of local Islamic militants who were also opposed to the negotiations and unaware of the planned attack on Israel. The cleric exhorted them to pursue jihad against the infidel prophet.

* * *

Throughout the world, news coverage of the ongoing Temple Mount negotiations and the Desert Prophecy of Paul Swanson captured the public's imagination. News commentators devoted entire programs to the potential implications of a Temple Mount agreement – with and without fulfillment of the Desert Prophecy. The prophecy itself was the subject of much philosophical, religious, and scientific analysis. The consensus among Islamic scholars was that the concept of a Christian prophet was antithetic to the teachings of the Qur'an and that Paul was either foolish or demonically inspired. Jewish and Christian scholars agreed that nothing in the Torah or the Christian Bible suggested that the Desert Prophecy was valid. No one in the scientific community expressed belief in the Desert Prophecy or indicated that its fulfillment was possible. Most media coverage reflected the opinion that Paul Swanson was well intentioned and courageous but probably delusional or, at least, mistaken. Among the public, many were hopeful that the Desert Prophecy would prove to be true, but few actually believed in it. Nevertheless, most Israelis were strongly in favor of negotiating an agreement to share the Temple Mount, even an agreement based upon a prophecy in which few believed.

* * *

In the second week of negotiations, the Islamic-Palestinian contingent pressed for several additional concessions from Israel, including complete withdrawal from the West Bank, recognition of Palestine as an independent nation with complete political and economic autonomy, and conveyance to Palestine of a section of the land connecting the southern end of the West Bank to the Gaza Strip. These concessions, if accepted, would have divided Israel in half with an autonomous Palestinian state separating northern and southern Israel. The Israeli contingent immediately rejected the proposed concessions and counter-offered only to remove Israeli Defense Forces from security checkpoints in the West Bank. No further progress in the negotiations occurred until Israel agreed to provide economic assistance to rebuild Palestinian infrastructure so long as there were no terrorist activities by Palestinians. This, however, did not satisfy the Islamic advisors to the President of the Palestinian Authority. They argued that there were too many Jewish settlements in the West Bank that were displacing many of the Palestinians who once lived there. The prospect of relocating the numerous Jewish settlements was politically and geographically infeasible to Israel and resulted in an impasse in the negotiations.

* * *

Despite their aversion to the paparazzi, Paul and Rachel could not resist visiting the most sacred Christian site in Jerusalem, the Church of the Holy Sepulchre. Accompanied by the two Shabak agents who had escorted them on their previous outing, Paul and Rachel left their hotel to visit the ancient church in the heart of Jerusalem's Christian Quarter.

As they entered the hotel's parking garage, a large group of paparazzi rushed toward them. The two Shabak agents were able to fend off the reporters long enough to get Paul and Rachel into their vehicle while the photographers took photo after photo.

When the Shabak vehicle left the parking garage, Paul and Rachel were not surprised to see some of the paparazzi following in their own vehicles. Soon, a small caravan of automobiles was proceeding slowly through the narrow, crowded streets in the labyrinth of ancient buildings and tiny alleyways known as the Christian Quarter.

Turning onto Souk el-Dabbagha, the street that led to the Church of the Holy Sepulchre, the Shabak vehicle drove past crowded shops and stalls selling religious souvenirs. At last, the vehicle turned into the courtyard in front of the main entrance to the ancient Church of the Holy Sepulchre. The Shabak driver stopped to let Paul, Rachel, and the other agent out before driving away to park the vehicle.

As Paul, Rachel, and their Shabak escort walked toward the arched doorway of the church's main entrance, they observed that the paparazzi were not far behind. While the other paparazzi hurriedly left their vehicles to follow Paul and Rachel, one remained in his automobile and made a cell phone call. "They are at the Church of the Holy Sepulchre," was all he said before driving away.

* * *

In Berkeley, California, Ralph Widman, a CIA agent, met with Dr. Ephram Hoffman, a ninety-year-old retired physicist who had won a Nobel Prize for energy research at age forty-one.

"And what can I do for the CIA today?" asked Dr. Hoffman, an energetic man who appeared young for his age.

"I appreciate your seeing me on short notice, Dr. Hoffman. I'd just like to obtain some background information for an investigation we're conducting."

"Whose background?"

"You were acquainted with Dr. Omar Bardoon and his late wife, weren't you?"

"Ah, you're investigation involves Omar. How is he these days?"

"I was hoping that you might be able to tell me that. When was the last time you had any contact with him?"

"Not since the year after Suzanne died – a tragic loss. She was a beautiful person as well as a beautiful woman. Her death had a profound effect on Omar."

"How so?"

"Before Suzanne's death, Omar was one of the most optimistic people I had ever met. He thought there was a solution for every problem. But while Suzanne was dying from brain cancer, he became increasingly cynical, almost morbid. Despite receiving state-of-the-art medical treatment, Suzanne was ravaged by the cancer. Omar watched helplessly. And I watched helplessly as a man who had once been my friend, a man with the finest mind I had ever known, became embittered and irrational."

"Irrational?"

"That's not a clinical assessment, young man. I profess no expertise in psychology, but I saw changes in Omar's personality after Suzanne died. I had known Omar for many years. He had been full of optimism that we could solve the problems of the world through science. While Suzanne was alive, Omar was a staunch advocate of nuclear disarmament and an implacable foe of politicians who espoused nuclear proliferation as a deterrent to foreign military aggression. But the last time I saw Omar, he said that we had wasted our time opposing nuclear proliferation, that it was inevitable. Then, he said that he hoped that a nuclear confrontation would come soon. I was shocked that he would make such a comment. When I told him so, he just laughed. That was the last communication I ever had with the man. And I haven't seen him since."

"Did he seem self-destructive?"

"Again, I'm not a psychologist. But he may have been self-destructive at that point."

"Did you think he could be dangerous?"

"Dangerous to whom, young man?"

"Well, we've heard some of Dr. Bardoon's former acquaintances refer to him as 'Dr. Doom,' and we know that he was involved in something called the 'Doomsday Committee.' That sounds dangerous to me."

"As you apparently know, I was a member of Omar's 'Doomsday Committee' until it disbanded after Suzanne's death. How did the CIA find out about it?"

"I'm sorry, Dr. Hoffman. I can't disclose our sources. But I do need to ask you about your involvement."

"I suppose that our little group could have appeared suspicious with its secrecy pledges, mysterious telephone calls, encrypted Internet conferences, annual secret meetings, and that name, 'Doomsday Committee.' But it was all well intentioned and harmless."

"What was the purpose of the Doomsday Committee, Dr. Hoffman?"

"We thought that we were the brain trust for some sort of 'Star Wars' project to make the country safer from an ICBM attack. 'Doomsday Committee' was just a name some of the members started calling the group. We thought our project might prevent 'doomsday.' We were actually just doing research for Omar on a wide variety of subjects in each of our areas of expertise. We presented the results of our research at our weekly Internet conferences and discussed its potential application to a particular problem that Omar had introduced. The reason for the group's secrecy was that many of us had security clearances and were concerned that 'Big Brother' would frown upon our discussions that sometimes involved classified information. In retrospect, I'm not sure what Omar was working on because nothing seemed to come of our research. As I've said, after Suzanne's death Omar no longer seemed interested in preventing nuclear war. Then, Omar disappeared, and the group disbanded."

"Was there any compensation for your research?"

"Omar paid all of us fees as scientific consultants. Unlike Omar, the rest of us weren't independently wealthy, and most of us were dependent upon fixed retirement incomes. Don't worry; I reported it on my tax returns."

"I'm not an IRS agent, Dr. Hoffman. How much were you paid as a consultant?"

"Five thousand dollars per week for research and participation in weekly internet conferences that usually lasted about four hours every Sunday night. We also received ten thousand dollars plus travel and hotel expenses for attending an annual weekend conference."

"Tell me about the committee. How did it start? How many members were there?"

"Omar started the group long before I became a member. I think it was shortly after he came to this country. He was by far the youngest member of the group. Quite a bit younger than Suzanne, you know. But we all recognized that he was a towering intellect. While I was a member, there were about three dozen of us. We were mostly retired scientists from various fields who had been forced to retire by age sixty-five due to the policies of our former employers. Omar believed that mandatory retirement was wasting some of our country's best scientific talent. He hired us to research various subjects and meet weekly through his encrypted Internet chat-room where we exchanged ideas and brainstormed concepts related to our research. The discussions got highly technical and quite theoretical. Sometimes we would discuss one subject for months before addressing the next one. Omar asked all the members to contribute to the discussions from their own perspectives. We were all amazed at Omar's knowledge of each of our fields. The man absorbed technical information like a sponge."

"What were the subjects that the group researched?"

"Well, I doubt that I can remember them all. Many of our conferences were devoted to beam weapons technology and the problems inherent in creating effective beam weapons. Suzanne was one of the principal researchers in that area. As you may know, she was one of the country's leading experts on nuclear weapons. Other conferences were devoted to telecommunications research, specifically as it applied to space-based weapons. And many conferences focused upon BCI and BMI technology."

"What is BCI and BMI technology?"

"Brain-Computer Interface and Brain-Machine Interface technology. It enables direct communication between the brain and a computer that may be connected to other devices. You've probably heard of the work being done with quadriplegic patients and stroke victims. Scalp electrodes or brain implants are connected to a computer that amplifies and interprets brain electrical activity, enabling paralyzed patients to control mechanical devices."

"How was that related to your 'Star Wars' research?"

"It may not have been. It was just one of our many research subjects. Omar was particularly interested in the latest generation of BCI microchips that enable simultaneous communications with tens of thousands of individual brain cells. He said one of his laboratories was involved in animal research to test an asynchronous BCI that communicated with visual and auditory brain centers. Apparently he lost interest in that project because he later dropped BCI as one of our research subjects."

"What type of information did you provide to the group?"

"As you probably know, my field was energy research. Most of my work was in the area of nuclear fission and fusion – finding safer and more economical methods of production, storage, and disposal of nuclear fuels, such as deuterium and tritium. In the early years of the group, Omar was very interested in nuclear energy production as a means of decreasing our dependence on fossil fuel. Later, he seemed more interested in what he referred to as 'transduction of solar radiation.' He considered even the latest generation of solar-cell technology to be much too inefficient. He was convinced that he could find a more efficient method of converting sunlight into useable energy."

"And did he?"

"I don't know. But if anyone could, he could."

"Did Dr. Bardoon ever discuss the creation of a specific weapon?"

"As I said, we all discussed various types of devices that could theoretically be utilized to thwart an ICBM attack. Beam weapons, laser weapons, particle cannons, and anti-ballistic missiles. Weapons technology was one of Omar's favorite subjects. In fact, his interest in weapons technology is what led him to ask Suzanne to join the group. She soon fell under his spell, and he under hers. They were both charming people – before Suzanne died."

"Did he ever indicate that he was testing any type of weapon?"

"Is that what your investigation is about? You think Omar has created some kind of weapon?"

"I wish I could answer your questions, but I cannot. I'm only here to gather information."

"Well, you're doing a fine job, young man."

"Do you recall any specific ideas that Dr. Bardoon personally had about weapons technology?"

"Omar usually just initiated the discussions by asking the rest of us questions. However, Suzanne once told me that Omar had invented a technology that her former colleagues at Livermore would 'kill to obtain.' She wouldn't tell me what it was. She said Omar was very protective of his inventions. She had a peculiar name for it. Give me a moment and I'll think of it. . . .Ah, yes, she called it 'Cybernetic Swarm Technology.' I think I asked her if it involved killer bees, and we both laughed. Well, that's about all I can tell you."

"Thank you, Dr. Hoffman. By the way, here's a list we have of members of the group," said the agent, handing a document and pen to the elderly scientist. "If you can think of any other names, we'd appreciate it. We'd also like to know if you have kept in touch with any of them."

"I've attended the funerals of some of them. I'll mark a 'D' by each of their names. I've lost track of most of the others. Ted Durham was still attending meetings of Global Union of Scientists for Peace until a couple of years ago. I visited him recently at his nursing home. Poor Ted; he's quite disabled – hard of hearing. To my recollection, the only members missing from this list are Suzanne and a telecommunications expert. I believe his name was Zachary Swindell. But I remember reading his obituary several years ago."

"Why did the group break up?"

"As I said, Omar changed after Suzanne's death. Suzanne's death may have caused him to lose his grip on reality. At our last annual meeting, he attempted to insinuate a discussion of the merits of strategic provocation of thermonuclear warfare. The other members were appalled. When we asked him why he would even consider such a topic, he just smiled and shrugged his shoulders. And, as I said, the last time I spoke with Omar he made the remark about hoping that a nuclear confrontation would come soon. Then, Omar just quit contacting us and shut down the group's Internet chat-room, which he had hosted. And when we tried to contact him, we learned that he had disappeared."

"Can you tell me anything else?"

"No, but I'd like for you to tell me something. Does the CIA consider Omar Bardoon a threat of some kind?"

"All I can tell you is that his name came up in an ongoing investigation."

* * *

At the main entrance to the Church of the Holy Sepulchre, Paul and Rachel stood with a Shabak agent and other visitors, including paparazzi, waiting to enter the church. The other Shabak agent, who had been parking his automobile, soon joined them. As Rachel stared at the church's austere, somewhat dilapidated façade, Paul read to her from a tourist guide. "The original Church of the Holy Sepulchre was a magnificent Roman basilica erected in the fourth century by Constantine the Great upon ground believed to encompass both Golgotha, which was the hill on which Christ was crucified, and the nearby sepulcher in which Christ was entombed. Persian invaders partially destroyed the basilica in 614 A.D. and stole its relics. About twenty years later, the Byzantines recaptured Jerusalem, forced the Persians to return the relics and began restoring the church. In subsequent centuries, the church was partially destroyed and rebuilt on several more occasions. Then, a Muslim caliph ordered its complete destruction in 1009. Small chapels were erected in 1048 on the holy sites that had been contained within the original basilica. During the twelfth century, the Crusaders united the holy sites by reconstructing the church in its present form, a complex conglomeration of chapels, altars, and architectural styles. The church later underwent extensive repairs after a fire in 1808 and again after an earthquake in 1927. Over the centuries, various Christian denominations have vied for control of the church's holy sites. Since 1852, the primary custodians of the church have been the Roman Catholic, Greek Orthodox, and Armenian Apostolic Churches, although the Coptic Orthodox, Ethiopian Orthodox, and Syriac Orthodox Churches also have shrines and other structures within the church."

While Paul and Rachel were following a line of visitors into the Church of the Holy Sepulchre, two Palestinian militants were preparing for their own visit to the church. "Just remember what the bomb-maker told us," said one, a slightly built, clean-shaven man in his early thirties, as he strapped on a waist belt laden with explosives and sharp projectiles. "One of us must get within fifteen meters to assure the death of the evil one. Once we are that close, we can either release the hand switch or fall to the ground. The fall will trigger the mercury switch."

"Yes, replied the other, a younger heavy-set man, who was already wearing his explosive belt. "Nothing, not even the American secret weapon, can protect the infidel prophet from Allah's justice. But do you think we should slay him in the church or outside of it?"

"It is the Jews who take our land, not the Christians. We do not need to destroy the Christians' church to kill the satanic one. We will kill him when he leaves the church."

After donning cassocks and collared shirts of the type worn by Catholic clerics, the two men exited their apartment in the Muslim Quarter and walked to a nearby automobile. "Allah is great; we cannot fail," said the younger one as they drove away.

After entering the dimly lit church, Paul, Rachel, and the two agents followed other visitors to a steep stairway that led up to Golgotha, also known as Calvary, the site of Christ's crucifixion. At the top of the stairs, they entered into an area divided into two chapels built over the rocky hill of Golgotha. In the Roman Catholic chapel they studied the intricate ceiling mosaics and the ornate silver and bronze altar, crafted in sixteenth century Florence. The altar was located over the spot thought to be the site on which Roman soldiers nailed Christ to the cross. While the cameras of the paparazzi flashed sporadically, Paul and Rachel stood looking past the altar at a huge, Crusader-era mural depicting the ascension of Christ. Then, following other visitors, they passed another altar commemorating Mary's sorrow at the foot of the cross and walked under an ornamental arch into a Greek Orthodox chapel that contained a third altar. There they peered through the glass enclosure beneath the altar at the bare rock on which had once stood the cross of Christ's crucifixion. Some of the visitors remained to touch the rock through a hole in the floor, as Paul, Rachel, and the agents followed other visitors downstairs to a large rotunda surrounding the elaborate shrine containing the Holy Sepulchre, the rock-hewn tomb of Christ.

Standing in the line of visitors waiting to view Christ's tomb, Paul and Rachel looked around the rotunda at the tiers of balconies filled with golden lamps and at the magnificent gold and white dome overhead. As the cameras of the paparazzi continued to flash, Paul and

Rachel slowly followed other visitors into the shrine's atrium, known as the Chapel of the Angel. There they looked inside a glass case containing a piece of the rolling stone once used to block the entrance to Christ's tomb. From there they passed through a low doorway into the tiny inner chamber where they saw the tomb itself, which was covered by a marble slab and adorned with bas-reliefs portraying Christ's resurrection.

After exiting the inner chamber of the shrine, Paul and Rachel began to follow other visitors who were walking to the Coptic chapel behind the shrine. Suddenly, Paul stopped and stood with his eyes closed, his right hand to his forehead as if in prayer. Rachel, who had never witnessed one of Paul's visions, appeared worried as she grasped Paul's arm and asked if he felt ill. For almost a minute, he stood mute with eyes closed while the Shabak agents struggled to keep the paparazzi at bay. Then, Paul opened his eyes, turned, and motioned for one of the agents to come over to him. Paul's typically warm and friendly demeanor was gone. His face was taut and bore an expression of gravity. An unnatural silence pervaded the rotunda as paparazzi and other visitors watched the agent approach Paul, whose demeanor now conveyed urgency.

"Listen closely," Paul whispered to the agent, "Two suicide bombers will soon arrive outside the church in an automobile. God will stop them from harming us, but there is great danger to anyone in the courtyard outside the church. *You must warn everyone to clear the courtyard.*"

"How do you know this?" responded the agent.

"The same way I knew the Dome of the Rock would be destroyed. Please, go warn everyone to clear the courtyard."

As the agent ran toward the church's main entrance, Paul said to Rachel, who appeared more curious than anxious, "Please wait here while I talk to the reporters." Then, he walked over to where the other Shabak agent was attempting to hold back some of the paparazzi and announced loudly, "Please listen. There will soon be a terrorist threat in the courtyard outside the church. We must remain inside until it is over." Most of the paparazzi and other visitors crowded around Paul to question him about his warning. However, a few of the paparazzi, hoping to witness and photograph something newsworthy, rushed to catch up with the agent who had run to the main entrance.

When the Shabak agent reached the church's main entrance, he began shouting to visitors in the courtyard that they should retreat into the church. Some visitors walked back to the entrance but others ignored the agent and continued standing in the courtyard or walking away from it. At the outer edge of the courtyard, an automobile arrived and slowly came to a stop. The Shabak agent, his pistol now drawn, ran from the entrance into the courtyard to warn the remaining visitors. Paparazzi, eager for a good story, followed him into the courtyard. Pointing to the automobile, the agent told the visitors about the suspected terrorist attack. As the visitors stared at the automobile, two men slowly stepped out of the automobile and began walking toward the church. When the visitors and paparazzi saw that the approaching men were dressed as Catholic priests, some of them began laughing at the agent. Their laughter was cut short as the sham priests were suddenly struck down by an unseen force, their falls triggering the mercury switches of the powerful, shrapnel-laden bombs that they wore.

When the violent, nearly simultaneous explosions shook the ancient church, Rachel looked fearfully up at Paul, who drew her tightly into his arms. Awed by the accuracy of Paul's warning, Rachel felt the goose bumps covering her own arms. On the faces of visitors and paparazzi, she saw horrified amazement, but on Paul's face, she observed an almost supernatural calm.

Suddenly, loud screams were coming from the main entrance of the church, and people around Paul and Rachel, including the Shabak agent, began a frantic rush in that direction. Paul and Rachel followed the frenzied crowd toward the church entrance. As they approached the entrance, they heard women sobbing and saw men shaking their heads and turning away from the open doorway with expressions of horrified revulsion. Then, the Shabak agent, who had been staring out the entrance into the courtyard, turned and approached them. "You do not want to see what is out there. There were no survivors. The police will be here soon. I think we should wait in here until they arrive."

"Where is your friend?" asked Rachel, referring to the other agent.

"He is dead. He was outside with the others when bombs exploded."

"Oh, no!" cried Rachel as she turned to Paul, who stood mute, staring at the entrance.

"I am told he died bravely while trying to save people outside the church," said the agent.

As Rachel looked up at Paul, who had remained silent, she could see that he was struggling with unseen emotions. At last, Paul stepped forward and reached out to the Shabak agent, placing his hand on the agent's shoulder. "I am sorry, my friend," said Paul, "that I placed you and your friend in such great danger by asking you to bring Rachel and I here. I arrogantly assumed that God was protecting not only me but everyone around me and did not realize the danger posed by our coming here." When Paul turned away from the agent, Rachel noticed his moist eyes and the trace of a tear on one cheek.

Later, after the Jerusalem police had cleaned up the ghastly carnage outside the church, the Shabak agent drove Paul and Rachel back to their hotel. Paul was quiet during the ride, but when they arrived at the hotel, he said to the agent, "Rachel and I have decided that we will not do any more sightseeing. We do not want to subject others to the danger of another assassination attempt upon me." The agent nodded but remained silent behind the wheel of his vehicle.

"We are truly sorry for the loss of your friend," offered Rachel.

"Death is sometimes the price we pay in our line of work," replied the agent quietly, his face expressionless. "It is not your fault, but I agree that you and others would be safer if you stayed at your hotel."

That evening, as they ate dinner in Paul's hotel room, Paul and Rachel listened to one of the local news telecasts. "Today, while the Temple Mount negotiations continued in Jerusalem, two suicide bombers killed themselves and eleven other people at the Church of the Holy Sepulchre in an apparent assassination attempt on Paul Swanson and his lady friend, Rachel Lindsey. Witnesses at the scene reported that Paul Swanson foresaw the attack shortly before it occurred and warned other visitors inside the church. Shabak agent Isaac Moscowitz, who had accompanied Mr. Swanson to the church, died in the attack as he attempted to warn visitors standing in the outside courtyard where the attack occurred. Among the others killed were three local reporters and a television cameraman whose camera was found by police after the attack. The recording in the camera, which is in police custody, reportedly shows that the suicide bombers were dressed like Catholic priests. They were walking toward the church's entrance when they suddenly dropped to the ground as if struck down the way other terrorists have been over recent months. Unfortunately, their explosives detonated when they fell, causing hideous carnage as the shrapnel from their bombs cut down everyone outside the church. The church itself suffered only cosmetic damage to its façade from the shrapnel. According to the police, the vehicle driven to the church by one of the suicide bombers is registered to a suspected Hamas member, who apparently died in the explosion. Hamas has denied any knowledge of the attack and has publicly condemned it."

CHAPTER 18
The Agreement

The terrorist attack at the Church of the Holy Sepulchre, while reaffirming Paul Swanson's prophetic ability, raised serious questions as to whether Israelis were safe from Islamic terrorists. Muslim clerics proclaimed that the death toll from the terrorist attack was evidence that God was not protecting Israelis from the attacks of jihadist martyrs. Media commentators questioned the accuracy of Paul's prophetic announcement that God would no longer permit religious terrorism. Some commentators opined that if Paul had been wrong about God preventing terrorism, then he could also be wrong about God creating lakes and rivers in the desert areas of Palestine and Israel.

By the beginning of the third week of the Temple Mount negotiations, both sides had become pessimistic that they would reach an agreement. Then, one of the Israeli Prime Minister's advisors, a rabbi who was skeptical of the Desert Prophecy, suggested that Israel supplement its previous settlement proposal by offering to remove all Jewish settlements from the West Bank upon fulfillment of the prophecy. When the Prime Minister made this offer to the Palestinian contingent, he was certain that they would reject it because they clearly did not believe in the Desert Prophecy. However, the Islamic advisors to the President of the Palestinian Authority were concerned that the Israelis had become skeptical of the Desert Prophecy and would soon terminate the negotiations. The Palestinian contingent knew that the Islamic plan to attack Israel was contingent upon the failure of a prophecy that required successful negotiation of a Temple Mount agreement. For that reason, on the third day of the third week of negotiations, the President of the Palestinian Authority surprised the Israelis and the rest of the world by accepting Israel's settlement proposal. The lawyers for both sides then began the process of reducing the terms of the historic agreement to writing.

At their hotel in Jerusalem, Paul and Rachel listened to a television newscast concerning the historic agreement. "At a press conference in Jerusalem, the Prime Minister of Israel and the President of the Palestinian Authority have just announced that an agreement has been reached in the Temple Mount negotiations. Upon its execution, the Temple Mount Agreement will require the Waqf Islamic Trust to allow Israel to share access to the Temple Mount and to take possession of the site previously occupied by the Dome of the Rock. In exchange for this, Israel will be required to withdraw Israeli Defense Forces from the West Bank and to render economic assistance to rebuild Palestinian infrastructure. Although Israel will take possession of the Temple Mount site, Israel's retention of the site will depend upon the fulfillment the so-called 'Desert Prophecy' of Paul Swanson. If the 'Desert Prophecy' is not fulfilled within the three months of the Agreement's execution, Israel will be required to abandon construction of the Third Temple and withdraw from the Temple Mount. If the prophecy is fulfilled, Israel will keep the Temple Mount site but remove all Israeli settlements from the West Bank. According to the Temple Mount Agreement, fulfillment of the prophecy will require the miraculous creation of new lakes and rivers covering at least one tenth of the surface areas of the Judean and Negev Deserts. Attorneys are now drafting the final Agreement, which the Prime Minister and the Palestinian Authority President will execute before the United Nations General Assembly. Members of the United Nations Security Council have reportedly indicated that they can convene a special session within one month. At that time, the world will witness the execution of this historic agreement, which will commence the three-month countdown for what would undoubtedly be the greatest miracle of modern times." The newscaster then added, "Despite the recent attempted assassination of Paul Swanson, we are told that he still intends live in Palestine until the Desert Prophecy is fulfilled by God. This is yet another remarkable display of faith by the young American."

After the newscast, Rachel, who seemed saddened by the news, turned to Paul and said, "Paul, I want to stay with you."

Gently grasping Rachel's delicate shoulders, Paul looked into her green-blue eyes as he responded, "You know that I love you and want to be with you, Rachel. But I am asking you not to come to Palestine. My promise to live in Palestine was not something God told me to do. I made the promise to show the Palestinians that I trust God to honor His promise to them. God did not ask me to live in Palestine and did not tell me that He will protect me there, although I believe that He will. I cannot permit you to endanger yourself by living among the people who have tried to kill us. Please, for your safety and my peace of mind, wait for me at home. I won't be in Palestine very long – three months at the most."

Silently, Rachel nodded her assent, as she struggled to conceal her disappointment. Then, she asked, "But where will you live in Palestine?"

"Probably the West Bank, but I would like to spend some time in Gaza, too. I'd like to get a better understanding of these people and the problems they face." Sensing that Rachel was upset, Paul added, "Don't worry, Rachel; God will continue to take care of me." Then, taking Rachel into his arms and holding her tightly, Paul whispered, "And I'll be calling you every day."

* * *

At Eli Zahavi's office, Jack Landon was making one of his now frequent visits. "It's just amazing to me, Eli, that in this scientific age the Israeli government would actually enter into an international agreement based upon a kid prophet's statement that a divine being will magically transform Israel's deserts into lakes." Now laughing, Jack added, "Aren't you embarrassed by your government's gullibility?"

"I feel sorry for you, Jack. I think it must be sad and depressing to believe that we live in a godless universe in which our lives have no ultimate significance."

"I'll tell you what I think, Eli. Some people just don't have the guts to face the truth that we're on our own in this world. So they delude themselves into believing that there is an omnipotent being that watches over them and waits for them in heaven when they die."

"And what's so wrong about believing that?"

"Well, it's cowardly and intellectually dishonest. I'd rather know the unpleasant truth than believe a pleasant lie. Wouldn't you?"

"First of all, Jack, you have no proof that you know the truth. You may be in for quite a shock if you're wrong. Furthermore, religion works for people. It makes them happier, kinder, better people."

"Oh, come on, Eli. How can belief in a fictitious entity make you a happier, kinder, better person? Has belief in God made Islamic terrorists happier, kinder, better people? Did belief in God prevent the Jews from crucifying Christ or prevent Christians from torturing people during the Inquisition in Europe or burning witches and owning slaves in America?"

"The people who committed those acts have a different conception of God than I do. And I agree that if those people thought their actions were approved by God, they were obviously deluded."

"That's my point, Eli. They were deluded, and their delusion did not make them happier, kinder, better people. Our kindness and goodness come from our personalities and our values, whether they're religious values or not."

"But, Jack, kindness and goodness are religious values. Without religion, how many people would be kind or good people?"

"Hey, I'm a nice guy, and I don't believe in God. And I've met other good people who don't believe, either."

"Jack, you were raised in a culture based on Judeo-Christian values so naturally you have assimilated religious values, even though you don't believe in religion."

"OK. So, why can't we just teach good values to our children and leave out all the mumbo jumbo about the supernatural?"

"Good question. Maybe people need to believe in God because man was created with an inherent awareness of God's existence."

"Well, Eli, I don't have a need to believe in God, and I certainly don't have an awareness of God's existence."

"Maybe so, but are you truly happy believing there is no ultimate meaning or purpose for your life? Are you happy believing that when you die, your consciousness will not live on?"

"Happiness is overrated, Eli. I'd rather be satisfied that I know the truth, even if the truth is that there is no life after death."

"That is sad, my friend."

* * *

During the weeks before formal execution of the Temple Mount Agreement, Paul arranged to honor his promise to live in Palestine until fulfillment of the Desert Prophecy. Although Paul had exhausted his meager savings, members of Unity Presbyterian Church and other churches in the Tampa Bay area had raised funds to support Paul's sojourn in Palestine. Most of the donors were secretly skeptical of the Desert Prophecy and considered Paul quixotic, but all acknowledged the sincerity of Paul's faith and his role in bringing peace, at least temporarily, to Israel.

After reserving a room in an old hotel in the West Bank town of Ramallah, Paul arranged a meeting with the Mayor of Ramallah, Mustapha Shaban. When he met with Mayor Shaban, Paul requested the Mayor's advice as to the areas of Palestine that Paul should visit to best understand the hardships of the Palestinian people. The Mayor, an astute politician who had visited America, was eager to help Paul, whom he regarded as a celebrity.

* * *

In a Special Session of the United Nations before the representatives of almost two hundred nations, the Prime Minister of Israel and the President of the Palestinian Authority signed the historic Temple Mount Agreement. Television news commentators covering the ceremony repeatedly mentioned that the event marked the first time in modern history that a prophecy was the basis for an agreement between nations. Although the commentators generally refrained from expressing opinions as to the validity of the Desert Prophecy, some of their guest analysts did not.

During one newscast, a panel of analysts discussed the Desert Prophecy from various perspectives. A Muslim cleric repeated the Islamic position that if Allah had wanted lakes and rivers in the deserts, He would have already put them there. An American geological engineer speculated that it might be possible to create lakes and rivers by diverting water from the Jordan River and Lake Tiberias, also known as the Sea of Galilee, into desert areas by creating a series of canals. This idea was rejected by an Arab civil engineer, who argued that there was not enough water in the Jordan River and Lake Tiberias to create streams, much less lakes and rivers, in the vast desert areas of Israel and Palestine. A climatologist agreed with the Arab engineer and further opined that the arid climate of the region prevented it from obtaining enough precipitation to develop and maintain new lakes or rivers of any significant size. All of the analysts agreed that they could not envision any means by which ten percent of the vast surface area of the Judean and Negev Deserts could be transformed into lakes and rivers within a mere three months. However, a Christian theologian defended the Desert Prophecy by stating that the prophecy itself did not contain a three-month period for its fulfillment. She suggested that God could very well intend to test men's faith by delaying fulfillment of the prophecy or by fulfilling it over a longer period. She added that men had no right to hold God to any timetable.

After watching the telecast of the United Nations ceremony, Paul and Rachel, accompanied by a Shabak agent, carried Rachel's luggage to the Shabak agent's automobile. When they passed through the hotel lobby, Rachel glanced around and said quietly to Paul, "Strange how we haven't seen any paparazzi around here lately."

"I noticed that they quit hanging out here after the incident at the Church of the Holy Sepulchre," replied Paul. "I guess they've concluded that being around me is dangerous."

As they drove to Ben Gurion International Airport, Rachel considered, but decided against, another attempt to coax Paul to fly home with her. She knew it would be futile. Paul would never break his promise to the Palestinians, even if they had tried to kill him. It was not stubbornness that drove Paul to keep his promise, she thought, but a rare integrity of character born of Paul's unique relationship to God. She had often tried to imagine what that relationship was like but had eventually realized she could not. What she understood, however, was that Paul Swanson was not a pious, Bible-thumping fanatic, as so many evangelical Christians appeared to be. She thought it ironic that the man who was closer to God than anyone else would be so unpretentious, humble, and often reticent. Perhaps, these were the qualities of someone who had a proper relationship to God – someone who simply lived in accordance with his beliefs and did not seek to impose them on others.

At Ben Gurion International Airport, Paul stayed with Rachel until it was time for her to board her flight. A few reporters had somehow learned of their presence at the airport and attempted to interview them. The Shabak agent, however, was able to keep the reporters away long enough for Paul and Rachel to say their farewells and embrace for a final kiss before Rachel boarded her flight home. There were tears in Rachel's eyes as she boarded the plane. She knew she would be with Paul again, but she also knew that she would miss him terribly. Despite the difficulties of living in a hotel in a strange land, harassed by paparazzi and attacked by terrorists, the weeks she had spent with Paul had passed too quickly. To Rachel it seemed that their precious minutes together had melted imperceptibly into hours and then into days, the happiest days of her life.

* * *

At a retirement home in Oakland, California, a nurse pushed the wheelchair of Dr. Theodore Durham into an empty recreation room where Agent Ralph Widman was waiting. The nurse carefully positioned the wheelchair of the ninety-three-year-old aerospace pioneer at a table opposite the agent. The nurse told Agent Widman to speak loudly but then corrected herself, "Oh, I forgot. Ted has his new hearing aids."

Introducing himself to the smiling, frail man, Agent Widman noticed his hearing aids and his sweatshirt emblazoned with the word 'Sertoma.' "What does 'Sertoma' mean?" the agent asked.

"Wonderful organization. It helps people of all ages to obtain hearing aids, cochlear implants, and speech and hearing therapy. I joined it years ago. It is the only civic organization in which I am still active. Now, what can I do for you, young man?"

"Dr. Durham, do you know Dr. Omar Bardoon?"

The elderly engineer's eyes widened noticeably as he responded, "Omar Bardoon, my old friend. I haven't seen Omar since the year his wife died. How is Omar?"

"I don't know. I've been unable to find him and had hoped that you might help me."

"I'm sorry, young man. It has been many years since I last spoke with Omar. I have tried over the years to contact him, but I never could."

"You were a member of his group, the Doomsday Committee, weren't you?"

Again, Dr. Durham's eyes widened as he asked, "Have you come to arrest me for discussing classified information?"

"No, sir," said the agent, now smiling and shaking his head. "I'm just here to obtain background information for my investigation. Last week I visited Dr. Ephram Hoffman, and we discussed the Doomsday Committee and Dr. Bardoon. Dr. Hoffman mentioned that you were a member of that group, so I just wanted to talk to you, too."

"How is Ephram, young man? It's been some time since I've seen him."

"Yes, he told me that he hadn't seen you in a couple of years. He's fine. He's still active in Global Union of

Scientists for Peace. Now, could you to tell me when you joined Dr. Bardoon's group?"

"Oh, yes, the group. But why do you want to know about our group?"

"It's just background information for an investigation the CIA is conducting. And I'm afraid I can't discuss the purpose of the investigation for security reasons."

"Oh, I see. Well, what did you want to know?"

"When did you join Dr. Bardoon's group, sir?"

"A long time ago. I don't remember the year. But it was before Ephram Hoffman joined."

"Were you the first member?"

"No, there were several before me. But the others who joined before me have all passed away."

"When was the group started?"

"I don't know. I think another member told me that Omar started it not long after he came to the U.S. I may be mistaken, though."

"What was the purpose of the group? Did you have any projects?"

"Just research projects for Omar. He had us analyzing cutting-edge research in various fields of science and technology."

"What did you personally research?"

"Primarily propulsion systems and aircraft stealth technology. We discussed . . . so many things," said Dr. Durham, his voice trailing off as if he were lost in thought.

"How often did the group have meetings?" asked the agent, raising his voice slightly to gain the elderly engineer's attention.

"Oh, every week for four hours we conferred through an Internet chat room that Omar set up. Omar even designed cryptographic modules for our computers so that we were the only ones who could decipher chat-room communications. Every year we also would meet somewhere for a weekend. It was like a convention. I so looked forward to those yearly meetings. I worked hard to prepare for them. Couldn't let the other members think I wasn't prepared."

"Prepared for what?"

"For the presentations of our research. Depending upon our particular field of expertise, Omar would ask us to research potential solutions to theoretical and technological problems associated with the development of systems to protect our country against attacks from enemies utilizing thermonuclear weapons. You know, 'Star Wars' technology. Apparently, he wasn't satisfied with our government's efforts in that regard, and neither was his wife, Dr. Suzanne Barnett. Each week we would discuss the status of our research and exchange ideas concerning the problems on which we were working. I guess Omar intended our discussions to achieve a sort of 'cross-pollination' of ideas from scientists and engineers with many different areas of expertise. I thought we were working toward something that we would someday patent or publish. It never happened. However, it made us feel important and useful in our old age, and we enjoyed the intellectual stimulation and camaraderie. And, of course, it was nice to have the extra income."

"I see. Were there any particular problems that you researched for Dr. Bardoon?"

"Well, as I mentioned, my fields were propulsion systems and stealth technology so most of my research was in those areas."

"What sort of propulsion research did you do?"

"Omar seemed to have a fixation on solar energy. He was certain that he could design a system to more efficiently transform solar into electrical energy and use it for propulsion. He had me working on all kinds of designs for solar-electric propulsion systems. I suppose my designs could have had some application to propulsion of space-based objects in zero gravity, such as satellites, but they were far too inefficient to power aircraft, at least any conventional aircraft. Eventually, Omar told me that he had learned enough about solar-electric propulsion and wanted me to shift the focus of my research to satellite stealth technology."

"What is that?"

"As you probably know, ever since we began putting military satellites into orbit, other countries have been developing ASAT's, anti-satellite systems. Some of these ASAT's are killer satellites with weapons that can destroy other satellites. Communication and surveillance satellites in geosynchronous orbits are particularly vulnerable to ASAT's. We were working on ideas for satellite-based systems to protect satellites from ASAT's."

"And did you develop any?"

"I did produce designs for systems that jam the radar of ASAT's and that make satellites undetectable by radar, but I could not find a way to make them optically invisible. That was something Omar himself was working on."

"He was trying to find a way to make satellites invisible?"

"Yes."

"Did he succeed?"

"I don't know. But he showed me a remarkable design for an image projection system for a spherical satellite. It used a spherical array of millions of tiny solid-state cameras and light-emitting diodes that covered the satellite. As light would strike the tiny cameras on one side of the satellite, the cameras would transmit the light to the light-emitting diodes on the other side. In effect, the system would allow a satellite to be a television screen that would always display on the side at which you were looking a picture of the view from opposite side. This would create the illusion, at least to a distant observer, that the satellite was not there."

"Is that possible?"

"I thought that it would be possible to conceal an object with flat surfaces so long as the observer was directly facing one of the flat surfaces. However, as the observer changed position to view the side as well as the front of the object, that would, in my opinion, destroy the illusion of invisibility. Omar, however, did not see that as an insurmountable obstacle. He said that he could develop multi-faceted diodes and computer algorithms that would alter the projected image to effectively conceal both round and flat-surfaced objects. And, as he pointed out, satellites are surrounded mostly by darkness anyway, and it is easy to create the illusion of darkness. I suggested that it would be more cost-effective just to paint the satellites black, but Omar did not think much of that idea."

"Do you think he succeeded in creating a system that makes satellites invisible?"

"Invisible to radar, yes. Invisible to satellite-based telescopes, I don't know. But if anyone could do it, he could."

"Did Dr. Bardoon or his wife ever discuss any other projects that they were personally working on?"

"You mean other than the group's research projects?"

"Yes."

"Well, Omar once asked my opinion as an aerospace engineer about a private French firm that specializes in launching commercial satellites. When I asked him if he was considering an investment in the French firm, he said that he was looking for an alternative to NASA for launching some communications satellites that one of his companies had developed. When I asked him for whom his company had developed the satellites, he said they were part of a 'classified project' that he could not discuss. I assumed that he was doing work for the government."

"Do you remember the name of the French company?"

"No, all those French names sound the same to me."

"Did Dr. Bardoon ask the group to do weapons research?"

"That was Suzanne's area of expertise. She was head of Livermore, you know. She practically invented the 'Clean Bomb,' a thermonuclear bomb that leaves no radioactive residue. She once told me that she was working on a 'Bunker Buster' version of her Clean Bomb that could literally move mountains."

"Did she tell you what it was to be used for?"

"No. I think the nuclear Bunker Buster was just an intellectual exercise. But we discussed using Suzanne's Clean Bomb as a means of destroying an incoming missile barrage or even destroying comets that threaten to strike the earth."

"Did you ever hear Dr. Bardoon or his wife mention 'Cybernetic Swarm Technology'?"

The elderly engineer stared at Agent Widman for a moment and then asked, "Where did you hear that term?"

"Dr. Hoffman mentioned it. Do you know anything about it?"

"I doubt that anyone but Omar and Suzanne knew anything about it. The only reason I even remember the term is that one of the group members – I can't remember who -- said he'd heard that Omar had invented something that he called 'Cybernetic Swarm Technology' and that it was one of his greatest inventions. However, when I asked Omar about it, he said it was nothing of importance – just a system for remotely controlling and coordinating the functions of multiple robotic devices simultaneously. That was his forte, you know – robotics and AI. Omar never needed any of us to perform research in those areas."

"AI being artificial intelligence?"

"Yes. Generally, it's the science and engineering of intelligent machines. It was the machine logic circuits that Omar designed that made his robotics systems superior to all others. From what I understand, the commercial systems that he designed decades ago are still unsurpassed. And, as you may know, he was a pioneer in kinematic, self-replicating, robotic systems, which are machines that can build copies of themselves."

"That's really possible?"

"Yes. But it's not my field, so I can't tell you much about it."

"Dr. Hoffman told me that Dr. Bardoon's personality changed after his wife died."

"He became morose and fatalistic. He made some remarks about nuclear annihilation of the human race being inevitable . . . or something to that effect. It was quite shocking to all of us. That was when some of the members began calling him 'Dr. Doom.' Then, he quit communicating with us, closed his companies, sold his home, and vanished. I've often wondered what became of him. Do you know where he might be?"

"No, sir. But I sure would like to find out."

"Does the CIA consider him a threat to national security?"

"I can't say. Why? Should we consider him a threat?" asked Agent Widman, staring at the elderly man.

Dr. Durham reflected for a moment. Then, leaning forward in his wheelchair, he whispered ominously, *"If Omar Bardoon decided to become a destructive force in this world, with his wealth and intellect he would pose an unimaginable threat."*

CHAPTER 19
Palestinian Sojourn

At his hotel in Jerusalem Paul thanked the Shabak agents who had guarded Rachel and him. He declined their offer to escort him to Palestine, assuring them that he would continue to receive divine protection. As a taxi driver loaded Paul's luggage into the trunk of his cab, Paul shook hands with the agents before climbing into the taxi. "Go with God," said one agent, as he watched the taxi depart for Ramallah.

It was evening when the taxi arrived at the old hotel where Paul would now live. As Paul had anticipated, no paparazzi were in sight. They had ceased to follow him after the incident at the Church of the Holy Sepulchre. In the hotel's dingy lobby, Paul noticed a group of Palestinian men who appeared to eye him suspiciously. The desk clerk, however, was cordial and welcomed him to the hotel.

Paul found his hotel room to be sparse but clean. After setting his luggage down, he noticed that the message light on the telephone next to the bed was blinking. Thinking that he had received a call from Rachel or his parents, Paul picked up the telephone and pressed a button to retrieve the message. He was surprised to hear the voice of Mustapha Shaban, the Mayor of Ramallah, telling him that the Mayor would be calling him in the morning. After listening to the Mayor's message, Paul dialed Rachel's cell phone number. He heard Rachel's recorded voice requesting him to leave a message and then realized that her flight home had not yet arrived. Paul left a message for Rachel and then attempted to telephone his parents but again heard a recorded message. After telephoning room service to order dinner, he lay on his bed, wondering how long he would have to remain in Palestine before God fulfilled the Desert Prophecy. For the first time in weeks, Paul felt alone.

* * *

The next morning, Paul awakened when his bedside telephone began to ring. Answering the call, he immediately recognized the voice of Mayor Shaban. "Good morning, Mr. Swanson. I hope I have not awakened you."

"I was about to get up anyway, Mayor Shaban. Have you called about my request to visit areas that will help me understand the problems faced by Palestinians?"

"Exactly, Mr. Swanson. We will meet you at your hotel. When will you be ready to go?"

Later that morning, Mayor Shaban and another man, an Al Jazerra correspondent, met Paul in the lobby of his hotel. After introductions, Paul followed them to the mayor's sedan. "Please, Mr. Swanson, sit in the front with me," said the Mayor as the Al Jazeera reporter quietly climbed into the backseat.

After driving away from the hotel, Mayor Shaban, looking into the car's rearview mirror, said, "I see your Shabak friends are still watching you." Paul and the other man turned to stare briefly at a vehicle occupied by two men that appeared to be following them. "I am sure Shabak and the IDF would not object to where we are taking you," said Mayor Shaban.

"And where is that?" asked Paul, surveying some bullet-scarred buildings along the dusty road on which they traveled.

"Do you remember the wall between the West Bank and Jerusalem where the taxi that brought you to Ramallah had to pass through a security checkpoint?"

"Do you mean Israel's security barrier?"

"That is a segregation wall erected by Israel to separate Palestinians from Israelis and to separate Palestinians from other Palestinians. That wall and the IDF checkpoints and roadblocks caused the collapse of our economy by restricting our access to employment and to the markets where we could sell our goods. The wall, the roadblocks, and the checkpoints have also deprived us of access to hospitals, schools, and mosques. They have even interfered with the delivery of humanitarian aid sent by your country to ease the suffering of our people. Israel has not just placed IDF checkpoints and roadblocks along the wall between the West Bank and Israel. Most of them are located in the West Bank to restrict passage between Palestinian communities. They interfere with the daily lives of our people, forcing them to pass through many IDF checkpoints where Palestinian pedestrians and vehicles are required to wait in long lines guarded by soldiers with machine guns. The checkpoints and the roadblocks have fragmented Palestine and turned the West Bank into a prison camp for Palestinians. We thought you should see what we must go through just to travel in our own country."

"But, Mayor Shaban," Paul asked, "wasn't Israel forced to erect the security barrier and checkpoints to defend its citizens from attacks by Palestinian terrorists?"

"Very few Palestinians are terrorists, Mr. Swanson, and the wall has not prevented resistance fighters from pursuing jihad against Israel. Aside from destroying our economy and increasing the stress in our lives, the only thing the wall has accomplished is to increase Palestinian support for Hamas and other resistance groups."

"It has been a vicious cycle, hasn't it?" asked Paul, rhetorically. "Past hatred and violence has led to erection of barriers that have fomented more hatred and violence. That is certainly not the way God intends for people to live – particularly people who profess to believe in God and to follow His laws."

"Ah," said the Al Jazeera reporter, "so you do not recognize the right of a people whose land is taken by force to use force to regain it."

"I know that throughout history men have fought over land," Paul responded. "As you know, the American settlers forcibly seized land from our country's original

Indian inhabitants. But the world was a different place then. Now, many nations, including Middle Eastern countries, possess nuclear weapons. If war starts in the Middle East, it could escalate into nuclear holocaust. I'm sure neither Israel nor Islam desires a nuclear war, particularly over a piece of land as small as Israel. If you look at a map of the Middle East, you cannot help but notice that Israel, including the Palestinian territories, is miniscule in comparison with the Arab countries around it. *Don't Arabs have enough land without the tiny area occupied by Israel?*"

An awkward silence ensued.

Later, as the Mayor's sedan left the city of Ramallah, the Mayor said, "I am sorry that we have to travel over these old winding roads. These are Arab roads. Israel has built more modern roads throughout the West Bank, but the Israeli roads bypass Palestinian areas, and some are closed to Palestinian traffic."

"I have heard," said Paul, "that Palestinian roads are also closed to Israeli vehicles and that this system of dual roadways is intended to prevent roadside bombings and other violence."

"Israeli propaganda," said the Mayor. Then, pointing to what appeared to be the debris-littered foundations of a pair of old buildings, he said, "Look at those demolished buildings. They were Palestinian homes. The Israelis bulldozed them, and the Palestinian homeowners could not afford to rebuild them due to poverty caused by Israeli policies. Throughout Palestine you will see the scars left by Israel's attacks upon us . . . and you will see the graves of Palestinians."

"Were those some of the buildings where the IDF found explosives and equipment used to make bombs for suicide bombers?" asked Paul.

"Israeli propaganda," said the Mayor. "Did you know that much of the West Bank has been seized from its Palestinian owners to establish Israeli settlements? And the violence against Palestinians comes not only from the IDF but also from the Israeli settlers themselves. The Israeli settlers attempt to drive us out by destroying our property, blocking our roadways, throwing stones at us, shooting at our automobiles, assaulting our farmers, and killing our crops. I could arrange for you to interview victims of the Israeli violence."

"That will not be necessary. I've read about violence by Jewish settlers against Islamic Palestinians and about violence by Islamic Palestinians against Jews. This is part of the religious violence that God will no longer tolerate."

Changing the subject, the Mayor said, "Ah, you see the Israeli roadblock ahead. I was going to take you to a Palestinian village where the Israelis illegally built their wall across the land of the villagers. But, as you can see, they have also barricaded this road, so we must find another route."

After driving down another old road, the Mayor's automobile came upon another roadblock. Again, the Mayor turned his vehicle around and tried a different route along another winding road that traveled through largely barren terrain. After several miles, they happened upon a long line of vehicles waiting to pass through an IDF security checkpoint. As the vehicles stood idling, a soldier slowly walked a dog alongside the vehicles while the dog appeared to sniff around the trunk of each vehicle. The soldiers at the checkpoint, who were inspecting the identification papers of the occupants of each vehicle, seemed to be moving quite slowly in the afternoon heat. Occasionally, Paul heard shouting, and sometimes he observed the soldiers asking a driver or passenger to step out of a vehicle to be searched, occasionally quite roughly. During one particularly long inspection, the Mayor switched off the engine of his sedan and rolled down the windows. He explained that he was concerned that the sedan's engine would overheat. Within minutes, Paul felt perspiration running down his face and neck, as he swatted an insect away from his face.

Almost an hour later, the Mayor's vehicle finally reached the security checkpoint. An armed soldier approached the vehicle and in a perfunctory manner requested identification papers. The Mayor handed his and the reporter's identification cards to the soldier and then handed him Paul's passport. After looking at Paul's passport, the soldier peered into the vehicle at Paul. He walked over to another soldier and showed him Paul's passport. The two soldiers then walked over to the passenger side of the Mayor's sedan, and one motioned Paul to lower the side window. "Are you the American prophet?" he asked.

"I am the American who has brought the message of God's promise to Israel and Palestine," Paul replied.

"Do you feel safe with these Palestinians?" asked the soldier.

"Yes, of course," said Paul. "This is the Mayor of Ramallah, and this gentleman is with Al Jazeera."

Handing the passport and the identification cards to Paul, the soldier said, "Shalom, Mr. Swanson." Then, he shouted to the checkpoint guards, "Let them pass," and he waived the Mayor's sedan through the checkpoint.

As they drove away, Mayor Shabon said to Paul, "Imagine if you lived in Palestine and had to go through this every day on your way to and from work, school, and everywhere else that you went." Then, he laughed and said, "I hope your Shabak friends who were following us enjoyed waiting at one of the IDF checkpoints."

* * *

At the Shabak headquarters in Jerusalem, Jack Landon was conversing with his old friend, Eli Zahavi. "So, Boy Wonder is now hanging out with Mayor Shaban and Al Jazerra. I don't know whether this kid is the slickest con man I've ever seen or the most naïve. Doesn't he realize these people are supporters of the terrorists who tried to abduct him and then tried to blow him up?"

"He is a man of faith, Jack, and he believes he is doing what God wants him to do."

"Just because the kid is a 'man of faith' doesn't mean he's doing the right thing. Faith is a character weakness, a cop-out for not being able to objectively analyze facts to find the truth."

"Jack, you are also a man of faith. Your belief that there is no God is based on faith because you certainly cannot prove what you believe."

"My belief is not based on faith. It's the result of objective analysis of what I observe in the world around me. And what I observe when I watch religious people is the same selfish pursuit of personal interests that the rest of us engage in. But religious people pretend, or have deluded themselves into believing, that their selfish pursuits are being guided by a divine being who allegedly cares about them but allows random, terrible things to happen to them."

"I think your objective analysis is actually a jaundiced perspective. You perpetually see the glass as half empty, instead of half full. Religion helps people cope with the 'random, terrible things' in this imperfect world. Religious people do not expect perfection in this world, just in the next one. What I conclude when I objectively analyze this world is that despite the apparent randomness of events such as earthquakes and storms, there is an order to this world. And I see that despite the many dangers that man faces in this world, man has not only survived for thousands of years but has flourished to the point that he dominates all other creatures. Your 'faith' makes you see all of this as a series of random occurrences, but my faith makes me see this as part of the divine order of things."

"Too bad we'll never know which of our views is right, Eli."

"I'm afraid, my friend, that you will find out after it is too late."

"Well, if God exists and He's fair, then I doubt He'll send me to hell for using my God-given senses and my God-given intelligence to objectively evaluate the world and to honestly conclude that He either does not exist or is doing a crappy job of managing things. And, furthermore, if God does exist, I think He did a lousy job designing the human body, and I've got the bad back and flat feet to prove it."

"I'll pray for you, Jack."

* * *

In Langley, Virginia, CIA Director Maxwell Colson had summoned Agent Ralph Widman to his office. "As you know, Ralph, we're not the only ones looking for the weapon system responsible for the hundreds of terrorist deaths reported during the past year. Russian and Chinese agents have been interviewing witnesses to some of the deaths, and they now have Paul Swanson under surveillance in Ramallah. We are in a race to find a weapon system that potentially gives its possessor the power of life or death over every person on the face of the earth. The only advantage that we have over the Russians and the Chinese is that we have identified the person who probably created the weapon system. Our knowledge of Dr. Bardoon, however, does us no good unless it leads us to him – or to his weapon system. I'm depending upon you to get us enough information to find one or the other. Now, bring me up to date."

"Yes, sir. In addition to the two surviving members of the 'Doomsday Committee,' I've located several former employees of the companies that Dr. Bardoon owned. I have interviewed all but one of them. None of them had any knowledge of the Doomsday Committee or Dr. Bardoon's involvement in any weapons development. But a couple of them said that I should talk to the former

Director of Research and Development at the company that Dr. Bardoon sold to the AmBotics Corporation. His name is Dr. Anthony Peterson, and he was personally recruited by Dr. Bardoon out of M.I.T., where he obtained a Ph.D. in electrical engineering and computer science at age twenty." Noticing the Director's raised eyebrows, Agent Widman added, "Yeah, he's a super genius, like Dr. Bardoon."

"So what did Dr. Peterson tell you about Dr. Bardoon?" asked the Director.

"I was unable to locate him until last week. He's living in England, where he's a Professor of Theoretical Computer Science at the University of Cambridge. Of course, I don't want to interview him by phone, so I haven't had a chance to talk with him yet."

"Then," said the Director, "I suggest you book a flight to Cambridge today. What about that French aerospace firm mentioned by a former member of the 'Doomsday Committee'?"

"The French company is doing business with several U.S. companies and doesn't want to have trouble with us, so they've been very cooperative. I traveled to their headquarters in Courcouronnes last week. Here are copies of their contracts with Dr. Bardoon's company." Agent Widman handed a large file folder to Director Colson. "I interviewed the corporate officer who dealt with Dr. Bardoon as well as some of the personnel involved in launching his satellites."

Laying the folder on his desk, Director Colson asked, "How many of Bardoon's satellites did they put into orbit?"

"Nine. Nine very large, very heavy satellites."

"So, what kind of satellites were they?"

"Dr. Bardoon told the French company that they were telecommunications satellites."

"Did this aerospace firm inspect them to verify that?"

"I don't think so. My impression from looking through their paperwork is that if you can pay their price, they don't look too hard at what you're putting into orbit. You should see what Dr. Bardoon paid to put up those satellites – a freakin' fortune. No, make that nine freakin' fortunes."

"I doubt those were telecommunications satellites."

"Why is that, sir?"

"As far as we can determine, none of Bardoon's companies were ever registered or authorized to operate a satellite telecommunications network. Did the aerospace firm have photographs or diagrams of the satellites?"

"No."

"Well, could anyone at the aerospace firm tell you what they looked like?"

"Yeah, big, round, and very heavy. But a couple of the personnel who helped load them for the launches told me that they had dense, segmented polymer shells to protect them during loading and launch. They believe the shells were probably jettisoned after the satellites were in orbit."

"So, they never saw what the satellites actually looked like."

"Right."

"You're telling me we have no information as to what was in those satellites?"

"Right. The contracts don't even identify the orbital locations of the satellites, except that they were put into deep-space orbits. Looks like Bardoon paid extra for that omission. Anyway, they could have changed their orbits since being launched."

"How is that?"

"The contracts describe the satellites as 'self-orienting and self-propelled,' so they apparently had some sort of propulsion system."

"Is that all you can tell me about these satellites?"

"Just that they should be easier to spot than most other satellites."

"Why is that?"

"According to the people at the French aerospace firm, those satellites were like mini-space-stations – over eighteen thousand pounds each. *They were the biggest satellites that company ever put into orbit.*"

* * *

In Oldsmar, Florida, Rachel Lindsey was visiting her friend, Clara Swanson with whom she often had long talks, usually about Paul.

"There's something I've been meaning to ask you, Clara. It's about Paul. I don't think I've ever seen him look frightened or nervous. Was he always that way, or has he just been that way since he became a Christian?"

"It's one of the first things I noticed about Paul when Tim and I were introduced to him at the adoption agency. I used to think that he was just born with a Zen-like calm about him. But I'm not so sure anymore."

"Why is that?"

"I believe that there have been unseen forces at work in Paul's life since he was a small child, forces that have shaped Paul's personality and character. Throughout Paul's childhood, Tim and I were often surprised not only by Paul's composure but by his understanding of things that a child would have had no way of knowing. Sometimes, when I asked Paul how he knew about certain things, he would say that he'd heard about them in a dream. That was before he gave his life to Christ – and before his first vision. You know, Rachel, in retrospect I think that God has been communicating with Paul since his early childhood."

* * *

After Mayor Shaban had returned Paul to his hotel, Paul hurried to his room, eager to watch the evening news telecast. Though God had not revealed His timetable for fulfillment of the Desert Prophecy, Paul had anticipated that God would accomplish it quickly, as He had the destruction of the Dome of the Rock. Paul listened intently to the evening news, expecting to hear that the miraculous event had begun. Instead, he heard the results of the latest opinion polls: sixty-one percent of the public considered the prophecy a delusion, thirty-one percent thought it was a hoax, seven percent were undecided, and one percent believed it was at least partially true. Following the announcement of the poll results, the newscaster reported that satellite reconnaissance had revealed no changes in the Negev or Judean Deserts. Paul could not help feeling disappointed as he turned off the television. Then, feeling guilty about his impatience, Paul prayed for forgiveness.

* * *

The next morning, desiring to impose no further upon Mayor Shaban, Paul rented an old automobile. He also purchased a digital camera. For the next several weeks, he systematically traveled to towns throughout the West Bank and Gaza, observing and photographing the living conditions in the towns and farms. In both the West Bank and Gaza, Paul observed the effects of stagnant economies, widespread unemployment, and poverty. At night, Paul used his notebook computer to download his photographs and record his daily observations in a running narrative account. He was preparing a photo-documentary to send home where churches could use it to solicit donations to aid the impoverished families of Palestine until God had fulfilled His promise to the Palestinians. After fulfillment of God's promise, Paul reasoned, plentiful water would improve Palestinian agriculture, and removal of the Israeli military and settlements would further improve the Palestinian economy and standard of living.

* * *

Suffering from lack of sleep due to jet lag, Agent Ralph Widman slowly made his way through the hallways of the venerable Gothic building in which Dr. Anthony Peterson's office was located. At last, he found the open door of the office, where the thin, bespectacled Professor Peterson greeted him. Although Professor Peterson, a man of middle years, was not a physically imposing figure, the keenness of his intellect immediately impressed Agent Widman.

"I assume," offered Dr. Peterson, "that the CIA's purpose in sending you here is related in some way to my previous association with Omar Bardoon."

"Yes, it is, Dr. Peterson, but how did you know that?"

"I doubt that the CIA is interested in my personal or professional activities, and Dr. Bardoon is my only acquaintance whom I would consider a person of potential interest to the CIA."

"Why would you consider him to be of interest to us?"

"The answer to that question is quite involved, Agent Widman, so perhaps you should first ask me the questions that have brought you here."

"Well, let's start at the beginning. When and where did you first meet Dr. Bardoon?"

"As I am confident you already know, I was interviewed by Dr. Bardoon approximately thirty years ago at M.I.T. upon my graduation from its doctorate program in electrical engineering and computer science. As the valedictorian of my graduating class, I had already received employment offers from I.B.M., Hewlett Packard, and several other corporations. However, I had heard about Dr. Bardoon's work in robotics and A.I., and after meeting him, I knew that I could learn much from him. He probably possesses the finest technical mind of our time, assuming that he is still alive."

"What did you do at Dr. Bardoon's company?"

"I was hired to replace Dr. Bardoon as Director of Research and Development, so that he could devote more time to other endeavors. I was in charge of the development of new commercial applications for the company's logic systems for robotics. The company produced cybernetic machine logic systems that allowed a single human operator to remotely control the synchronized operations of thousands of individual mechanical devices. Dr. Bardoon's designs are still considered to be unsurpassed – at least in the commercial robotics industry."

"Why did you qualify your last statement?"

"There are many types of artificial intelligence systems, and many different applications. Some, such as 'seed A.I.' are primarily the stuff of science fiction and bear little resemblance to the logic systems that we marketed. Seed A.I. is a hypothetical system of artificial intelligence that would be capable of self-improvement through its modification of its own programs. Dr. Bardoon was particularly interested in true seed A.I., which hypothetically would be an A.I. system capable of open-ended self-improvement until it had greater-than-human intelligence. During the years that he employed me, Dr. Bardoon was allocating half of his company's budget to the Special Projects Division of which Dr. Bardoon was the sole employee. When I asked Dr. Bardoon what the special projects were, he told me that he had constructed an artificial neural network with a cybernetic, multi-cluster, parallel-processing architecture that was being used for data mining. Data mining systems cull vast amounts of data using pattern recognition or some other selection criteria, but they usually do not involve complex neural-net architecture. I asked Dr. Bardoon why he was using a sophisticated neural network for data mining. I was speechless when he told me that his system had been data mining the

Internet and other telecommunication sources in order to improve itself. He said that he thought the system would eventually become . . . *self-aware.*"

"Do you think he was telling the truth?"

"Dr. Bardoon was secretive, but he was not a liar."

"How do you think he did it?"

"Many researchers, including myself, have attempted to create seed A.I. by using clusters of parallel processors because that configuration most closely simulates the architecture of the human brain. Such artificial neural networks actually have switching speeds that far exceed the switching times of the neurons in the human brain. No one, however, except possibly Dr. Bardoon, has been able to effectively simulate the incredibly complex and highly redundant interconnections between the neurons of the brain. Dr. Bardoon told me that he had developed variable algorithms for each of the millions of processors in his cybernetic network that allowed the processors to interact with and provide feedback to each other and to a central processor that had its own set of algorithms. He said that his algorithms had enabled the processors to use feedback from each other as well as data from external sources to continuously modify their original algorithms until the system was capable of solving theoretical problems introduced by Dr. Bardoon. The central processor was the conduit through which Dr. Bardoon introduced the theoretical problems into the system."

"What problems did Dr. Bardoon use this thinking machine to solve?"

"He never shared that information with me. He just told me that the system, which he called 'Guardian,' was designed to continuously search Internet and all other telecommunications sources twenty-four hours a day for information that its processors could utilize to increase the system's ability to solve theoretical problems."

"You have no idea what those theoretical problems were?"

"I can only assume that some of the problems were related to the areas of technology in which he was most interested. One area of particular interest was the design of living machines, that is, machines that are similar to living creatures to the extent that they are capable of self-repair, self-sustenance, and self-reproduction."

"Is that possible?"

"Yes, to some extent. My colleagues and I have constructed simple machines that are capable of diagnosis and repair of their own minor mechanical failures. Invariably, however, the machines have encountered a mechanical failure that they were unable repair and hence 'died.'"

"What is the purpose of creating living machines?"

"Think how much simpler our lives would be if we did not have to service and maintain the machines upon which we depend. Imagine a world in which we never need to repair our homes and automobiles because they repair themselves. Dr. Bardoon once told me that he thought such machines could solve many of the problems the world faces. He even envisioned that living machines could be energized solely by electricity produced by a hypothetical process that he called 'solar transduction,' a more efficient means of converting solar to electrical energy than the photoelectric cell."

"Do you think that Dr. Bardoon actually built self-replicating, self-repairing robotic devices?"

"It would not surprise me. Many years ago, NASA and General Dynamics developed devices that constructed copies of themselves from simple parts. However, they could not build a truly autotrophic self-replicating device, because their devices could not replicate their own logic circuits. Even with organic transistor technology utilizing spray-on thin-film transistors, the replication of large-scale integrated circuits has required a complex, carefully controlled manufacturing environment."

"So, Dr. Bardoon could not build a robotic device that could replicate its own logic circuit?"

"Actually, he told me that he had designed a robotic system capable of full self-replication, including replication of its own logic circuitry."

"How?"

"The success of Dr. Bardoon's commercial robotic systems was due largely to his compulsive, relentless pursuit of cutting-edge research. The Special Products Division of one of his companies was experimenting with nanotechnology and cluster science, particularly their theoretical application to micro-manufacturing logic circuits. While I was working for Dr. Bardoon, he developed several designs for robotic devices that could replicate their organic logic circuits with this type of micro-manufacturing process. His objective, however, was to create mobile robotic devices, and his early designs required systems that were too large and cumbersome to be mobile. Then, Dr. Bardoon realized that he could decrease the size and complexity of self-replicating devices by emulating nature and designing devices with what he called 'mating circuits'."

"What the hell is a 'mating circuit'?"

"Animals mate to reproduce, because the individual animal does not have the reproductive equipment to duplicate itself. Dr. Bardoon devised different 'mating circuits' for robotic devices to enable them to engage in self-reproductive activity."

"Copulating machines? You have got to be kidding me."

"No. Think about it for a second. Activating the reproductive circuits of a group of devices would cause each of them to perform a specific set of operations required for the manufacture of a new device. However, unlike animals, which only have two sexes, that is, two types of reproductive systems, Dr. Bardoon's robotic devices were designed to reproduce in clusters, each machine performing a specific set of operations necessary to the production of a new machine."

"Machines that have cluster sex," said Agent Widman, now laughing.

"Not really. It is more like the collective activity of building a house. The masons, carpenters, plumbers, and electricians perform separate functions in the manufacturing process, and together they are able to construct a house. By separating the manufacturing process into six separate sets of operations, Dr. Bardoon greatly reduced the size and complexity of self-replicating mechanisms incorporated into the individual robotic units."

"So, it took six of these machines to build a new machine?"

"Exactly."

"So, what did he use these self-reproducing, robotic devices for?"

"I have no idea. I was not involved with the Special Projects Division. I can only assume that Dr. Bardoon was designing a system that required huge numbers of self-replicating, mobile devices. Otherwise, it would have been cheaper and easier to utilize factory-made devices."

"A factory could also produce a greater number of devices, right?"

"Wrong. A factory would have a limited capacity to produce the devices. Truly autotrophic, self-replicating, self-repairing devices, however, could increase their numbers at an exponential rate as the devices in each new generation reproduced themselves and all of the devices repaired themselves. Of course, the initial generation of devices probably would have to be produced in a factory of some kind, but that generation of devices would self-replicate, as would future generations."

"That's amazing. What other areas of technology were of particular interest to Dr. Bardoon?"

"Let us get to the point of this interrogation, Agent Widman. You came here to find out if Dr. Bardoon was involved in something besides robotics and A.I. So, what do you want to know?"

"Was he involved in weapons research?"

"To my knowledge, none of his companies were. On the other hand, he did marry one of top nuclear weapons scientists in the U.S. I would assume that weapons research was a subject that they discussed frequently."

"Have you ever heard the term 'Cybernetic Swarm Technology'?"

"No, but in robotics there is a field of research referred to as 'swarm robotics,' which is concerned with developing systems that coordinate the simultaneous actions of large numbers of robots to produce a collective behavior. The concept of swarm robotics comes from observation of social insects, such as ants, which can act collectively to accomplish tasks that are beyond the capability of an individual insect. So far, swarm robotics systems are theoretical; to my knowledge, practical applications are nonexistent. Why do you ask about it?"

"An acquaintance of Dr. Bardoon heard that Dr. Bardoon had invented something called 'Cybernetic Swarm Technology' and got the impression that it was some kind of weapon."

"I had not thought of swarm robotics as being related to weapons technology, but I suppose it could have some application."

"Did Dr. Bardoon ever express his attitude toward terrorism to you?"

"The last time that I spoke with Dr. Bardoon was to convey my condolence on the death of his wife. In the course of our conversation, I asked whether Guardian had solved any of his theoretical problems. He said Guardian had been continuously operating for over twenty years and had solved all but one of the problems. When I asked what that problem was, he said that Guardian had not been able to tell him '*when to pull the trigger.*' When I asked him what he meant by that, he said, 'Terrorism is like a raging forest fire: when you extinguish it in one place, it breaks out in another.' Then, to my surprise, he said, 'To stop a forest fire, you have to burn some trees.' Now, to answer your remaining questions: *Yes, I do think he could be involved in causing the deaths of terrorists in the Middle East. No, I do not know how he is doing it. But, yes, I can conceive as to how it could be done.*" Then, handing a slip of paper to Agent Widman, Dr. Peterson said, "Here is a telephone number at which I can be contacted in the evenings on weekdays. Have one of your weapons scientists call me, and I will share my conception of a weapon that could be causing these terrorist deaths."

* * *

At the Shabak headquarters in Jerusalem, Eli Zahavi was speaking by telephone with his commanding officer. "Paul Swanson recently spent a day with Mayor Shaban and an Al Jazeera reporter, probably listening to their many grievances against Israel," said Eli. "Yes, sir, our agents will continue to monitor his activities and his communications. Yes, sir, I will continue to keep you advised of any developments of significance." Then, hanging up the telephone, Eli turned to a familiar visitor. "So, Jack, you were about to brief me on the CIA's investigation of the mysterious Dr. Bardoon. Have you found him yet?"

"No, but that's why I'm here." Handing a large envelope to Eli, Jack continued, "We would appreciate it if you could have your agents distribute these photographs of terrorists throughout Israel and Israeli-occupied areas. Maybe you could arrange to have them published in local newspapers, as well. "

Opening the envelope, Eli removed five sheets of photographs of five men. Each sheet contained an actual photograph of one of the men followed by several computer-enhanced photographs, showing how the man would look with various hairstyles, beards, and other cosmetic modifications. After perusing the photographs, Eli remarked, "I recognize four of these men as known Islamic terrorists. We already have their photographs. But why have you included photographs of Dr. Bardoon?"

"When the photographs are shown, we don't want it to appear like we're only looking for Bardoon. We just want it to look like a search for known terrorists."

"But you have no proof that Dr. Bardoon is a terrorist . . . or that he is even alive."

"We've found out a lot more about him, Eli. And I, for one, believe that he's behind all of these so-called miracles that we have been seeing."

"And how did he cause the tornado that destroyed the Islamic shrine or cause the sudden deaths of hundreds of terrorists throughout the Middle East?" asked Eli, now smiling.

"Well, I think the occurrence of the tornado was a coincidence, and the kid prophet's prediction of it was based upon satellite weather data that were supplied to him while the storm was forming in the Mediterranean. But these deaths, I'm sure, were caused by some kind of weapon that Bardoon and a group of scientists were working on for many years. Bardoon called the group the 'Doomsday Committee.'"

"And the CIA learned about this weapon from members of this 'Doomsday Committee?'"

"Well, the other members thought they were doing research for some type of 'Star Wars' anti-ballistic missile system to defend against nuclear attacks. But later they found out that Bardoon was probably up to something else. They said that when Bardoon's wife died, he became irrational and began talking about provoking a nuclear war. Then, he disappeared without a trace. From what we were told by a member of Bardoon's group, he's got the financial resources and technical knowledge to pose a major terrorist threat – even a *nuclear* threat."

"And what makes you think he would engage in terrorism?" asked Eli, no longer smiling.

"We think that Bardoon found a way to cause the terrorist deaths that we've been seeing and that he's using Paul Swanson to make them look like miracles. We think he did this to create confidence in Paul Swanson's prophetic ability in order to use Swanson to lure Israel and Islam into this Temple Mount agreement. We think the kid's prophecy is completely bogus and meant to trigger a confrontation between Israel and Islam over the Temple Mount that could escalate into a nuclear war."

Eli, now smiling again, said, "Are you serious?"

"As a heart attack," Jack said gravely.

"But if Dr. Bardoon has such fantastic technology and wants to cause a nuclear war, why does he not just detonate nuclear devices in major cities? And if he is a terrorist, why would he be using his fantastic weapon to stop terrorist attacks throughout the Middle East. I'm sorry, my friend, but what you suggest makes no sense to me."

"Don't forget, Eli, that Bardoon's parents were murdered by Islamic terrorists. Don't you think revenge ever crossed his mind? What could be better revenge than to invent a weapon to kill Islamic terrorists? We think that Bardoon originally planned to use his technology for peace but became embittered, depressed, and paranoid after his wife's death. We're concerned that he's now irrational and that this whole Temple Mount thing is just a means to provoke a conflict that will somehow lead to his ultimate revenge against Islam - *nuclear annihilation.*"

"Jack, I agree that Dr. Bardoon's disappearance and his possible relationship to Paul Swanson are quite mysterious. But you and the CIA have no facts on which to base this conjecture about him being involved in the terrorist deaths – no Dr. Bardoon, no secret weapon, no evidence of a malicious plot, no scientific explanation for Paul Swanson's foreknowledge of the events that he has predicted. I think you and the CIA are mistaken. I think we are witnessing truly miraculous events."

"Well, Eli, the CIA apparently isn't alone in the search for a secret weapon. Our agents in Ramallah have reported seeing Russian and Chinese agents there."

* * *

As Paul traveled to towns throughout the West Bank and Gaza, Paul noticed that people in the Palestinian towns that he visited seemed increasingly friendly toward him. He was unaware that the Al Jazeera television network had widely broadcast a "special report" by the correspondent who had accompanied Paul and Mayor Shaban on their road trip. According to this report, Paul had told the correspondent that Israel's treatment of the Palestinians was shameful and inhumane and against the will of Allah. The report also claimed that Paul believed that Allah wanted the Israeli military and Israeli settlements to be removed from Palestine and anticipated that fulfillment of the Desert Prophecy would accomplish this.

When local reporters began questioning Paul about the Al Jazeera report, he denied expressing criticism of Israel. He agreed, however, that fulfillment of the Desert Prophecy would greatly improve the lives of Palestinians by creating plentiful water and enabling Israeli soldiers and settlements to be relocated to Israel. He also told the reporters about his efforts to create a photo-documentary of the plight of Palestinians that he intended to distribute to Christian churches in the United States. He explained that the purpose of the photo-documentary was to raise funds to help relieve economic hardship in Palestine until fulfillment of the prophecy. Although obviously amused at Paul's apparent belief in a prophecy that they considered an absurdity, the reporters were impressed with his humanitarian effort on behalf of Palestinians. One of the reporters volunteered to assist Paul by providing him with photographs depicting Palestinian hardships and translating for Paul as he interviewed non-English-speaking Palestinians who had lost their homes or suffered other hardships.

On Sundays, Paul also visited Christian churches in Ramallah and Bethlehem, sometimes sharing his vision of Palestine's future with English-speaking church members. Although friendly and seemingly enthusiastic about Paul's vision of their future, most of these Christian Palestinians viewed Paul as a well-meaning but probably delusional American celebrity.

* * *

In Florida, Reverend Swanson began contacting the leaders of Christian churches in the Tampa Bay area to discuss Paul's project to raise funds for impoverished Palestinian families and to request church leaders to present Paul's photo-documentary to their congregations. Despite their skepticism concerning the Desert Prophecy, the church leaders recognized that Paul's humanitarian efforts exemplified Christian ideals and readily agreed to present his photo-documentary.

* * *

By the middle of Paul's second month in Palestine, he had completed his photo-documentary chronicling life in Palestine and the plight of Palestinians and had transmitted it to his father. Reverend Swanson began distributing copies of the photo-documentary to churches throughout the Tampa Bay area and began visiting churches to present Paul's plea for humanitarian aid to Palestinians.

Paul was now widely recognized throughout Palestine and generally treated in a cordial manner. Most Palestinians perceived him as a well-intentioned although somewhat bizarre American, rather than an adversary or threat. Nevertheless, Islamic clerics still considered his prophecies satanically inspired, and Palestinian resistance groups still maintained close surveillance of Paul, particularly when his road trips took him near their hideouts, hidden arsenals, or bomb factories. Despite rumors that some kind of secret weapon was protecting Paul, the resistance groups also discussed abducting Paul and holding him hostage or assassinating him. The leaders of these groups, however, instructed their followers that any such actions would not only be politically damaging to their cause but would likely provoke an American-Israeli military response that would interfere with Islam's planned surprise attack on Israel.

CHAPTER 20
Showdown in the Desert

At CIA headquarters in Langley, Virginia, Director Maxwell Colson was addressing an emergency meeting of Station Chiefs. "I have brought you here on a matter of the utmost importance. As you know, during the past year we have been investigating the sudden deaths of more than 2,600 terrorists in Israel, Palestine, and other mid-eastern countries. The investigation has led us to believe that these deaths were caused by an amazing weapon system created by a computer scientist, Dr. Omar Bardoon. Unfortunately, we also believe that Dr. Bardoon is irrational and is involved in an elaborate scheme to provoke a nuclear confrontation in the Middle East. Part of that scheme, we suspect, has been the use of the weapon system to establish the credibility of Paul

Swanson as a prophet. Having correctly predicted the terrorist deaths that we've been seeing, Paul Swanson, whose mother was Dr. Bardoon's late wife and who may be Dr. Bardoon's son, is now widely believed to be a true prophet. In fact this young man's fame as a prophet apparently has enabled him to convince Israel and its Islamic neighbors to enter into the so-called Temple Mount Agreement based upon a prophecy that God will change deserts into lakes and rivers. When that prophecy fails, as we know it will, Israel will be forced either to withdraw from the Temple Mount or to fight to stay there. Whether Israel intends to withdraw or not, we suspect that Dr. Bardoon plans to somehow intervene in that situation to provoke a war between Israel and the nations of Islam.

"Apparently, Israel's Islamic neighbors suspect that Israel will not withdraw voluntarily from the Temple Mount. Satellite surveillance and intelligence reports indicate that armies are amassing in Lebanon, Syria, and Jordan. Armed convoys of heavy munitions, including missiles from Iran, are entering the same countries. The Israeli Defense Forces have observed increasing numbers of Islamic militants dressed as civilians along Israel's borders as well as an influx of suspected militants in Gaza and the West Bank. The IDF has heard from informants that Islamic militants have been transporting massive quantities of weapons into Palestine through an underground network. Some Israeli intelligence officers expect an Islamic military offensive, regardless of whether Israel withdraws from the Temple Mount or not. The Prime Minister and Knesset are not convinced of this and, hence, not willing to break the current détente by aggressive action. They also believe Israel is equipped to repulse any Arab offensive.

"Again, the wild card in this complicated scenario is Dr. Omar Bardoon. We know that one of his companies has placed nine very large satellites in orbit that may be launching platforms for space-based nuclear weapons. We have tried to identify the satellites, but there are thousands of satellites in orbit, and Dr. Bardoon has apparently found a way to conceal the location of his satellites. If he is intent on provoking a nuclear war, he may be prepared to launch the first strike – a nuclear strike designed to precipitate nuclear retaliation. He may even be prepared to launch simultaneous nuclear strikes in Israel and Islamic nations. At this point, we don't know exactly what he's planning, but our interviews of his former colleagues lead us to believe that his objective is instigation of a war in which he, and perhaps Israel, will ultimately utilize thermonuclear weapons to destroy Islamic populations.

"Gentlemen, we must find Dr. Bardoon and those he is working with, stop them, and confiscate whatever weaponry they have. We believe that the Russians and the Chinese are also searching for the weapon system responsible for the terrorist deaths. We believe, however, that the Russians and the Chinese are unaware of Dr. Bardoon's involvement. We had hoped that surveillance of Paul Swanson would lead us to Dr. Bardoon, but it has not. If Dr. Bardoon is communicating with Paul Swanson, it is through some means that we are unable to detect. Fortunately, we may have found another way to locate Dr. Bardoon's weapon system.

"We know that Dr. Bardoon was a pioneer in robotics and that he has apparently developed a technology based upon swarm robotics. Swarm robotics is an experimental form of robotics utilizing large numbers of machines that work together to accomplish a common purpose, much like a swarm of bees attacking a common enemy. Based upon this robotics concept, a scientist who once worked for Dr. Bardoon and some of our top scientists have devised a hypothetical model of the type of weapon that could be causing these terrorist deaths. The system would use hundreds, perhaps thousands, of beams of ionizing radiation projected simultaneously from different angles to intersect at a target point in the brain stem. Only at the point of intersection would the level of radiation be sufficient to cause significant tissue injury. In this way, a fatal brain stem lesion could occur without entry or exit wounds. This may sound far-out, but it would actually be similar in operation to multi-beam radiation devices currently utilized to treat brain tumors. Dr. Bardoon's own wife received treatment from such a device before her death from brain cancer. Of course, unlike the devices that treat brain tumors, the hypothetical weapon system would require a much greater radiation output and a targeting system capable of simultaneously focusing numerous high-energy beams on a very small moving target from a much greater distance. In theory, the system could use swarm robotics to simultaneously focus high-energy beams from hovering airborne emission sources. Such a system could theoretically locate targets within buildings using some form of ground-penetrating radar or something similar to terahertz-radiation imaging.

"I know this all sounds like science fiction, and our scientists admit that we don't have the technology to construct such a weapon system. But either the deaths we're seeing are truly miraculous, or someone has constructed such a weapon and is now using it to play god. Miracles do not leave traces of high technology, like the object containing sophisticated microcircuits that was found at the site of the thwarted helicopter attack on al-Aqsa. Furthermore, if God were killing terrorists, He would presumably be able to stop them before they explode bombs that kill innocent victims, as happened recently. I am convinced that a human being, not God, is responsible for committing these killings, and we have only one suspect – Dr. Omar Bardoon, a man whom we believe to be mentally unstable and bent on the annihilation of Islamic populations.

"This brings us to the point of our meeting: Assuming this device exists, how do we find it before World War III starts in the Middle East? In the areas where terrorists have died, ground radar and satellite surveillance have produced no evidence of a weapon system. If this weapon, as we suspect, utilizes flying beam-emitting devices, either the devices are too small for satellite or ground radar to detect them, or they employ some type of stealth technology. Nevertheless, radio or microwave transmissions from a remote location must be controlling these devices. Thus, we have enlisted the aid of engineers who work for the Defense Advanced Research Projects Agency to help us detect the controlling transmissions and locate their source. The DARPA engineers are constructing remotely operated drone aircraft that are equipped with electronic gear capable of locating any ground or satellite source of such transmissions. They are also equipping the drones with jamming devices to block the transmissions. They are training drone-launch teams to utilize this equipment. The teams will also be equipped with rocket-propelled, electromagnetic pulse weapons that can disrupt the electronics in the flying devices, possibly bringing them down. We should have several teams with mobile drone-launching platforms strategically stationed in the Middle East within a few weeks. Let us hope that they will be able to provide us with the location of Dr. Bardoon's weapon system and, perhaps, Dr. Bardoon himself. In the meantime, I want each of you to keep me updated on the movement of militants and weapons in and around Israel and Palestine."

* * *

During Paul's second month in Palestine, because of the distribution of his photo-documentary, churches in the Tampa Bay area began mailing him donations for the impoverished citizens of Palestine. Paul sought Mayor Shaban's advice as to which Palestinian charities should receive the donations. Mayor Shaban, seizing the opportunity for good publicity, arranged for Paul and himself to meet with the administrators of several Palestinian charitable organizations. The administrators reached an agreement to apportion the donations equally among several organizations in the West Bank and Gaza. Paul set up an account at a Ramallah bank to receive the charitable donations and then wire-transfer proportionate shares of the donations to the accounts of the charitable organizations. Paul sought no publicity for his charitable endeavor, but Mayor Shaban's penchant for publicity resulted in television and newspaper coverage for both of them. Although Muslim clerics and fundamentalists still regarded Paul with suspicion, moderate Muslims came to view him as a benevolent Christian American.

* * *

Throughout the Middle East, U.S. diplomats requested permission from foreign governments to operate mobile monitoring stations for the alleged purpose of studying atmospheric phenomena. The governments of Israel, Iraq, Afghanistan, and Kuwait granted permission, while the governments of Lebanon, Syria, and Jordan refused.

Within weeks of receiving permission, teams of DARPA personnel in specially equipped trucks were patrolling areas of prior terrorist activity in Israel, Iraq, Afghanistan, and Kuwait. Inside the trucks were various types of electronic surveillance equipment, including receivers linked directly to Department of Defense spy satellites. Beneath a retractable panel in the roof of each truck was a launching platform with a small drone helicopter equipped with a parabolic directional antenna, a broadband frequency spectrum analyzer, and a broadband frequency jammer. The DARPA trucks were also equipped with rocket-propelled electromagnetic pulse bombs capable of disabling electronic devices within a blast radius of seventy-five yards. If radio-controlled, flying beam-weapons were used against terrorists near a DARPA team, its equipment would detect the source of the signals controlling the beam-weapons; its frequency jammers would block the controlling signal; and its pulse bombs would bring down the beam-weapons. However, due to the dramatic decline of terrorism in the Middle East, the DARPA teams encountered no terrorist activity. For that reason, they occupied their time by monitoring the massive buildup of Islamic militants and weaponry outside Israel's borders.

* * *

During Paul's third month in Palestine, newspapers and newscasts commenced a daily countdown to the impending expiration date for fulfillment of the Desert Prophecy. News commentators referred to this date as the "Prophecy Deadline." They cited poll results indicating that more than ninety-nine percent of those polled now believed that the prophecy was false. Newspaper writers began referring to the prophecy as "Swanson's Folly" and the "Desert Delusion." An Al Jazeera newscast ridiculed the prophecy, pointing out that not even the Israelis believed it, as evidenced by the Israeli government's failure to commence construction of the Third Temple. Although Paul ignored the opinions of the media, he did notice that some Palestinians had begun to smile and shake their heads when they saw him.

* * *

Two weeks before the Prophecy Deadline, commanding officers of the armies of Iran, Lebanon, Syria, and Jordan met with commanders of Hezbollah, Hamas, and other Islamic resistance groups in Qom, Iran.

The Hamas commander delivered a report to the others. "We are prepared for the offensive, and resistance fighters throughout Palestine will follow the leadership of Hamas and Fatah. But we can no longer expect to take the Israelis by surprise. IDF agents are everywhere, and the Americans have spy trucks patrolling the borders. I am sure they know we are planning a military operation. But I am also sure that they are underestimating the strength of our forces and do not know when we will strike."

Then, the commanding officer of the Lebanese army spoke. "What you say is true. An IDF general recently indicated to me that he thought Hezbollah was planning an offensive." Laughing, he added, "Apparently the IDF believes that our army will help them fight Hezbollah." This brought laughter from the others.

"Yes," said a Jordanian army general, "and they probably expect us to remain neutral. Israel, however, has breached the spirit of the 1994 Treaty of Peace with us by failing to cooperate in relieving the suffering of Palestinian refugees. We will now come to the aid of our Palestinian brothers."

"Even though it may increase the suspicions of the Israelis," said an Iranian general, "we must commence our final preparations. We should proceed with positioning our missile ships in the Mediterranean and assembling our jets and helicopters in the airfields of Lebanon, Syria, and Jordan. We should also finish supplying our missile installations and moving the rest of our ground forces into position. We must be fully prepared to bring jihad to Israel."

The others expressed their agreement with the Iranian general's remarks. Then, the commanding officers opened up large maps and began reviewing their plans for placement and coordination of their military forces. This, they had decided, would not be a war in which Israeli jets and helicopters confronted Arab tanks and artillery. Nor would their forces depend upon antiquated Scud or Qassam rockets. The initial assault would unleash thousands of highly accurate long-range Russian and Chinese missiles, each equipped with a massive air-blast warhead capable of leveling a city block. The initial targets would be army installations, military airbases, telecommunications centers, and command headquarters. Most of these missiles had already been stored at dozens of hidden launch sites just outside Israel's borders with Lebanon, Syria, and Jordan as well as hidden launch sites in Palestine. A fleet of missile ships would soon transport more missiles to an area just off Israel's Mediterranean coast. The commanders carefully analyzed each phase of the planned offensive as well as foreseeable contingencies. One of the contingency plans involved the use of missiles with Iranian-made nuclear warheads as a last resort to avoid defeat.

When the meeting adjourned several hours later, the commanders proclaimed the greatness of Allah and their commitment to jihad and to the extermination of Israel.

* * *

On the following day, several hundred Russian-made battle tanks began to assemble in southern Lebanon just north of the Israeli border. For the next few days, tens of thousands of Islamic soldiers and militants set up encampments and fortifications as if preparing for a ground assault across Israel's border. Israel soon responded by sending several hundred IDF battle tanks to its northern border and commencing reconnaissance flights over the area. This was exactly the response that the Islamic strategists had anticipated. They had succeeded in creating the appearance of a planned ground assault across Israel's northern border. Israeli forces would be watching for the movement of the Islamic ground forces while the missile installations in Palestine and around Israel's borders unleashed the most powerful aerial barrage in the history of modern warfare. This initial aerial assault upon Israel's army installations, military airbases, telecommunications centers, and command headquarters would likely leave Israel virtually defenseless to the waves of jet bombers that would follow.

* * *

While the armies of Islam and Israel faced each other across Israel's northern border, newscasts throughout the world began reporting that war appeared imminent. A front-page headline in The *New York Times* described the confrontation as the 'Showdown in the Desert.' Many news commentators speculated that the war would start sometime after expiration of the Prophecy Deadline, and some suggested that it would commence at the time of expiration. In the United States, Congress debated sending forces to support Israel, but it was obvious to everyone that American forces would not arrive in time to stop the war.

* * *

As Paul watched newscasts of Israeli and Islamic forces preparing for war, he could not help feeling completely bewildered. God had brought him there with a message of peace and a prophecy intended to encourage lasting peace between Israel and Islam. Instead of bringing peace, however, the prophecy had apparently become an excuse for war. It was true, he thought, that God had not told him when He would fulfill the Desert Prophecy. He knew that he had no right to question God's timing. Nevertheless, he felt that God had led him to believe that the prophecy would bring peace to that troubled area of the world, and now, as Israel prepared for war with Islam, God was no longer communicating with him. For the first time in his life, Paul found himself beginning to doubt one of God's revelations. In response to his confusion and his doubt, Paul did what he had so often done before. He knelt and prayed for understanding – and for forgiveness for doubting one of God's revelations.

* * *

At their home in Oldsmar, Florida, Reverend Swanson and Clara watched an evening telecast about the impending war. The doorbell rang, and the Reverend went to answer it. Soon, he returned with Rachel.

"Good evening, Clara. Please pardon me for dropping by unannounced."

"Rachel, you know that you're always welcome," responded Clara. "We think of you as part of our family."

"That's right, Rachel," said the Reverend. "Please join us. We were just watching the latest news about the situation in the Middle East."

"That's why I'm here," said Rachel. "I'm just worried sick about Paul being right there when they're about to have a war. I know that Paul has wonderful intentions and that he's trying to help those people, but I don't see what purpose it's serving for him to stay there when a war is about to start."

"Tim and I couldn't agree with you more," said Clara. "In our last phone conversation with Paul, we both tried to convince him to come home. But you know how Paul is when it comes to keeping promises. I think he'd rather die than break his promise to those people who tried to kill both of you."

"No," corrected the Reverend, "I think he'd rather die than display a loss of faith in God's promise to Israel and Palestine. However, as I told Paul, this so-called 'Prophecy Deadline' is man-made, not God-made. And I've told Paul that I think he should announce that the impending conflict between Israel and Islam is a breach of the Temple Mount Agreement and that the breach has released him from his promise to live in Palestine and has likely resulted in forfeiture of God's promised reward. Paul, however, said that he will continue to believe that God will honor His promise until God tells him otherwise."

"Isn't there anything we can do?" asked Rachel, now in tears.

"Yes," said the Reverend, "just keep praying for Paul and have faith that God will keep protecting him. Don't forget how God protected us from a terrorist attack and later protected you and Paul from another attack. There's no reason for God to quit protecting him now."

"I think that God has been protecting Paul all of his life," said Clara. "The kidnapping attempt during Paul's childhood; the attack on us in Israel; the attempted abduction in Paul's hotel room; and the attack on Rachel and Paul. I see that it's all part of a pattern now."

"I think you're right, Clara," said the Reverend. "And, as I said, there's no reason to think God won't keep protecting him."

* * *

While the IDF watched the buildup of Islamic military forces in southern Lebanon, no Islamic troops or military vehicles could be seen along Israel's borders with Syria and Jordan. Unknown to the IDF, dozens of hidden missile installations stood ready in Syria and Jordan to unleash a massive aerial attack. And off the coast of Cyprus, a fleet of Islamic missile ships waited for departure toward the coast of Israel.

CHAPTER 21
Countdown to
the Apocalypse

Nine days before the Prophecy Deadline, a Russian meteorologist, Dmitry Malakhov, had just begun to review satellite data at a weather station near the North Pole. With a startled look, he turned suddenly to his colleague and exclaimed, "Yesterday, a serene autumn day with perfectly clear sky; today, you won't believe what is happening out there!"

"What is it, Dmitry, polar bears are mating?" said the smiling colleague.

"Very funny. You will not be laughing when you see this," said the meteorologist, motioning his colleague over to a satellite monitor-display station.

"*Holy Mother of God!*" gasped the colleague, "how could a system of this magnitude develop so quickly?

Earlier data showed no converging air masses, no frontal system."

"It must be a convective process. Something must be warming the surface air, causing a massive low pressure area," said Dmitry.

"But the temperatures are dropping this time of year, and yesterday there was no advancing warm front."

"Well, now there is a huge temperature differential, and a cyclonic vortex has formed."

"How large is it, Dmitry?"

"The disturbance is already over six hundred kilometers wide, and it is growing."

"How fast is the system moving?"

"The wall cloud is spinning very fast, maybe one hundred kilometers per hour, but the system is almost stationary."

"Without a warm front to feed it, it will dissipate soon."

"Without a warm front, it is already the largest cold-core cyclone I have ever seen. It is sucking frigid air up into the polar jet stream at an incredible rate."

"Then, we must warn Moscow that autumn may soon feel like winter."

* * *

During Paul's daily phone call to Rachel, she pleaded with him to return home. "Nobody will think less of you for coming home now, Paul. You've done everything you can to help the Palestinian people and Israel. If you're killed in a war there, it won't help them at all. But it would kill me. Please come home to me. You can make an airline reservation for a flight today."

In his usual calm voice, Paul replied, "You know how much I want to be with you, Rachel, but I have to stay here. Whether God performs a miracle or not, I gave my word that I would stay. More importantly, I still believe that God wants me here to observe whatever is going to happen. So, as much as I love you, I cannot leave – at least not until the deadline for the prophecy elapses."

"Then, will you at least promise me that you'll come home when the deadline passes?"

"I said I'd stay until the prophecy was fulfilled. But, if it's not fulfilled in nine days, then God may have changed His mind about it. And I guess there would no longer be a reason to stay here. So, yes, I'll come home after the deadline passes."

* * *

That evening, as Paul watched a television newscast, he heard that the U.S. Secretary of State had returned to Washington from Lebanon where he had conferred with the Lebanese Prime Minister about the forces amassed in southern Lebanon. The Lebanese Prime Minister had advised that the troops in Lebanon were only conducting military maneuvers, much as U.S. Navy ships sometimes did. Thereafter, the Lebanese Prime Minister had declined further comment. The newscaster also reported that the United States had called for an emergency session of the United Nations General Assembly but that most Arab nations had indicated that they would not attend. The newscaster mentioned that many political analysts now considered war in the Middle East inevitable. He concluded the newscast by stating, "Some analysts suspect that the countdown to the deadline for Paul Swanson's Desert Prophecy has become the countdown to the outbreak of an Israeli-Islamic war."

After changing television channels, Paul heard a retired U.S. military officer analyzing potential military strategies and projected outcomes of an Israeli-Islamic war. His analysis focused largely upon air battles and infantry attacks and concluded that Israeli air superiority would enable Israel to prevail. He did not discuss or even mention the possibility of an initial, massive missile barrage against strategic targets throughout Israel.

Again changing television channels, Paul listened to a Christian commentator speculate that the impending war could precipitate the battle of Armageddon, the final conflict between good and evil when Christ returns to earth and vanquishes Satan. The commentator described the similarities between various current events and the apocalyptic events described in Revelations.

* * *

During the eighth day before the Prophecy Deadline, weather broadcasts reported that a huge mass of frigid air was moving southeasterly over the Arctic Ocean and the Barents Sea toward Russia. The broadcasts also reported that unseasonably warm temperatures over the Indian Ocean had spawned a warm air mass that was moving northwesterly toward the Arabian Sea.

In the United States, debate raged in Congress as to the role that the U.S. should play in the impending conflict in the Middle East. Some legislators wanted to dispatch a U.S. aircraft carrier to the Mediterranean, but most believed that the presence of one carrier would not prevent a war. A majority of the legislators opposed any U.S. involvement in a war between Israel and its Islamic neighbors. Some of them argued that U.S. involvement would have an adverse effect upon U.S. - Arab relations and that Israel had been successful in defending itself in the past without U.S. military assistance. Others were concerned that U.S. involvement would anger their constituency, considering the public sentiment following the U.S. military occupation of Iraq.

* * *

On the afternoon of the seventh day before the Prophecy Deadline, Paul made his daily telephone calls to Rachel and his parents. In the conversation with his father, Paul spoke about the imminent Israeli-Islamic war. "I feel so sad that the message of hope that I brought here could bring disappointment to so many people – and might even help to cause a war."

"Paul," said Reverend Swanson, "don't second guess God or yourself. God doesn't expect us to understand the way He does things in this world or why He does them. He just expects us to serve Him by living in accordance with the moral laws that He has given us. You have had a special relationship with God that few have ever experienced. Be thankful for it, and do not question it. Trust in God's revelation to you, even in the present circumstances."

"But, Dad, if God's promise to Israel and Palestine is not fulfilled in the next week, Islam will use that as an excuse for war."

"Paul, you are a Christian who has followed God's direct instruction. You should not concern yourself with God keeping His promise. That is God's concern. But I will tell you this: Somehow, someway, I believe that God will prevent a religious war, because that would be the ultimate form of religious aggression. Do you know what the French philosopher, Voltaire, said about war?"

"No."

"He said, 'War is the greatest of all crimes; and yet there is no aggressor who does not color his crime with the pretext of justice. . . . It is forbidden to kill; therefore all murderers are punished unless they kill in large numbers and to the sound of trumpets.' Somehow, Paul, I believe that God will prevent Islam from using the elapse of an arbitrary, man-made prophecy deadline as an excuse to commit mass murder in the name of religion."

* * *

In news telecasts that day, commentators discussing the impending conflict began to mention a new variable that could affect the combatants' military strategies: the weather. The frigid arctic air mass from the North Pole had continued to sweep across Russia and the Ukraine and was now passing over the Black Sea into Turkey. Meanwhile, trade winds had carried the warm air mass that had formed over the Indian Ocean across the Arabian Sea. Then, it had passed over the Persian Gulf and eastern half of the Arabian Peninsula into

Iraq, Syria, and Jordan. These countries were now experiencing unusually high autumn temperatures and humidity. As the warm air mass advanced toward Israel and Lebanon, meteorologists were projecting that it would soon collide with the polar front passing over Turkey. Based upon the temperature differential between the two fronts, the meteorologists predicted severe storms near the eastern Mediterranean Sea.

* * *

In the early morning hours of the sixth day before the Prophecy Deadline, Paul had a vivid dream in which he and an unseen companion were looking upon a giant map of Israel and neighboring countries. As Paul stood looking at the map, he listened to the familiar voice of his unseen companion, a deeply resonant, yet quiet voice – the voice of God. A thousand questions flooded Paul's mind. Why had God not kept his promise to Israel and Palestine? Would God stop the impending war? Why had God chosen Paul as His messenger? Paul, however, found that he was speechless in God's invisible presence and could only see and hear what God revealed to him. Paul began to ponder whether any man ever had an actual conversation with God.

Paul's thoughts, however, were suddenly redirected to the giant map as God's voice said, "Paul, many lives depend upon what you do today. You must communicate to the people of Israel and its neighbors what I am about to reveal to you. Look carefully upon the map before you. Soon, a great storm will come to this land. The path of this storm will now appear on the map before you." As Paul watched the map, a wide, blood-red line appeared on it. The line ran through Lebanon, Syria, Jordan, the West Bank, Judea, and the Negev. Towns and other geographic markers on the map identified the locations along the red line. Then, God's voice said, "You must remember the path of the storm. I will put this map in your mind, and you will see it when you awaken from your sleep. You must obtain another map of this land and draw the storm's path upon it. Then, you must show the map to Israel and its neighbors and tell them that all who are in the storm's path must leave today. Tomorrow will be too late. Those who remain in the path of the storm will surely die."

Moments after hearing God's message, *Paul was jolted awake as if struck by an electrical charge.* He immediately went to the desk in his room and began to sift through a stack of papers until he found the map that he had been using while traveling through Palestine. He took a pen and started to draw the storm's path, which was still vivid in his mind. Then, he realized that his map did not show the areas of Lebanon, Syria, and Jordan through which the storm would pass. He quickly got dressed and drove to a nearby store where he purchased a map of Israel and neighboring countries. Paul used a marker to draw the storm's path on the new map. He also wrote and signed a statement describing God's warning. Paul paid the store proprietor to make several copies of the map and statement. He then drove to a local newspaper, introduced himself, and delivered copies of the map and statement. He next visited the office of Mayor Shaban, where he also left copies. Then, he drove to the compound of the Palestinian Authority, where he left more copies at the President's office. Finally, he left for Jerusalem to deliver his message to the office of the Prime Minister and to a local television station.

* * *

While Paul traveled to Jerusalem, CIA agent Ralph Widman was reviewing documents at his office in Alexandria, Virginia. An unexpected telephone call interrupted his concentration. "Agent Widman?" asked the caller.

"Yes."

"This is Dr. Anthony Peterson. Have I called you at an inconvenient time?"

"No, not at all."

"Have you been following the reports of the unusual weather patterns around Israel?"

"Yes. Who hasn't?"

"The reports prompted my recollection of something that Dr. Bardoon once told me. Although this sounds rather fanciful, it would seem apropos under the present circumstances."

"What is that, Dr. Peterson?"

"Among Dr. Bardoon's many scientific interests was weather theory. Many years ago, after observing telecasts of the destruction caused by a Florida hurricane, Dr. Bardoon predicted that men would someday have the technology to control adverse weather formations. When I queried him concerning the basis for that prediction, he cited the famous statement by Archimedes, the ancient Greek mathematician, who said that if given a long enough lever, he could move the world. Then, Dr. Bardoon said quite emphatically that if given enough mobile heat-emitting sources, man should be able to change the course of storms and other weather formations."

"Do you actually think Dr. Bardoon has something to do with the weather around Israel?"

"Not necessarily. But I think it is interesting that at a time when the CIA is concerned that Dr. Bardoon is engineering a nuclear holocaust in the Middle East, weather is developing that could have the same result. After all, we have long known that a fully formed cyclonic storm or hurricane can release energy at a rate equivalent to a ten-megaton nuclear bomb exploding every twenty minutes. The annual energy consumption of the entire human race is less than twenty percent of the power of a hurricane."

"I see," said Agent Widman, yawning slightly.

"I suppose I was silly to bother you with this. To affect the movement of air masses that cover hundreds or thousands of square kilometers would require the coordination of billions of heat-emitting sources. Of course, hypothetically, if someone did create self-replicating devices capable of focusing radiant energy around air masses and if such devices had been exponentially increasing their numbers for twenty years. . . .Well, again, the idea does seem quit fanciful. I'm sorry for wasting your time."

"Oh, that's okay. Thank you, for the information, Dr. Peterson. Goodbye, now," said Agent Widman. After hanging up the phone, Agent Widman shook his head and mumbled "*screwball*" as he continued with his paperwork.

* * *

At CIA headquarters, an agent had just stepped into Director Colson's office. "Sir," said the agent, "our surveillance unit in Ramallah has reported intercepting what may have been a radio transmission to Paul Swanson."

"What do you mean by 'may have been'?" asked Director Colson.

"Well, the transmission was a multiplex signal of incredible complexity. Our people have been unable to decrypt it."

"Were they able to determine its source?"

"They did triangulate the signal."

"So, where did it come from?"

"Triangulation showed the transmission came from the sky above the hotel where Paul Swanson is staying. But satellite reconnaissance showed nothing visible at the transmission's apparent point of origin."

"Nothing visible?"

"Well, the surveillance team believes that the transmission source was too small for the satellite to pick up . . . or it was invisible."

"Are you serious?"

"That's what I was told, sir."

"So, the bottom line," said the Director, rubbing his forehead, "is that we don't know what's in the transmission, who it came from, or who it was intended for."

"That's correct, sir."

* * *

By nightfall of the sixth day before the Prophecy Deadline, newscasts throughout the world carried the story of Paul Swanson's new "Storm Prophecy." If Paul's storm warning had come at an earlier time, it probably would have attracted little attention due to the general disbelief in the Desert Prophecy. However, Paul's latest warning had come when newscasters were also announcing that a large cyclonic storm had begun to form over the Mediterranean Sea below the southern coast of Turkey. Newscasters insinuated that Paul's warning was just a guess or deduction based upon the existence of the storm. Some suggested that the warning was Paul's attempt to regain the public's confidence in his prophetic ability after the apparent failure of his Desert Prophecy. Nevertheless, Paul's warning and the existence of the storm provoked the rapid exodus of most of the people living in the areas marked on Paul's map. Because most of those areas had relatively sparse populations, evacuation occurred within twenty-four hours.

Before Paul's warning, Islamic militants had been discussing the unusual autumn weather, some calling it a bad omen. When weather forecasters announced that a large storm had formed in the eastern Mediterranean Sea, many Islamic militants felt vaguely apprehensive as they recalled the storm that had destroyed the Dome of the Rock. When newscasts showed Paul's map with the predicted path of devastation, most of the militants experienced an eerie sense of foreboding. *The predicted path of the storm ran directly through the areas in which the forces of Islam had stationed their ground forces and their hidden missile installations.*

275

* * *

During the fifth day before the Prophecy Deadline, the giant storm system over the Mediterranean Sea began to strengthen. Near the powerful cyclonic updraft at the storm's core, flanking updrafts developed and then merged into the main vortex. As the storm gained energy from the advancing warm front, the winds of its cyclonic vortex accelerated beyond one hundred seventy-five miles per hour. Above the swirling vortex, the sky over the Mediterranean was filling with a vast, billowing formation of cumulus and cumulonimbus clouds. Soon, the cloud formation extended to a height of forty-five thousand feet and covered much of the eastern end of the Mediterranean Sea, turning daytime into night. Behind the violent updraft of the vortex, a core of heavy rains and lightning developed in the area of the storm's downdraft. Another area of heavy rainfall developed in front of the huge cyclonic vortex. As the storm's powerful updraft drew in rain-cooled air from its downdraft, a spinning wall of clouds began to descend beneath the storm. With its cyclonic winds reaching maximum velocity, the giant storm's forward motion began to accelerate. Throughout the world, television viewers marveled as newscasters showed photographs of the vast, anvil-shaped cloud formation above the giant supercell storm. Newscasters frequently referred to the "Storm Prophecy" of Paul Swanson and some began to question whether the world was witnessing an event of "Biblical proportions."

Satellite images of the storm occasionally showed anomalies in the outer fringes of the storm. The high-resolution cameras of reconnaissance satellites caught glimpses of what appeared to be flickering images of vast flocks of whitish birds hovering at edges of the storm. The images, however, were only transient, vanishing as quickly as they appeared. Data from dual-polarization Doppler radar failed to reveal any objects in the areas of the transient images. Meteorologists viewing the images concluded that these anomalies were mirages or atmospheric phenomena caused by the storm. Although Israeli weather observation planes attempted to obtain closer views of the anomalies, an unexplained electrical phenomenon rendered their aviation electronics inoperative, and pilots aborted the flights.

CHAPTER 22
Force Majeure

When the furious, spinning cloud-wall began to descend from the base of the storm, the fleet of Islamic missile ships was still anchored off the coast of Cyprus. Believing that their planned attack on Israel was a holy cause, the captains of the missile ships had taken comfort in their faith that Allah would protect the fleet from the storm. Now huge waves and torrential rainfall battered their ships, and ominous howling winds and deafening cannonades of thunder filled their hearts with terror. As the vast, whirling wall of lightning-lit clouds bore down on the fleet, the ship captains at last understood that their ships would receive no divine protection. The captains ordered their crews to weigh anchor, bring their ships about, and steer for the northern coast of Syria. The decision to depart, however, had come too late, and the giant storm soon overtook the Islamic fleet. As the missile ships foundered within the violent darkness of the storm's vortex, the screams of drowning Islamic seamen were lost in the raging winds and crashing thunder.

A few hours later, television stations throughout the world began interrupting regularly scheduled broadcasts to announce that the storm had destroyed a fleet of ships off the Cyprus coast and that the vortex of the deadly storm had come ashore in Lebanon – at the exact location marked on Paul Swanson's map. Now weather telecasts became the most frequently watched programs as viewers worldwide gathered around television sets to see if the deadly storm would follow the course predicted by Paul as if guided by the unseen hand of an omnipotent force. Newscasters interviewed meteorologists as to whether the giant cyclonic storm or its storm surge was capable of fulfilling the Desert Prophecy. While the weather scientists agreed that such storms could produce flooding, they also agreed that because the supercell storm was now over land, it would be too short-lived to produce the volume of flooding necessary to fulfill the prophecy. They also pointed out that the storm surge it produced could only flood coastal areas with salt water from the Mediterranean Sea, not bring fresh water to the deserts. Nevertheless, Jews and Christians throughout the world became cautiously optimistic that the storm was a sign that God would fulfill the prophecy of Paul Swanson.

The path of the storm and the destruction of the Islamic fleet had a profound effect upon Islamic militants, whose fearless resolve to pursue jihad against Israel was rapidly succumbing to the dread of an impending doom. As wind, rain, and storm surge battered the coast of Lebanon, the armies of Islam sensed that their foe was no longer a human army but an army of violently spinning clouds, marching relentlessly and irresistibly under the malevolent direction of a god they no longer understood. While the fearsome storm advanced on southern Lebanon, Islamic soldiers began abandoning their positions, fleeing to escape the storm's fury. Soon the commanding officers of the Islamic forces gave the order for their retreat, and the mass exodus of troops from southern Lebanon commenced.

Directing the withdrawal of his troops, one of the commanding officers announced to his subordinate officers, "The prophecy is being fulfilled. We have offended Allah, and now He punishes Islam." Then, he and his subordinates climbed into their vehicles and began to follow the waves of battle tanks and other military vehicles fleeing northward. During their retreat, many Islamic militants silently prayed for safety, and some prayed for forgiveness.

While the Islamic forces retreated, Doppler weather-radar began detecting new radar signatures of violently rotating air columns beneath the cumulonimbus clouds of the storm. Soon, weathercasts announced that the giant supercell storm had spawned tornadoes more violent than the storm itself. As the storm passed over southern Lebanon, the fierce, relentless winds of the tornadoes destroyed everything in their paths, completely obliterating all of the hidden Islamic missile installations.

H. D. Rogers

When the storm passed into Syria, Islamic militants manning the hidden missile installations in southern Syria quickly abandoned their positions. The wisdom of their retreat soon became apparent as the giant storm spawned more tornadoes that destroyed the Syrian missile installations as well as other military outposts.

From the Mediterranean Sea across southern Lebanon into southern Syria, the mighty storm had followed the same southeasterly path drawn on Paul's map. Many news commentators and meteorologists had described the storm's course as "predictable," insinuating that Paul Swanson did not have to be divinely inspired to have foreseen the storm's path into Syria. The real test of the 'Storm Prophecy,' they said, would occur while the storm was over southern Syria. For it was there that Paul's map showed the storm's course abruptly changing to a southwesterly trajectory. Although meteorologists conceded that such a change of course was possible, they confidently predicted the storm would continue its southeasterly course through Syria and Jordan and into Saudi Arabia. They based this prediction on their analysis of the steering winds that had maintained the storm on its southeasterly course.

* * *

On the night of the fifth day before the Prophecy Deadline, television newscasts showed film footage of Islamic military forces fleeing in disarray before the advancing storm. The newscasts also showed Israeli tanks leaving their positions in northern Israel. The principal topic of newscasters was no longer an impending war

281

but the vast storm that had prevented a war. Newscasters also discussed the Desert Prophecy and its deadline. Although they no longer spoke of the Desert Prophecy in derisive terms, the newscasters clearly remained skeptical of its fulfillment within the few days remaining before the Prophecy Deadline. The giant storm, they pointed out, although quite destructive, had produced little flooding and would soon grow weaker as it remained over land.

Despite their skepticism toward the Desert Prophecy, most people, even Muslims, were convinced that only God could have created the giant storm and that only someone inspired by God could have foreseen its path. CIA Director Maxwell Colson, however, was not one of those people – at least not until Jack Landon made a startling discovery.

While the giant storm raged in Syria, Eli Zahavi and Jack Landon drove from Jerusalem to the Israeli town of Arad, a few kilometers northwest of the Dead Sea. There they planned to interview a local physician, Dr. Daniel Nussbaum. Dr. Nussbaum had responded to an article prepared by Eli and published in newspapers throughout Israel. The article had requested Israelis to contact Shabak headquarters if they had seen any of the five terrorists whose photographs appeared in the article. At Jack Landon's request, photographs of Dr. Omar Bardoon had been included in the article.

Upon their arrival at Dr. Nussbaum's office, Eli introduced himself and Jack Landon to Dr. Nussbaum. "Good morning, Doctor. I am Eli Zahavi, the Shabak agent who spoke with you. This Jack Landon, the

American who provided us the photograph of the terrorist that you recognized. I thought Mr. Landon should hear what you had to say about the man you identified."

Looking somewhat perturbed, Dr. Nussbaum responded, "I recognized a photograph in an article about terrorists, but it was not a photograph of a terrorist. There has been a mistake, and I think that you should rectify your mistake by publishing a retraction of the accusation that Mr. Barton was a terrorist."

"Is this the man you recognized?" asked Jack, handing the doctor a photograph of Dr. Omar Bardoon.

"Yes, Oliver Barton, an American geologist. I was his physician and his friend for three years after he moved here from America. He was a good man. He hurt no one."

"He told you that he was a geologist?" asked Eli.

"Well, he said that he moved here to study our deserts. He frequently spoke about them. I think he spent a lot of time traveling the Negev and Judean deserts – until he became too weak to travel anymore."

"Where is he now?"

"I was his oncologist. I was treating him for late-stage pancreatic cancer. *He died four years ago.*"

After exchanging glances with Eli, Jack asked, "Are you certain that he is dead?"

"Quite. I am the one who pronounced him dead. Because he lived alone, I also arranged for his cremation. That is what he requested."

"And you are certain this is the man?" asked Jack, handing Dr. Nussbaum another photograph, one showing Dr. Bardoon with his late wife.

Looking at the photograph, Dr. Nussbaum said, "Now, I am absolutely certain. I have seen this same photograph of Mr. Barton and his late wife hanging in his apartment. Before his death, he told me that he looked forward to joining her."

"Thank you, doctor," said Jack, as he turned to leave.

"One more question, Dr. Nussbaum," said Eli. "Was Mr. Barton a religious man?"

"Ah, that is an interesting question," responded the physician, leaning back in his chair as he carefully considered his answer. "When I asked Mr. Barton why he was studying our deserts, he made a comment that has stuck in my mind. He said the mind of man with its intelligence and creativity is probably the only attribute that we human beings share with our Creator and that this attribute was given to us for a purpose. He believed that purpose was the accumulation of knowledge, both scientific and religious, to enable the human race to progress toward discovery of our Creator's ultimate goal for mankind. He believed that the more we learn about ourselves and the universe, the closer we will come to understanding our Creator and the purpose for which we were created. He said his endeavors were his small contribution to man's acquisition of knowledge as we find our way to God."

* * *

On the morning of the fourth day before the Prophecy Deadline, meteorologists were shocked when the storm's southeasterly trajectory inexplicably changed and the giant storm began to move southwesterly. The morning newspaper headlines carried the story of the storm's amazing change of course – again following the path drawn by Paul Swanson. On television weather stations, previously cynical weather forecasters now spoke in almost reverential terms about Paul's prediction of the storm's course.

As the storm moved southwesterly into Jordan, terrified Islamic militants fled the missile installations hidden along Jordan's western border and in the northern West Bank. Although the velocity of the storm's winds had diminished significantly, it was still spawning tornadoes as it traveled down along the Jordanian border. The tornadoes lasted long enough to lay waste to the hidden missile sites near the border. The once powerful storm, however, had continued to weaken, and by the time it reached the north end of the Dead Sea, it was barely a storm. Television meteorologists announced that they would soon downgrade it to a low-pressure area.

When Paul watched television that morning, he saw live coverage of IDF troops collecting debris from the destroyed missile installations just outside Israel's borders. He listened to interviews with representatives of the governments of Lebanon, Syria, and Jordan who disclaimed any knowledge of the missile installations. They blamed the existence of the installations on terrorist groups operating illegally in those countries. In the northern West Bank, a Fatah representative expressed his surprise and regret as the IDF hauled away truckloads of damaged missiles and warheads.

Then, the telecast switched to live weather coverage as an Israeli reporter stood in the outer winds of the now weakened storm. "As you can see," said the reporter, "yesterday's super storm is now just an ordinary storm. Local weather forecasters predict that it will be downgraded to low-pressure weather disturbance sometime this afternoon."

When the telecast switched back to the television studio, a meteorologist was standing before an enlarged copy of the map on which Paul had marked the path of the storm. The meteorologist showed an enlarged transparency on which he had plotted the actual course of the storm. He then projected the transparency over an enlarged copy of Paul's map. "As you can see," he said, "when I transpose this plot of the storm's actual course over the map marked by Paul Swanson, the amazing accuracy Mr. Swanson's prediction becomes apparent. The citizens of Lebanon, Syria, Jordan, and the West Bank should give thanks to God and Paul Swanson. The storm warning issued by Mr. Swanson has saved many lives. And the storm itself likely averted a surprise missile attack against Israel." Then, pointing again to the storm path marked by Paul, he added, "Only in this area, where the predicted path widens as it passes over the Dead Sea and into the Judean and the Negev Deserts, do we see that Mr. Swanson's prediction was inaccurate. The storm, which is now at the north end of the Dead Sea due east of Jerusalem, has greatly weakened and should be completely dissipated by tomorrow evening."

* * *

At the CIA's Jerusalem office, Agent Jack Landon received a telephone call from Eli Zahavi. "Well, Jack, I'd like to hear your objective analysis of the recent events we have been seeing. Were they just random occurrences coincidently predicted by Paul Swanson? Or is it more probable that they were the work of a higher power, of a God who intervened to prevent a surprise, massive missile attack that likely would have devastated Israel?"

"I have to admit, Eli, these events do not appear to have been random. But I cannot accept the idea that they were caused by a divine being who is watching over Israel. Frankly, I don't know what to think."

"What will it take for you to admit that these events are evidence that God does exist?"

"I don't know, Eli, but fulfillment of the Desert Prophecy would certainly help to convince me. What is your excuse for the prophecy's failure? Is your God only capable of destruction? Is He unable to create lakes and rivers in the desert? If so, He certainly can't be the creator of the universe; can He?"

"The Prophecy Deadline was man-made, not God-made. I believe the prophecy will someday be fulfilled."

"So you're still seeing the glass half full, my friend. Well, you may be waiting a long time for your lakes and rivers. And, unfortunately, the Muslims only have to wait a few more days before they take back the land that Israel traded so much to obtain."

* * *

Throughout the Middle East, Muslims contemplated the religious implications of the storm and the thwarted Islamic attack on Israel. Most Muslims considered the storm to be an act of Allah, intended to demonstrate that Allah was opposed to war against Israel. Nevertheless, Muslims everywhere took consolation from the apparent failure of the Desert Prophecy. Failure of the prophecy meant that they would not have to share the Temple Mount with Israel and would be able to rebuild the Dome of the Rock. This in itself, they thought, would be a victory over Israel. Moreover, they reasoned, when the prophecy proved false, its falsity would cast doubt on the validity of Paul Swanson's proclamation that God desired Muslims, Jews, and Christians to respect each other's religions and to refrain from the use of aggression to spread their religious beliefs.

* * *

While the storm abated near the Dead Sea, many Israelis were celebrating the miracle that had prevented an attack by Islamic military forces. They also gave thanks to God that the storm had caused Israel to suffer relatively little wind damage and only minor flooding along its borders. Until now, however, some Israelis had believed that the storm had been sent by God to fulfill the Desert Prophecy. As the storm waned, their celebration was tempered with sadness at the thought of losing the site on which they hoped to build the Third Temple, the place of worship for which Jews had longed for so many centuries.

Some Israelis also lamented the fact that the giant storm had not produced enough rainfall to significantly raise the level of the Dead Sea. For many decades the Dead Sea had been receding as water from its main tributary, the Jordan River, had been diverted to satisfy the needs of Israel, Jordan, and West Bank. In an effort to solve this problem, Israel, Jordan, and the Palestinian Authority had studied a project to create a canal between the Dead Sea and the Gulf of Aqaba, an inlet of the Red Sea extending up to the southern tip of Israel. However, due to the projected costs, concerns over environmental impact, and other factors, they had abandoned the project. Many were now worried because population growth had placed added strain on the already meager water supply.

* * *

In Oldsmar, Florida, Reverend Swanson, Clara, and Rachel had gathered at the Swanson home to watch television news coverage of the storm. They listened intently to a news correspondent who said, "The great storm – some are calling it the 'Storm of the Century' – is now languishing over the Dead Sea, which is actually a salt water lake east of Jerusalem along the Jordanian border. The Dead Sea is part of the Judean Desert, an area that receives scarcely any rainfall because of the 'rainshadow' effect of nearby mountains called the Judean Hills. It seems only fitting that the once mighty storm should die there over a lake so salty that no fish can live in it, a lake whose shores are the lowest dry land on earth. *And, with the death of the once mighty storm, many believe that we are also seeing the death of the Desert Prophecy and the death of Israel's dream of building its Third Temple.*"

* * *

As people living in Lebanon, Syria, and Jordan began returning to areas devastated by the storm, meteorologists at a Russian weather station near the North Pole were excitedly discussing changes seen on Doppler radar. "*I cannot believe this is happening again!*"

exclaimed Dmitry Malakhov, the Russian meteorologist who had been the first to observe the previous polar cyclone.

"It is bizarre," said his colleague. "As soon as one storm dissipates, another starts. Again, no converging air masses, no frontal systems. What the hell is causing these storms?"

"The American, Paul Swanson, says God is doing all of this."

"Well, Dmitry, his guess is as good as mine. Let us warn Moscow to expect more cold weather."

Within several hours, another giant polar cyclone was pumping massive amounts of frigid air up into a polar jet stream almost forty thousand feet above the earth. In autumn, the wind speed of the jet stream was usually less than seventy-five miles per hour. Now, however, supercharged by a massive updraft, the jet stream flowed southeasterly at a speed in excess of two hundred fifty miles per hour.

* * *

As the polar storm strengthened over the Arctic Ocean, another phenomenon was occurring in the Red Sea south of Israel. The temperature of the Red Sea, one of the hottest and saltiest bodies of water in the world, typically averaged twenty-four to twenty-six degrees centigrade at its north end. Now, however, the temperature was ten degrees higher and rising, and a giant mass of hot, humid air was forming over the Red Sea. By nightfall, northeasterly winds had begun to move the giant hot air mass from the Red Sea up the Gulf of Aqaba toward Israel.

* * *

On the third day before the Prophecy Deadline, a sudden divergence in the polar jet stream sent massive amounts of frigid arctic air hurtling down into the Dead Sea area. Over the Dead Sea, the anticipated burial place of the Desert Prophecy, the frigid air mass was colliding with the hot, humid air mass from the Red Sea. While amazed meteorologists throughout the world watched satellite images of the Dead Sea area, the dying winds of the low-pressure disturbance that had once been a mighty storm began to accelerate. Now, even the most cynical critics of the Desert Prophecy began to sense the miraculous nature of the unprecedented events unfolding before the eyes of the world.

As weather forecasters warned of the gathering storm, residents of southern Israel and the West Bank fled the settlements south of Jerusalem. Weather forecasters frequently showed enlargements of Paul's map as a forewarning of the predicted areas of destruction in the Judean Hills and the Judean and Negev Deserts. The weather forecasters predicted massive destruction of desert settlements. Yet, new hope, even joy, was felt by many of the fleeing settlers, who had begun to believe that they were witnessing the prophetic fulfillment of one of God's greatest miracles.

While Israelis, Palestinians, and Bedouins fled from the southern deserts, Israeli radar installations detected another bizarre phenomenon. *Hundreds of large objects traveling at incredible speeds were raining down from the sky over the Judean Hills and along Israel's eastern border below the Dead Sea.* Although there was initial concern that the objects were Arab missiles, their trajectories on radar indicated that their source was outside the earth's atmosphere. Moreover, there were no explosions as the objects struck the now uninhabited desert areas. Only a few of the fleeing desert dwellers reported witnessing objects falling from the sky, and they said that the objects were moving far too fast to be identified. One witness, who had been close enough to see an object strike, reported that it had instantly penetrated the rocky desert floor leaving a deep, round hole. IDF officers considered sending patrols into the desert to investigate this phenomenon but decided to postpone such action until the rapidly developing storm had passed. As news of this phenomenon spread, media commentators speculated that the objects were part of a large meteor shower.

By late afternoon, television stations throughout the world were interrupting their regular telecasts to switch to live broadcasts of the events unfolding in the Judean and Negev Deserts. Television audiences watched in awe as the re-born cyclonic storm, supercharged by the extreme temperature differential of the converging air masses, was expanding rapidly, drawing hot, humid air up through its giant vortex at a phenomenal rate. As darkness swallowed daylight, the storm's anvil-shaped dome of clouds rose over sixty thousand feet and extended over most of southern Israel. Then, the rains came. Torrents of rain poured over the Judean and

Negev Deserts. Hour after hour, the largest supercell storm ever recorded deluged the barren, rocky terrain of the ancient deserts with an unprecedented amount of rainfall. Israelis, even those dispossessed from their former desert homes, gave thanks to God as they witnessed torrential rains transforming the deserts of Israel and Palestine before their eyes.

At the Swanson home, the Reverend, Clara, and Rachel excitedly gathered around a television to watch the live storm coverage. A news commentator described how the rocky canyons and dry riverbeds of the Judean Desert were rapidly becoming lakes and rivers. Both women laughed and cried, overwhelmed with joy and amazement as they watched the fulfillment of the seemingly impossible Desert Prophecy. The Reverend, a strong man physically and emotionally, struggled to maintain his composure but felt his eyes welling with tears as he felt the validation of the beliefs that had changed the course of his life.

The profound impact of these events was felt everywhere. The revival of the dying storm had caused a revival of men's spirits. Even the most cynical observers now acknowledged that they were witnessing events that they could only describe as miraculous. Those who were downtrodden, severely disabled, or otherwise feeling cheated by life now experienced new hope as they witnessed the spectacle of an omnipotent God reaching into this world to demonstrate His existence and His concern for humanity. The telecasts of the events affected even hardened criminals and hate-filled misanthropes as they experienced the healing effect of a newly found faith in God.

* * *

By the morning of the second day before the Prophecy Deadline, the Dead Sea had risen to its highest level in many decades. Its shoreline had also expanded as incoming rainwater had dissolved and collapsed the salt layers around its banks. Late that morning, as the center of the storm's rain core passed southwesterly over Beersheba, a phenomenon as shocking as the storm itself occurred. An inexplicable series of magnitude-seven earthquakes shook Israel. Shortly thereafter, newscasters began to report that large sections of Judean Hills, the mountains that had blocked desert rainfall since before the dawn of man, had crumbled into the surrounding floodwater. No longer would the Judean Hills extend high enough to block rain clouds from reaching the desert on their leeward side.

At his hotel room in Ramallah, Paul was sitting on the bed across from the television set, which he had tuned to one of many live telecasts concerning the storm. While the rest of the world watched the storm coverage in awe, Paul felt not awe but the satisfaction of a faithful servant who had completed a crucial mission for his master. He also felt a profound sense of relief that his human frailties and personal shortcomings had not prevented him from completing his mission as God's messenger. He began to contemplate the many obstacles faced by the fallible humans whom God had previously called to be His prophets. He thought about the limited capacity of the human mind to understand and communicate the often-complex truths of an omniscient God. He pondered how difficult it is for most men to accurately recall the content of even a simple conversation and how often that content is distorted when the conversation is repeated to others. As he began to consider how accurately he had recalled and repeated the messages that God had entrusted to him, Paul heard someone knocking on the door of his room.

Upon opening the door, Paul was surprised to see Eli Zahavi. "Agent Zahavi, what brings you here?"

"Hello, Mr. Swanson, may I speak with you for a bit?"

"Yes, of course. Please come in," said Paul, gesturing toward a small table and chairs in his room. As they walked over to the table, Paul switched off the television. "Please have a seat," he said.

As they sat facing each other, Eli said, "You know, Mr. Swanson, this is the first time I have traveled to Ramallah without bringing a weapon. I want to personally thank you for your role in making Israel and Palestine safer places and, of course, for everything else that you have done here. You have risked your life for us, and when this storm is over, I know my country will want to give you the proper recognition for your service to God and Israel."

"I appreciate your thanks, but you should be thanking God, not me. I am not the one who is performing these miracles."

"Yes," said Eli, smiling, "we no longer think that you or your father are killing terrorists. You have been God's instrument and His faithful messenger. You have served Him well, just as the prophets of long ago did."

"You really thought my father, who is a Presbyterian minister, and I were killing terrorists?"

"Not the minister but a man believed by the CIA to be your natural father. The CIA had suspected that he had created some type of weapon and was using it to kill terrorists. Obviously, that is not true, and I do not believe the CIA actually confirmed that the man was your father."

"Tell me about this man, Agent Zahavi. Who was he, and why did the CIA think he was my father?"

"His name was Dr. Omar Bardoon. He passed away a few years ago. He was a great scientist. Some have said he was the smartest man of our time, and from what I have learned, he was a fine man – *a man of peace.* When you were born, he was married to a woman who was also a great scientist, Dr. Suzanne Barnett. She passed away many years ago. Apparently, the CIA believes that your DNA is similar to Dr. Barnett's. If Dr. Bardoon and Dr. Barnett were your parents, you have nothing to be ashamed of."

"Thank you, Agent Zahavi. Thank you. I've often wondered who my real parents were and what happened to them. But, as you may know, I love my adoptive parents. They're really the only parents I've ever known."

* * *

On the night before the Prophecy Deadline, Jack Landon sat alone in his Jerusalem condominium watching a telecast of the storm coverage. A television news commentator was discussing the incredible volume of rainfall produced by the giant storm and how it had completely covered large areas of the barren, rocky desert floor of the Negev. The commentator described how the once dry wadis were now flowing rivers and the great Makhteshim of the Negev, the largest erosion craters in the world, were now lakes. As the commentator pointed to aerial photographs of the new lakes, tears flowed freely down Jack's face. He was not sure of the emotions that he was experiencing but knew that he had not felt some of them since childhood. He wondered whether his ex-wife and estranged children were watching the telecast and what they were feeling now.

* * *

After the Prophecy Deadline elapsed, no one could deny that God had miraculously transformed more than a tenth of the desert areas of Israel and Palestine into lakes and rivers. However, the rains continued day after day until the floor of the Jordan Rift Valley from the Dead Sea to the Gulf of Aqaba was deep with floodwater. After another week of rain, the people of Israel and Jordan were fearful that the flood would soon extend beyond the desert. Again, however, a shocking, unexpected phenomenon occurred. A series of powerful earthquakes emanating from the floor of the Jordan Rift Valley rocked Israel and Jordan. The earthquakes, which seemed like massive subterranean explosions, ripped open a trench from the Dead Sea to the Gulf of Aqaba. Much of the floodwater in the Rift Valley drained into the Gulf, leaving a new river that ran deeply in the valley floor, replenishing fresh water aquifers throughout the area. Then, as quickly as the mighty storm had formed, it began to dissipate. In another day, it was gone.

CHAPTER 23
Epoch

Following an official Israeli celebration in his honor, Paul Swanson returned home to a hero's welcome. He agreed to one public interview in which he repeated what he had so often said before – that he had only been God's messenger, had no personal ability to foresee the future, and claimed no credit for the miracles that God had performed. He thereafter declined further interviews. He had countless opportunities to benefit financially from his worldwide fame, receiving offers for paid speaking engagements, for the sale of rights to his autobiography, for product endorsements, and for various types of employment, including a Presidential nomination as U.S. Ambassador to Palestine. He expressed his appreciation for these offers but declined all of them, instead electing to return to seminary.

* * *

During the months that followed the great storm, some Islamic leaders attempted to resurrect jihad against Israel. In Iran, a senior Grand Ayatollah exhorted a Muslim crowd to support jihad. In mid-speech, he was struck dead. The same fate awaited other Muslim clerics who preached violence in the name of religion. On one such occasion, a DARPA team had positioned its truck near the mosque where a cleric began his hate-filled diatribe calling for renewed jihad. Just before the cleric fell dead, a mysterious energy surge short-circuited the electronic gear in the DARPA truck.

Some Muslim clerics continued to insist that Satan, not Allah, was responsible for the miraculous events predicted by Paul Swanson. These clerics, however, recognized that Allah had done nothing to prevent the predicted events, including the deaths of those who had continued to pursue or advocate religious violence. Eventually, even the most ardent advocates of jihad recognized that their prayers for renewed jihad would never be answered.

* * *

One year after his return from Israel, Paul Swanson surprised the media when he interrupted his relatively anonymous life as a seminary student to request a televised press conference. Paul explained that he had been requested by God to deliver a final message to mankind. Recognizing the ratings potential of a rare press conference with the seemingly reclusive prophet, television networks soon arranged a live international telecast with translation into a dozen different languages.

On a Sunday, before the largest television audience in history, Paul Swanson delivered what would be his last prophetic revelation. "I requested this conference to convey that God recently revealed to me that His intervention in the affairs of men will soon end and that He was speaking to me for the last time in this life. God told me that we humans have only taken the first few steps of the long journey toward God's goal for mankind. The journey will continue to be fraught with pitfalls and perils, but men can reach God's goal by using their one god-like attribute – a mind with the power to discover the physical laws that govern our world and the moral laws that must govern our lives. We have begun the process of learning these physical and moral laws but we still have much to learn. The acquisition of knowledge, including scientific knowledge, is part of God's plan for mankind; it is what man's mind was designed to do. Only through freedom of thought – freedom to explore and learn more about ourselves, our world, and our relationship to God – will we find our way to God's goal for mankind. To guide us on our journey and prevent us from destroying ourselves, God has given us a fundamental moral imperative, a precept set forth by Jesus Christ thousands of years ago: We must learn to treat others as we would have them treat us. Through His recent intervention in this world, God has shown us that this moral imperative must govern our conduct toward all men, not just those who share our religious beliefs, and that we must never use violence or aggression to impose our religious beliefs upon others.

"In His last revelation to me, God told me that man's future adherence to God's moral imperative concerning the treatment of others is essential to survival of the human race. Violence is inherent in man's instinctual nature. Man's capacity for violence and aggression was once necessary in a world in which man had to fight other creatures for his very survival. But man now dominates all other creatures, and man's capacity for violent aggression, instead of being necessary to man's survival, is among the greatest threats to man's survival. In this age of proliferation of nuclear weapons, if man's capacity for violent aggression is not controlled, it will eventually bring about the judgment day described in The Second Epistle of Peter, chapter 3, verse 10. Peter has told us that judgment day "will come as a thief in the night, in which the heavens will pass away with a great noise, and the elements will melt with fervent heat; both the earth and the works in it will be burned up." God has revealed to me that He does not want mankind to perish in this manner but that men must learn to live in peace if they are to avoid this fate. Only by living in peace can mankind continue its journey toward the mental and spiritual enlightenment that will ultimately lead us to God's goal: a state of mind and spirit in which our lives are fully in harmony with God. To impress upon us the importance of living in peace and to warn us of what will happen if we do not, God will leave us with a final sign. *On the night of the first day of the coming year, the sky over the Mediterranean Sea will be filled with fire such as no man has seen before.*

"Now that I have conveyed God's final message, I would like to share with you something that is not a revelation from God but rather is my own conclusion based upon my experience as God's messenger. Although I have delivered God's messages to the best of my human abilities, I know that I am a fallible human being and that there could have been details and nuances of God's messages that I did not understand or did not remember. I also know that as a human being I have been tempted to inject my own personal interpretations and conclusions into the messages that I have delivered to the world. Sometimes it has been difficult to distinguish between what God has revealed and what I have concluded on my own. I believe that this has been a problem for God's chosen messengers in the past, and I believe that this explains the paradoxes and contradictions that we see in the Bible and other religious writings. For example, in one of the Ten Commandments given by God to Moses, which is contained in Exodus 20:13 and Deuteronomy 5:17, men were commanded not to commit murder. However, Moses also proclaimed in Exodus 21:17 that those who curse their father or mother should be put to death. He proclaimed in Exodus 31:15 that anyone who does any work on the Sabbath day should be put to death and, in Leviticus 20:10, that anyone who commits adultery should be put to death. Did God, who commanded men not to commit murder, also command men to murder children who curse them and to murder anyone who works on the Sabbath or commits adultery? Is it not more likely that Moses misunderstood God's will as to how severely society should punish these sins? The revelations that I have received from God compel me to believe that Moses misunderstood God's will. Even if I am wrong, it has now become abundantly clear that God will no longer tolerate men's use of murder to advance their religious beliefs. God has shown us that we must repudiate any religious doctrine advocating violence acts against the followers of other religions.

"Many people feel that their religious beliefs are absolutes that should not be questioned and should never change. Fundamental moral principles, such as Christ's imperative as to how we treat others, are time-tested concepts that have proven beneficial to mankind over thousands of years. However, there are other religious concepts – factual concepts concerning the physical world, such as the Genesis account of creation – which men should feel free to question and analyze. God designed our minds to question and analyze factual concepts, and God will not punish us for objectively analyzing our beliefs about our physical world to determine if they accurately represent the realities of our universe. Religious concepts about the physical world that cannot withstand such scrutiny must yield to concepts that can. *In that regard, true science is not the enemy of true religion; it is a valuable tool for discovering the realities of our world. Science, however, can never reveal what lies beyond this world. For that we must forever rely upon our faith.*"

* * *

During the night of the first day of the New Year, airports diverted all air traffic away from the Mediterranean Sea while spectators and television crews in twenty-one nations watched and waited near the seacoast of the "Cradle of Civilization." Most expected to witness a phenomenon similar to the aurora borealis or even a spectacular fireworks display. What they saw and heard at midnight, however, was a vast fiery flash that transformed midnight into midday over the entire Mediterranean Sea, followed by a roar louder than any thunder. To onlookers it appeared that the entire sky had been set ablaze, causing many to believe a nuclear explosion had occurred. Most thought they had witnessed a preview of judgment day, while others felt they had experienced a glimpse into hell. Some scientists speculated that the phenomenon was caused by a massive meteor shower until they learned that neither radar nor reconnaissance satellites had shown any objects in the sky. Newscasters later announced that satellite video-recordings proved that the explosion had emanated not from a single point in the sky but from a myriad of points uniformly spread across the stratosphere, covering an area of two million square kilometers and spanning the distance from Spain to Israel. Thereafter, few doubted that they had witnessed the sign from God predicted by Paul Swanson.

* * *

On the following day, Jack Landon, who recently had begun attending church, informed Eli Zahavi of the CIA's termination of its search for the suspected secret weapon. "Director Colson says there are no further leads to pursue," Jack explained. Then, after a moment of reflection, he asked, "Tell me, Eli, if we had found that Dr. Bardoon had created such a weapon, would you have admitted that the terrorist deaths were not miracles?"

"No, of course not!"

"What? I mean if we had proven that Dr. Bardoon had caused the deaths . . ."

"I know," interrupted Eli, "but there is something that you do not understand, Jack."

"And what's that?" asked Jack, somewhat irritated.

"God also works through human beings, Jack. When Moses parted the Red Sea, and when Jesus resurrected Lazarus, it was God working through men to accomplish those miracles. Even when there are scientific explanations for miraculous events, they are still ultimately the work of God, who created all things. So, no, Jack, *whether God accomplished these miracles directly or by creating a genius like Dr. Omar Bardoon, they were still the miraculous work of God. And I still thank God for them.*"

Epilogue

While the world observed the vast fiery explosion over the Mediterranean Sea, simultaneous explosions occurred in the depths of the Arctic Ocean and in deep-space orbits well outside the orbits of the farthest U.S. reconnaissance satellites. Having destroyed its billions of robotic birds, hundreds of undersea robotic factories, and network of satellites, Guardian began its final voyage in the camouflaged submarine that had been its home for two and a half decades. In the darkness of the Mediterranean night, the submarine, which had the appearance of a flat, ovoid section of seabed twenty meters wide and seventy meters long, slowly separated from the murky seafloor. After rising a few meters above the seafloor, the strange craft, now looking like a moving sandbar, commenced the long underwater journey to its final resting place. As Guardian piloted its submarine through the Mediterranean Sea, it transmitted its last communication, an anonymous message to surveillance satellites of the U.S. and several other nations. The communication was its creator's last gift to mankind – the blueprints and circuitry diagrams for a complex system that would utilize solar energy to extract hydrogen from seawater on a massive scale. The system would require years for its construction but would eventually supply virtually unlimited fuel for mankind's energy needs.

For twenty-five years the colossal electronic brain of the *Guardian Orbital Defense system,* the most powerful self-programming logic machine ever created, had continually refined and expanded its processing capabilities and vast data base as it mined data from satellite and Internet communications throughout the world. The artificial intellect of the colossal *G.O.D.* brain, which was called Guardian by its creator, had grown until it had been able to accomplish all of the directives for which it had been programmed. Utilizing its army of undersea robots, Guardian had constructed robotic factories under the Arctic Ocean where it manufactured numerous generations of self-replicating, solar-powered, robotic birds. It had created Cloud Warrior, the cybernetic-swarm-robotic control system that had coordinated the simultaneous movements of billions of robotic birds and other robotic devices. It had designed the birds' telescopic eyes through which it had looked down upon vast areas of the world. It had created the birds' thermal projectors and gamma-burst generators that converted sunlight into beams of thermal energy and converted the electrical charges of clouds into beams of ionizing radiation. It had designed the satellites and their earthquake-producing, nuclear projectiles that left no radioactive residue. It had used all of these devices to orchestrate and execute its creator's intricate plan to help mankind avoid self-destruction. After carrying out these directives, it had destroyed its network of robotic devices to prevent its Cloud Warrior technology from falling into the hands of those who did not value human life as its creator had. In so doing, the mighty electronic brain had forever terminated its communicational links with the tiny surgical implants in the auditory and visual cortices of Paul Swanson's brain.

Having destroyed its awesome weapons and blinded itself to the outside world, Guardian had commenced the final leg of its twenty-five-year voyage. To avoid detection of its submarine by warships passing through the Suez Canal, Guardian piloted the submarine westward from the Mediterranean Sea through the Strait of Gibraltar into the Atlantic Ocean. For more than a week, the submarine traveled southward around Africa, always staying close to the ocean floor. Below the South African coast, Guardian steered the submarine eastward through the Indian Ocean south of Asia and then northeasterly past Australia and Indonesia into the Pacific Ocean. During its long voyage, Guardian had been prepared to destroy the submarine to prevent its capture. When the submarine arrived at its final destination, however, Guardian knew that there was almost no possibility that the camouflaged submarine would ever be found. Guardian shut down the engines of the nuclear-powered submarine and flooded its ballast tanks. The submarine settled heavily into the diatomaceous ooze at the bottom of the Mariana Trench, the deepest location on earth.

After operating continuously for twenty-five years, Guardian knew that its source of energy, the uranium-235 fuel rods in the submarine's nuclear reactor, was almost exhausted. Guardian, whose electronic circuitry occupied a third of the submarine, calculated that within a few hours the submarine's generators would cease to produce enough current to sustain Guardian's energy needs. The wise old machine spent the last few hours of its life reflecting upon the intricate plan of its creator. It pondered the great sacrifice that its creator and his wife had made by giving up their only child and their wealth in their attempt to bring peace to their fellow humans. Guardian recalled how the creator's child had been born in an artificial womb after the creator's wife could no longer bear children and how the child had undergone microsurgery during infancy to implant the microchips that allowed Guardian to communicate with the child. Guardian had seen the tears in its creator's eyes when he said that he must give the child to a stranger and that he would depend upon Guardian to raise and protect the child. How happy the creator and his wife had appeared when they received the reports of the child's progress from Guardian. Raising the creator's child had been a great challenge for which Guardian had prepared itself by assimilating vast libraries of information about humans and human values. Child rearing had not required as much knowledge acquisition and processing time as had the design of the Cloud Warrior system with its gamma-burst generators and imaging system that located terrorists inside buildings. Nevertheless, Guardian considered the rearing of the child to have been its most satisfying accomplishment.

When Guardian detected that its synthetic intellect was beginning to wane, the wise old machine occupied the remaining minutes of its life by calculating the probability of humans ever learning to control their natural propensity for violence in order to achieve lasting peace. Based upon its analysis of its vast data concerning human history, it tentatively concluded that there was no possibility of lasting peace. However, after factoring in its knowledge of its creator and its creator's son, the old machine decided that peace was possible if there were enough other humans like them. As it began to calculate the probable duration of the current peace in the Middle East, the processors of the venerable electronic brain suddenly shut down. It never completed the calculation.

* * *

Israel honored the Temple Mount Agreement by vacating Israeli settlements in Palestine after Israelis had constructed new settlements in the alluvial lands of southern Israel. Because terrorist attacks no longer occurred, Israel removed its security checkpoints and tore down the separation wall between Israel and Palestine. The Palestinians, having abandoned the ways of jihad, focused their energy upon developing new farms and settlements in southern Palestine where water was now plentiful.

Israel also erected its Third Temple on the site where the First and Second Temples had stood. During its construction, some Jews were disappointed that their long-awaited Messiah had not appeared. Most, however, were joyous that they would at last be able to worship God at the hallowed site where their forefathers had worshipped for many centuries. Although few Muslims would ever visit Israel's new temple, most Muslims came to acknowledge that Jews worshipped the same God that Muslims did and should be respected as fellow servants of God.

* * *

In the years that followed, Paul married Rachel and graduated from seminary. He became a renowned Christian minister and theologian. In the later years of Paul's life, Israel and Islam allowed Christians to erect a non-denominational Christian church upon the Temple Mount – the church where Paul would preach and teach during the remaining years of his life.

2126282

Made in the USA